QUARTET E[...]

THE S[...]

The Snake seems to be a colle[...]
in a brilliant denouement dis[...]
together to reveal the under[...]
Based on the author's experience of conscription,
Dagerman tells his story through the experiences of the
inmates of an army camp in Stockholm.

From the sexual fantasies of Irene, a young woman who
murders her mother by pushing her off a train, to the
ingrained anxieties of the elderly conscript misleadingly
nicknamed the Joker, a quarryman whose best friend
died in his arms after a mining accident, Dagerman
writes with equal skill from the point of view of both
sexes, and through them he examines wider issues of
social justice and the psychology of fear.

STIG DAGERMAN

Stig Dagerman was regarded as the most talented young writer of the Swedish postwar generation. By the time he was twenty-six, he had published four novels, a collection of short stories, a book of travel sketches and four full-length plays – an astonishing output which was brought to a tragic end in 1954 when, at the age of thirty-one, Dagerman committed suicide, cutting short a career of brilliant promise.

STIG DAGERMAN

The Snake

Translated and with an introduction by
Laurie Thompson

QUARTET ENCOUNTERS

Quartet Books

Published in Great Britain
by Quartet Books Ltd 1995
A member of the Namara Group
27 Goodge Street
London W1P 2LD

A catalogue record for this book is available from the
British Library

ISBN 0 7043 0241 1

Printed and bound in Finland by WSOY

Introduction

In 1945 Stig Dagerman and the majority of the Swedish people could be confident that the Second World War would end in victory for the Allies, and the threat of invasion by the Nazi army had all but vanished. Having been appointed Cultural Editor of the Anarcho-Syndicalist newspaper *Arbetaren* (*The Worker*) on 1 January, at twenty-two the youngest holder of such a post in Sweden, Dagerman's journalistic career had really taken off. It was not much more than three years since he had published his first article in the Syndicalist Youth journal *Storm*, having been introduced into the movement by his father, and his rise had been rapid. Almost every day he stimulated and provoked his readers with articles attacking what he saw as the restrictive and reactionary cultural attitudes of the day, besides reviewing a large number of books, plays and films. He also contributed an almost daily satirical poem, based on some controversial news item and criticizing or poking fun at conservative traditions: Dagerman soon built a reputation as a witty and perceptive defender of the underdog. Now that the war was almost over, intellectuals of the left could turn their attention to the society which was to emerge in its aftermath. And they wanted fundamental changes.

What most people did not realize was that Stig Dagerman's sights were set on goals higher than journalism: he was determined to become a novelist – and why not also a playwright and poet? Strindberg had proved himself a master of all genres, so why could not Dagerman? Legend has it that Dagerman's first novel, *The Snake*, was written at his desk in the newspaper office during occasional lulls in the frenzied hustle and bustle invariably associated with the meeting of deadlines. His first wife, Annemarie Dagerman, maintains that in fact most of it was written at home. No matter; what is indisputable is that *The Snake* reflected the ideas Dagerman was arguing for most energetically in his journalism. It is by no means exclusively a political novel, but there is certainly a political level to it.

Anarcho-Syndicalism was surprisingly strong in Sweden in the 1940s. Also known as Free Socialism, it echoes the social ideals of socialism while rejecting the central authority socialists believe is necessary to put those ideals into practice. Individual freedom is the key concept for Anarcho-Syndicalists, who believe power should be based in local groups – factory committees, union branches – so that every individual can have a say in policy-making; the idea that edicts can be handed down by some central authority is anathema to them. True socialists scoff at what they consider to be the impracticality, not to say naïvety, of the Free Socialists. Dagerman was well aware of such criticism, but commented in an article about anarchism, published in 1946, that: 'Being a politician of the impossible in a world where all too many are politicians of the possible is, in spite of everything, a role which can satisfy me personally as both a social being, an individual and the author of *The Snake*.'

As the Second World War drew to its close, Dagerman was alarmed by talk of 'getting back to normal'. It seemed to him most people meant by this the restoration of power and authority to the same old political parties, religious and philosophical movements, cultural values and so on that had held sway in the 1930s – but Dagerman was convinced this was a recipe for disaster. Was it not precisely those '-isms', those traditional beliefs and attitudes, which had brought about the war in the first place – or at the very least, been unable to prevent it? What was needed, he argued, was a serious, unprejudiced, in-depth analysis of what had gone wrong, and a determination to start all over again, rejecting all aspects of the past which had proved fatal for the future.

On a superficial political level, of course, this meant embracing the ideals of Anarcho-Syndicalism, ideals which most politicians ridiculed as being splendid in theory but totally impractical in the real world. Socialists were especially aghast at the way Dagerman seemed to be questioning the concept of the welfare state, the cornerstone of the Swedish Social Democratic government in the 1930s and destined to be developed much further in the post-war era. Of course, Dagerman was not in fact arguing against improvements in social conditions for the lower classes; he took it for granted that all right-thinking people were in favour of that and would do their best to squash any reactionary capitalists who sought to prevent it from happening. His objection was the tendency for the nanny state to relieve the individual of any necessity or even desire to think for himself and be responsible for his own fate. He felt citizens in a paternalistic welfare state were lulled into a false sense of security, all too keen to allow others to smooth their paths and create a world of constant happiness and harmony. Life is not like that, he argued, and every individual must learn to cope with adversity as well as with bliss. A world in which one is protected from reality is a fundamentally insecure world; an insecure individual is inevitably vulnerable, susceptible to angst, and incapable of dealing with it.

Dagerman found his ideal allegory for the fate of the angst-ridden invidual in the circumstances Sweden found herself in during the Second World War. Not having been involved in a war since 1814, Sweden declared her neutrality in 1939 together with her Scandinavian sister-countries. When the Germans invaded Denmark and Norway in 1940, Sweden found herself playing mouse to the German cat: would she be invaded next? When? Where? How? The Swedish army was in a constant state of readiness – theoretically, at least. As anyone who has seen a conscript army from the inside knows all too well, inactive soldiers, repeatedly told that it's their job to obey and not to think, soon become disillusioned, devoting all their energies to dodging the column while giving the appearance of enthusiasm and alertness. The powers that be try to counteract this by insisting on discipline, but are easily outmanoeuvred by the conscripts, who lapse into an almost trance-like state and drift from one day to the next, interested only in finding some pleasurable way of alleviating the boredom, and avoiding being caught by their superiors.

The second part of *The Snake* is set in a barracks—based on the Göta Livgarde barracks in Stockholm where Dagerman had been employed as a clerk during his own national service in 1943. The conscripts dodge and malinger their way through army life until one day, they are faced with a situation the military system and their ways of beating it cannot cope with: a snake has escaped and is at large somewhere in their living quarters. Just as Sweden was under a vague but constant threat of attack by Germany during the war, so the individual soldiers feel threatened by the snake, which might be hiding in their lockers, or in their boots, and if they are not careful might crawl into their beds. They cannot sleep at night, but distract their attention from the snake by telling each other stories, each of which features individuals placed in horrific situations, and has symbolic significance either for the way individuals can cope with life, or the society which brings about such situations, or both. They are greatly relieved when they can escape from the barracks with a late-night pass, but during their evening at large, several individuals are also confronted with horrific situations, and have an opportunity to recognize a truth about themselves or the social system in which they live. Back in the barracks in the early hours, the snake is found, dead. The crisis is over, and the conscripts return to their normal existence; no lessons have been learnt. Only middle-class, educated Gideon seems to have been changed by his experiences; but he has not yet learnt a lesson, merely had his eyes opened to the inadequacies of some of his preconceptions and assumptions.

The first section of *The Snake*, named after the main character, Irène, could be said to depict on a personal level what is portrayed in a more general social context in the second part. Irène is basically a 'good girl' who nevertheless has an urge to be abandoned, liberated and 'bad' like the many young people she sees around her. She has run away from home after an argument with her parents, and now works at the local army camp, living in. Her problem is one repeatedly encountered in Dagerman's work, and basically the author's own dilemma: she wants to be true to herself – but how can she be sure what she really is? She already has a bad conscience about leaving home, before coming across her mother on a train taking her to a birthday party planned to turn into an orgy, but after a heated argument she throws her mother off the train, presumably to her death. Or does she? Is the incident factual, or a figment of her heated imagination? In any case, the vague feeling of rebellion now has something specific to form the basis of her bad conscience, which is depicted in terms of a rat-like creature gnawing away inside her (together with a host of other images portraying Freud's theories of repression and the subconscious).

Stig Dagerman had a personal horror of rats and mice, which he traced back to a childhood incident on his grandparents' farm. A hole had been dug for a telegraph pole and left overnight; next morning, when the workers arrived to raise the pole under the eagle eye of the young Stig, they found a rat trapped at the bottom. They took a sharpened stake, teased the terrified creature for a while, then eventually tired and drove the stake through its eye and killed it. The rat's horrific scream as the stake pierced its eye remained in Dagerman's memory, and he was overcome by uncontrollable

5

fear whenever he encountered a mouse or a rat in later life. On one occasion a fellow-author invited for Christmas dinner jokingly remarked that he thought he had heard a mouse under the floorboards; Stig Dagerman hurried out of the room and did not return for several days.

He was also terrified of snakes. As a young boy he had been walking through the woods with his uncle when they suddenly came across an adder coiled on the path before them. Dagerman the author was of course well aware of the traditional significance of snakes as a symbol of fear, and of the sexual connotations; but the intensity of his personal fear had very real origins.

If the rat-like creature symbolizes the angst caused by Irène's bad conscience, her fear is given an external embodiment in the form of a snake. Bill, her tearaway, bullying boyfriend, captures a snake and uses it to terrify his sergeant – Bill is a conscript in a small-town provincial barracks. He is the tempter who makes Irène long to be sinful and abandoned, and her confusion comes to a head when, at the height of the orgy, Bill produces the snake, which slides over a table through a forest of empty bottles towards her. The rat-like creature inside her leaps out of her mouth in the form of a scream, and coincides with the snake: the symbols of her internal and external terror have combined, and she can no longer avoid the question at the heart of her dilemma. Did she in fact kill her mother? And beyond that are the deeper-seated questions she will have to face up to sooner or later: what is her true nature, and how can she live up to it? Confronting these questions will not cure her angst, for angst is a part of the human condition; but it will give her a better chance of living and coping with it.

Although we are not told specifically, it is implied that the snake caught by Bill is the same one that escapes in the Stockholm barracks. Men from the Göta Livgarde regiment have been based in the provincial camp while on manoeuvres; one of them picks up the wrong haversack and finds himself the new owner of the snake. Dagerman is thus able to link the psychological study of Irène with the more general social and political analysis of contemporary society embodied in the 'We Can't Sleep' section.

Although Dagerman was no scholar, he was well aware of contemporary trends in literature and philosophy, and it is not difficult to trace the influence of Kafka in his style, and the philosophy of Satre and French Existentialism. For a long time Dagerman was regarded in Sweden as their most typical writer of the 1940s and the high priest of angst (although it is recognized now that his message is universal and timeless). Like most of his contemporaries in the younger generation, he was radical in politics and an avid reader of fashionable foreign literature – deprived by war of the possibility of leaving Sweden, the young writers were fully abreast of trends in Europe and North America. Dagerman's *alter ego* in *The Snake* is Scriber, the conscripted writer who features in the last chapter of all, discussing with literary friends the contemporary cultural scene. Like Scriber, Dagerman argued that a writer had to be committed politically and socially: in 1945, no writer could afford to be a drawing-room entertainer, but was duty-bound to analyse the human condition in the context of contemporary society as the Second World War came to an end. There was a literary movement in Sweden, calling itself New Vitalism, which claimed that readers had suffered enough deprivation and horror during the war years. They deserved a break, and instead of being treated to difficult intellectual social analyses and political sermons, they should be served with more romantic fare in which characters sought happiness and pleasure, not least through sensual excess. To some extent Dagerman was parodying this school of thought in *The Snake*, especially in the 'Irène' section where the 'hard-boiled' approach of Americans like Caldwell and Faulkner is imitated but shown to be inadequate to deal with the inescapable problems of the post-war era. Angst cannot be repressed for long without disastrous consequences,

7

and modern man must come to terms with his personal self if he is to cope with modern life – just as modern society must undergo an honest and unprejudiced examination of its shortcomings before establishing its direction for the post-war years.

Significantly, Scriber's discussions take place in a hotel in Klara, the district of Stockholm which was traditionally the haunt of bohemians, artists, journalists and radicals. Its atmospheric buildings and streets were largely demolished in the 1960s, but in the 1940s it was still the corner of Sweden where conventions were undermined, dreams dreamt and Utopias envisaged. Most of the conscripts in *The Snake* spent their free time in accurately depicted areas of central Stockholm where bourgeois citizens lived their bourgeois lives; but Scriber has visions of a new and better Sweden – and because *The Snake* is universal in its implications, of a new and better world. Not necessarily a happier and easier world, but a more genuine and realistically based one. Just as the writers and artists must abandon old traditions which have proved to be inadequate to portray life as it really is, so politicians must abandon their worn-out creeds and start afresh. To demonstrate what he means, inspired by the many beers he has drunk in the course of the evening, Scriber climbs out of a window, declines to climb back into the same room through another window, but insists on progressing to a third window leading into a new and different room – but in doing so falls to his death.

Is Dagerman being so pessimistic, he implies that no solution to the modern dilemma is possible? Or is he suggesting that the role of the writer is to pose the questions, leaving the reader to answer them? It is for the reader to decide.

Laurie Thompson

If literature is a drawing-room entertainment, I will venture out into the twilight with blackened feet, and make friends with the snakes and the little desert rat. If literature is an essential part of life, don't forget your sandals, and watch out for mounds of stones! Now the snakes are after my heels, and the desert rat disgusts me.

(My friend Scriber)

Irène

1

It was so hot you could almost have roasted coffee on the rails. The gravel inbetween the sleepers glistened brightly, and on the other side of the railway slouched a field of half-ripe oats. Beyond the field was a cluster of red-painted wooden houses, and the sharp toothpick of a flag-pole towered up from the cluster. The station building, like a colossus, was bringing its weight to bear on the plain, and in the gravel square in front of it were little pillars of dust. In the far distance a train was approaching from out of the green infinity. Smoke came pouring out of the engine's funnel and small clouds settled like mushrooms along the track. It was nearly one o'clock, and the train drew up, giving the sleepy hamlet a dig in its flank.

On the bench outside the waiting rooms for ladies and gentlemen sat two old women, like sparrows perched on a telephone wire. One of them was squinting up at the sun, trying to give her warts a tan. The other was Nosy-Parkering around with her quick, rat-like eyes, noting instantly everything of interest within range. A lonely little suitcase stood on the concrete platform, its metal catches glinting in the sun. The case had a solid-looking leather handle, but, more notable, fastened to the handle was a lifeless bouquet of marigolds dangling down one side.

Just like a hanged man, thought old Rat-Eyes, poking her companion in the ribs. 'Nasty drought we're 'aving this year,' she said, taking a series of close-ups of her friend's face. It was in the shadow from the rim of her hat at present. Her eyes were blinking helplessly as her pupils groped around in the dark. Her eyelids were tight as a drum and a tear trickled out of the corner of her eye, groped its way down the bridge of her nose, watering a few warts on the way, and eventually joined up with the saliva oozing out of the side of her mouth. Her lips slid apart and the tip of her tongue swayed back and forth in the opening like the head of a snake. 'You can say that again,' she said. 'Good drying weather.'

'Tee, hee,' giggled Rat-Eyes, puffing up her cheeks. 'Tee, hee, there's some as never think of nowt but washing.' She took another series of close-ups of her companion's mouth. It was so quiet you could have heard a louse clambering around in the jungle of her hair, and the train cut into that silence like a razor blade.

As the old women got up from the bench, the door of the ladies creaked and footsteps crunched on the gravel. Rat-Eyes glanced quickly in that direction but looked away even more quickly, and the fat woman with the washing peered with her searchlight-eyes, then turned her beam on her friend and said: 'I reckon that lass of yours is out gallivanting.' Then she started waddling away towards the train. The other old woman picked up her dusty parcel from the ground and shuffled after her, just as if she were on skis. The old women climbed up into the train like timid mice and crept as inconspicuously as possible into the murky carriage. It was nearly empty, apart from a fat man glued to the wall, sweat pouring from his face and down on to the upholstery. It was very hot, but there were no windows open and a few flies were buzzing around in the cracks without being able to find their way out.

'This'll do, eh?' said the fat woman with the warts – she was the one taking the initiative now, and she pointed to the seat with a grand gesture of invitation. Her companion slumped down by the window, eased her hat off and felt a great sense of relief, as if she had just got rid of a crown of thorns. The fat woman started unlacing her boots and setting free her ample calves: it was like knocking the walls out of a kneading tray.

Somebody started to open the door to the compartment, and through the crack they could hear the sound of gunshot from up in the woods; but then the train from town came gushing past like a waterfall and drowned all the little drips of sound. Their train started moving.

'Hmm, so your daughter's on board, eh?' said the fat woman, driving a little wedge into the clammy silence. 'Where's she off to, then?'

The windows didn't quite close properly. A thin, clear breath of air wafted into her face. Not like this, she thought, not like this. Back at home somebody was closing an upstairs window. The church came gliding over the plain with its steeple on a lead behind it, and then they were in the cool tunnel of the forest. The sun was injecting sparks between the trunks. The warm gentleman by the window spread a handkerchief over his face, and it sucked up the dampness like blotting-paper clinging to his face like a death mask. Not like this, not like this.

'Ah, yes, Irène,' said Maria Sandström, feeling the crown of thorns digging into her forehead even though her hat was still lying on its seat, sweating.

2

When she woke up the paralysing heat had already managed to creep into the barrack room: the sheet felt like a wet swimming-costume round her body and the blanket had fallen on to the floor. The green curtains were still drawn across the open window, providing some resistance to the light – but not to the heat. There was a reverential half-light in the room, just like in church, she thought sleepily, and started peeling off the sheet. It was like getting out of the bath. Her feet were free now, and she waved to herself with her toes. The shroud slid away from her legs, which hadn't had time to get sunburnt yet; they were as white as candles, and made her think of church again. She drew up her knees so that the sheet stretched like a bridge over her upper body, and she just lay there for a while, without moving, as a feeling of anaesthetized peace and quiet contentment oozed through her body like strong liquor through blood. She was totally alone now; not even matron was around, although she was normally ever-present, just like the flies and mosquitoes. No, she was totally alone. The other seven beds lay there yawning like empty sacks, spreading a sickly-sweet aroma through the room. Nightdresses and damp blankets were hanging over head-boards, and down by the door was the matron's flowery dressing-gown, just as flowery and all-embracing as its owner.

The old bitch, thought the young girl as she lay there pumping herself full of sensuality. A slight, gentle breeze came dancing in through the curtains and a whole, long, marvellous holiday was lurking outside, waiting for her. She let the sheet slide slowly down to the floor and lay there for a while, naked, staring unseeingly up at the ceiling. In her mind she was picking her way through the coming day's offering of possibilities, just as one wanders through a market lined with tempting stalls. I'll start by cleaning up in the barrack room, she thought; I'll make the bed and then go and have some breakfast in the kitchen. Then I'll get dressed and go home to see how they're getting on. I'll march into the kitchen just as I always do and pretend nothing has happened. Hello, there, Mum and Dad, I'll say, long time no see, but everything here's just as it always was, I expect. I have a day off, so I thought I'd just call in and see how you're getting on. There's quite a lot to keep me busy down there, in fact. There's three hundred soldiers in the camp, so there's plenty to do. Hmm, no doubt they'd say something as well: maybe they'd ask how she was getting on and she'd say it was OK – not like being at home, of course, I mean, it's just barrack rooms, with bare walls and iron beds. But it's OK, she oughtn't to overdo it. Then they might ask her what had gone wrong, why she'd left and hadn't come home any more. She'd say, not too apologetically, of course, no fear, that she'd been a bit silly perhaps, well, a bit nervous, she'd say, that sounded much better, she'd been feeling a bit miserable, she'd say, that happens sometimes, I mean, Mum should understand that at least. Well, things would turn out OK, once they got talking a bit. Everything would be all right again. Everything.

She turned over, lifted up the mattress and pressed her head against the bed-frame; it was so hot in the barrack room that it felt like ice. She'd just stay there a little bit longer, just a little bit, and make the most of the delights that come from being on holiday. Then she'd get up and do what she'd been thinking about. Do just what she'd planned. Exactly that. Nothing would stop her. Nothing. She lay there, as if pressing her good intentions into her brain, and the cooling ache from the bed took possession of her whole body in the form of calm, cool resolve.

Suddenly she heard steps outside, rapid, purposeful steps over the pine needles that were lying everywhere; an iron-studded heel clashed against a stone and she realized breakfast must be over and the three hundred men would soon come pouring out of the mess and disperse into the barrack rooms and then they'd form platoons and troupes and run around in the woods, fling themselves down behind tree stumps or lie perfectly still, just as she was doing, and fire a few shots at the rifle range. The approaching footsteps were on their own, though, and they were heading straight for her billet, straight for her window, without a moment's hesitation, and it dawned on her who it was.

Bill, she thought, that bastard! No, I'm not going to get up, he can stand there and hang around for as long as he wants, he can coax and talk and whistle, but I'm not getting up. She lay there, quite still and quite naked, and there was no longer any sound of footsteps. He's here, she thought, he's standing outside, but he's not saying anything, he's standing outside without saying a word. She raised her head to listen and the bed creaked. Now he must realize I'm here, she thought in annoyance, straining her ears.

Then she thought she could hear somebody breathing outside and a puff of wind came in through the curtains; it was hot and it felt like somebody's breath, somebody's breath, a hot puff of breath flowing over her face, and suddenly it seemed as if somebody was breathing into her ear, whispering passionate words, and it was as if the wall wasn't there, as if the man outside had come in to her and was lying beside her, breathing into her ear. There was a pounding in her head, she was all dizzy and hot and on edge. I'll just pull the curtains and see if it's him, but I'm not going to promise anything, I shan't promise a thing, she thought to herself in confusion and quite pointlessly, and she raised herself on her elbow. Then she suddenly realized she was naked and grabbed the sheet from off the floor and wrapped it round her shoulders like a shawl. The chill from the damp sheet almost cooled her ardour, she was almost as cold as she'd been before, as she stretched up her arms hesitantly and pulled open the green curtains.

There he was outside, with the sunshine streaming down between the pine trees, but she couldn't see him properly at first in the dazzling daylight. She closed her eyes to protect them from the sun and could feel the heat creeping all over her, and then she opened her eyes again and there he was, quite close to her, smiling. His smile made his face look lopsided, as it always did, and she could see his yellowish teeth, his chapped lips and the dead cigarette hanging almost vertically down from his mouth. He was bare-headed, his beret stuffed into his belt like an Indian scalp, and his hair had flopped down over one of his eyes. He stepped back non-chalantly, fixed her with his gaze and said, the cigarette still dangling from his mouth: 'Listen, I've been thinking. I've thought up summat all by myself.' Then he screwed up his eyes and stared past her into the room and said: 'Hey, have you gorra match?' She got out of bed and as she stepped down she lost hold of one corner of the sheet and he caught a glimpse of her breast. Then she came back, holding the sheet very close to her, and tossed him a box of matches. 'What have you thought up?' she asked, trying to sound reluctant in order not to sound keen. 'Anything special?'

'Yeah,' he said, lighting the cigarette in the cup of his hand, 'we're going to have a little party, we're going to have a celebration.' 'What kind of a celebration?' she asked, not sounding too reluctant at all. 'Could be a birthday,' he said, flicking the matchbox over her head and into the billet. 'Could be my birthday, for instance.' 'You don't say,' she said. 'That'd be nice.' 'I'm not,' he said. 'Not bloody nice. But you're going to be there and that's what's nice about it, see.' 'Oh, I'm going to be there, am I?' she said, sounding almost servile by now. 'And where d'yer think you're going to go, then?' 'I've got my eye on a little cottage,' he said. 'At Älvsjö. There'll be a few of us. The old man of one of the lads who's coming owns it, and the old bastard's not around.' 'No, course not,' she said.

'Well, you see, I reckoned,' he said, coming up closer to her, as close as he could with the wall in the way, 'I reckoned you could go there in advance and sort out a few things.' 'You don't say, is that what you'd reckoned?' she said. 'What if I don't want to? If I say bugger that for a lark?' She backed away over the bed on her knees, trying to grow in stature as she moved away from him. He just took the cigarette from his mouth, though, and dropped it on the ground and looked at her without smiling at all, looked her straight in the eye, and she crept back up to the window and tried to stare at about the third button on his tunic. Then she suddenly saw his arm move and his hand shot down to his belt, shot back up again, and there was something in it; she saw him raise his arm and something whistled down on to the window-ledge and when she looked she saw a bayonet stuck in the wood between them.

'You will,' he said. He was smiling now, and as always it made his face look lopsided. She could see the bayonet trembling like a javelin that has just pierced the soil, she could see the sharp blade and the yellow oil sliding down it towards the point. She looked beyond the bayonet at the man behind the blade and suddenly everything was as it had been just before. So hot, so dizzy, so much blood in one place. Without a word she let the sheet fall and stood there naked in the window. She leaned her confused head over the top of the bayonet towards the man and he bit her mouth in a frenzy and as they kissed the bayonet fell over on the window-ledge and she cut her wrist on the sharp edge and it was like two bites: one in her mouth and one there. Then he let her go and she sunk back on to the bed while he took the blood-stained bayonet and slid it back into his sheath. Before leaving he leaned in over the window-ledge and said: 'See you in the café at twelve noon.' She nodded submissively and then she heard him striding towards the barrack square with firm, confident steps. That was when she felt she hated him. Then she heard the new day starting up and the buzz as the three hundred or two-hundred-and-ninety-nine men swarmed out of the mess. Somebody yelled, 'Get fell in!' and she heard the rattling sound of bolts being cocked in rifles. Then she got out of bed and started dressing her naked body, and she knew that this day was going to be very different.

3

The sun had just emerged from a cloud and oppressive heat

was bearing down on his back and neck. The whole of the clearing was bathed in relentless light and he curled up as tightly as possible in order to fit into the shadows cast by the stone. His forehead was beginning to drip with sweat, and he took off his beret, placing it stealthily on the stone. Then he raised his head like a lynx on the look-out until his eyes were level with the V-shaped notch driven into the rock like a wedge. He scanned the felled slope that descended in a series of gentle plateaux down to the railway line. The whole of the hillside was littered with ragged stumps looking like warts on the skin of the earth, and among the warts loomed blocks of stone at such regular intervals you almost got the impression you were in a graveyard. Behind every stone big enough to conceal a body lay a soldier stretched out, looking like a corpse, and most corpse-like of all was the sergeant, striking a pose in a hollow behind a stone on the front line.

The sunlight streamed down like hot rain, and the barrel of his rifle almost burnt him as he pulled the weapon towards him and slid the barrel into the notch. Then he got up on his knees and brought the butt alongside his cheek, closed his left eye and adjusted the rifle in a series of little movements, just as it said in the instruction manual, so that the sight was properly lined up, with the point settled in the middle of the V as if in a vice. Then he swung the barrel of his rifle slowly round and it struck him it was a bit like being in a theatre looking for actors on an empty stage with opera glasses. The whole of the scorched, hazy slope down below swung across his vision, and, just when the rifle began to come up against the side of the stone as he completed his sweep of the target area, he noticed the stage was not empty after all. The line running from his pupil along the barrel, through the sights and then leaping out boldly over the traps set all over the slope suddenly landed on the back of someone's neck; he saw straight away it was the sergeant's and as his finger felt its way inside the trigger-guard and crept towards the trigger he thought to himself: if there's such a thing as thought transference, Sergeant Bohman must be feeling a painful sting in the neck just now and he'll have to turn round and look over here, and if there was a live round in the breech and I pulled the trigger, the bullet would smash into his jaw just below his teeth and he'd fall forwards on to his knees with blood pouring out of the hole under his teeth and the hole would look just like a little round extra mouth.

Sergeant Bohman's neck didn't move at all, however, it just sat staring like a stupid fly under his forage cap and the whole figure behind the stone below was an expression of stupid, inert apathy.

At the very least he could be an enemy, he thought, openly hostile, and he tried pulling the trigger a few times; but the sergeant wasn't wearing a white band on his left arm, a necessary condition for an enemy soldier. He was in fact the leader of the platoon that had been lying in the hot sun for half an hour, waiting for the Svensson platoon, which, according to orders, ought to be advancing through the woods on the other side of the railway line. So far, though, there had been no sign of any left arms with white bands, and the platoon had been gripped by dull apathy, which increased in direct proportion to the heat. From a military point of view you could talk in terms of a decline in discipline. Soldiers not too close to the sergeant had unfastened vital buttons and from behind some of the gravestones small white columns of smoke were rising skywards, although no rest period had been announced.

Only Sergeant Bohman was still lying immobile like a dead mouse in its hole. He was staring relentlessly into the bushes on the other side of the railway line and was as tense as an archer's bow in readiness for the great moment when he would once again be the commandant, the power holding his men together, leading his troops through fire and water into battle with the enemy. His little eyes, well-disciplined under the well-groomed shrubbery of his eyebrows, were sniping at the edge of the woods, but the bushes were as preternaturally silent as ever, dripping with green disinterest. He ordered his gaze to march back to base, but just as it was about to come to attention in front of the stone, it paused in its final stride as if struck lame; his eyes rolled around a few times in their sockets and beads of swept crept out of his forehead like little animals. The whole of his body was convulsed into one big muscle of terror. The bushes came slithering towards the stone on their poisonous green bellies. Then they came to a halt in front of a patch of powder-dry twigs and the twigs opened up their belly and revealed a grey reptile with a hissing tongue. Snake, snake, snake went the message through his forehead, and it came to the boil and pressed hard against the top of his skull, the background melted away and only the expanding body of the snake existed. It swayed from side to side like the pendulum in an upside-down clock, sucking his eyes out of their sockets.

Just then his eye was caught by a flash of light from the edge of the woods and it dawned on him straight away that it was one of the scouts from Svensson's platoon prowling about in the bushes with an open map-case, its celluloid reflecting the sun. He tried to get a grip on himself so that he could forget the snake lying in the undergrowth six feet from his head, its tongue jerking in and out, but when he slid down behind the stone and out of sight for the scouts, the snake spread out like a long shadow and filled his field of vision, and he started panting as cramp closed in on his body like an iron ring.

I must do something, he thought feverishly, and his thoughts groped around the tree trunks like a drunk in a forest. I *must* pull myself together, he told himself, we *must* get ready for the battle. We *must* cross the railway line and try to creep up behind them. I *must* do something. I, I, I, the words pounded away inside his head and the iron ring tightened and he could feel the expectant looks from his platoon stabbing him in the back. *I must*: the words burned their way into his mind and he tried to wriggle out of the cramp as the threatening shadow of the snake riveted itself on his eyeballs and a sense of fiasco began to take possession of him. This feeling became so marked that eventually he imagined he could hear the hissing and the giggles and the roars of raucous laughter seeping into his ears.

But the twelve members of Bohman's platoon lay dozing in the shade of their stones and had lost all sense of taking part in a battle and only one of them, the one called Bill, had seen the careless scout with the open map-case flitting about on the edge of the woods, and as soon as he saw him he took out a fairly white handkerchief from his pocket, fastened it to the tip of his bayonet and then waved it about over his head so that the scout would get an eyeful of it. That was evidently what had happened – he'd signalled back using the reflection from his map-case, and after a while there was a rustling in the undergrowth on the other side of the railway line and it was evident Svensson's platoon was assembling, ready for the attack.

Bill lay stretched out and smug in the cool shade thrown by the stone, whistling softly through his teeth. Private 416 Matsson, who had been dozing with his cap over his eyes, woke up and turned to look at him. He reached casually for his rifle and aimed straight at Bill. He pulled the trigger, which made a clicking sound. Bill screwed his eyes up and peered contentedly at the sun, saying out loud: 'We won't have to lie here sweating much longer, thank God.'

There was a sound of cracking twigs down in the woods, and the undergrowth was swaying as if a hurricane was blowing through it. 'Why the hell doesn't Sarge do something?' wondered Bill, opening the breech of his rifle. 'Too bloody right,' said Matsson, staring hard at his stone. Sergeant Bohman lay as stiff as a felled log in his hollow, and seemed not to have noticed anything. 'For God's sake!' said Matsson. But Bill slid down from his position and grabbed Matsson's arm so violently he nearly fell over. 'Look,' he whispered, and there was something exultant, almost frightening, in the tone of his voice. 'Can't you see the snake?' They flung themselves down on their stomachs and watched the snake rise from the ground as if emerging from a hole, and they could see its slender body swaying almost melodically from side to side in front of the sergeant's head.

'Do you think it'll strike?' asked Matsson half-aloud, and he could feel little shivers rising like bubbles of air along his spine. Bill didn't answer, though, and Matsson stole a furtive glance at his face. He could see there was something special happening, and when Bill turned towards him his look was so sharp he nearly cut himself on it. 'He's scared,' said Bill and his voice sounded as if it was coming from only half a lung. 'Shit scared! Just look, eh!' Matsson just shivered as if he were freezing cold and crept back behind his stone and started loading blank rounds into his rifle.

Then they heard the train puffing away round the bend in the tracks, and thin little clouds of smoke wafted up through the tree-tops. The engine could be glimpsed here and there through the bushes as it chugged awkwardly along like an old man, the tender rattling along behind like a coffee-mill. The Bohman platoon came to life and waved casually at some young girls who were giggling in the window of one of the carriages. On the open platform of the last coach a captain was busy with his pipe, and just as the captain passed Sergeant Bohman, something unexpected happened. Bohman jumped up as if he had been bitten by the snake, took a few zigzag paces to one side and yelled, 'Single file behind me!' at his platoon, and when the twelve of them were lined up behind him in a compact group the first blank shots clattered out from the other side of the railway line.

In more realistic circumstances the effect would have been catastrophic and most of the platoon would have been mown down on the spot, but as it was, the salvoes merely had a catastrophic effect on Sergeant Bohman's humour. He turned to his men yelling, 'Attack!' and he raced off like a bolting horse followed by eleven men. The only one left behind was Bill, but he was not wounded, just a little sleepy at worst. He put his rifle down and eased off his haversack and then crept carefully towards the spot where shortly beforehand the snake had been swaying like a flower in the wind.

It had disappeared, but he thought he could see a dark shadow gliding in under the bracken and he started kicking at the dry twigs. Then he heard an angry hissing and the gliding stopped and before he really caught on to what was happening the reptile had wrapped itself round one of his boots and emptied its venom into his trouser leg. It seemed exhausted afterwards and clung listlessly to his leg, so he took off his beret, slid it over the snake's head and pressed hard, so that the snake was caught between his index finger and his thumb, as if in a vice. He pulled at the head until its body let go of his leg and the part that was free lashed around in the air. When he tried to force it through the opening of his haversack it resisted violently, but eventually it grew tired and slid into the hole and he pushed down his beret with the snake's head inside until he could almost feel the bottom of the haversack. Then he let go and whipped his beret out like lightning and pressed down the lid and sat on it and all the time he could hear the snake writhing around at the bottom of the bag, looking for a way out. After a while it was all quiet inside and so he got up, laced up the haversack securely, slung it over his shoulder, grabbed his rifle and lumbered off after the others.

By the time he got to the little clearing, however, the battle was already over and all the dead and wounded were lined up listening to a lecture on strategy by Sergeant Bohman, who, in accordance with all the rules of strategy, ought to have been dead seven times over by now.

The heat was cascading down between the tree trunks and everybody was sweating profusely. There was not the slightest breath of a breeze and the pine needles were bending almost double. The haversacks had turned the soldiers into hunchbacks, the rifle-bands were burning hot, and Sergeant Bohman's words fell to earth with dull thuds and aroused not the slightest response, like a tap dripping. Bohman gazed up into the bulging greenery in search of some kind of inspiration, but found as little reaction there as in the sullen, sweaty faces of his platoon. There was a crunching noise on the path from the railway line and when he looked in that direction he saw Private 362 Stenberg ambling towards them. I don't much like that laddie, he thought, and when he had finished thinking he realized that he must have somehow paused in his speech and he hadn't the slightest idea what he'd been saying, and so he wished 362 would get a move on so that he could start telling him off before the pause became too long.

At last.

'Private 362's a bit on the late side,' he said. 'Private 362 hasn't been with us, I fancy – it's a long time since I last saw Private 362. Perhaps Private 362 has been chasing butterflies?' He paused for a moment for the laughs, or at least the smiles, but he didn't get either, and so he continued, somewhat confused: 'Private 362 hasn't been paying these manoeuvres the requisite – lovely word, that, requisite – the requisite attention, has he? It's Wednesday tonight, isn't it? That means the company has a late pass, doesn't it? Well, those who haven't benefited from the lessons we've learnt today can't expect to reap the benefits of a late pass. Can they now? As for Private 362, perhaps we could have a cosy little tête-à-tête when we get home? Right, lads, let's get buttoned up and brushed down and on parade in three minutes from now. Officer Cadet Svensson will get you lined up and ready. Is that clear?'

'Yes, Sarge.'

He breathed a sigh of relief and withdrew into the fir trees for a few moments' contemplation in the cool shade. That's the way to do it, he thought to himself, that's the way, brief and to the point, like a good soldier, not a syllable too much, straight to the point. He glanced at his watch, which was dangling from his wrist like a hot dumpling. The three minutes were up and the officer cadet yelled out, 'Ten-shun!' He listened as the heels clicked together, then he stepped out of the shadows and announced loudly: 'OK, I'll take over now.' Then, 'Platoon . . . to the left . . . quick . . . march.'

Boots hit the ground with a dull thud. The platoon marched over the railway line, up through the clearing, then glided on to the road leading down to the camp. Their legs were hidden in a cloud of dust and their rifles hung over their right shoulders like dead weights. Bill had ended up next to Matsson, and he drew his rifle-butt to one side and nudged him. 'Hey,' he half-whispered, 'you're coming with us tonight, aren't you? I've had a word with Irène.' 'Hmm,' muttered Matsson, 'is Irène going as well?' 'Mmm, nice bit of stuff,' said Bill. 'She's going all right, I'll . . .' Somebody at the back of the queue shouted, 'Cut out the chatter up there,' and the leading group swung round towards the camp and Sergeant Bohman dashed up to the front and bellowed, 'Platoon halt! Stand at ease!' Heels crunched on the gravel; somebody stumbled against a tree stump and swore; it was so hot that sweat was seeping through the soldiers' tunics and their shoes were white with dust and there was an acrid smell enveloping their bodies. They'd come to a halt outside barrack room twelve, a halt more like a silent swoon, and then everybody supported his rifle on his left hip and removed the vital mechanical bits before dispersing in listless groups around the living quarters.

Only Bill stayed behind. He was standing a few yards away from Sergeant Bohman, who was busy imparting to Officer Cadet Svensson a few tactical subleties, and he took the opportunity of wiping the sand off his rifle with his fingers. Then he grasped the straps of his haversack and gave it a couple of jerks. He heard some rasping sounds from inside, and a soft hissing noise a bit like a jet of steam. Then the animal settled down and Bill strode the short distance towards his superiors, clicked his heels and announced: 'Sarge, Private 362 Stenberg reporting.' Bohman looked up, his mouth betraying a somewhat irritated grimace. 'Oh, yes, Private 362,' he said, giving the officer cadet a cursory nod and withdrawing into the shadow cast by the barrack-room wall. Bill followed close on his heels and when the sergeant turned to look him over he was a step or two too close and did not look at all like someone who had committed a breach of discipline.

There was something insubordinate about his whole attitude and the sergeant was about to say something sarcastic, but before he managed to say a word Bill came out with: 'Sarge, yer'll never guess what I've found, something extra-special. Want a look?' He put his haversack on the ground and took another step too close, loosened one of the straps, suddenly turned it upside down – and there was the sound of something sliding down and then something black and terri-fying came slithering into the opening and the sergeant stepped backwards and hit himself against the wall. Bill sidled even closer and when he was right next to him he said: 'It's a little snake. I caught him not long ago on the hillside. My old man collects all sorts of snakes in bottles, he's got loads of 'em.'

The sergeant pressed himself back against the wall and the paint came off all over his tunic; his eyeballs looked very lonely in their vast white oceans and his fingers twitched nervously at his lanyard. 'I see,' he said, and his larynx swelled up so much he couldn't manage any more than this 'I see'.

The snake was thrashing about inside the haversack and the tiny bit sticking out of the top looked horrible and menacingly active. You could clearly see its head darting around against the cloth of the haversack; it was like standing on a jetty watching a fish swimming about in the water. It slid up towards the opening and now Bill's hands became cautious. He pressed the wriggling creature back inside and quickly secured the haversack. Then he slung it back over his shoulder, and all the time they could hear the snake writhing around violently in its prison.

'Well, that's how it is,' he said, and it sounded as if what he was saying now was a continuation of his snake show, a sort of blackmail, it occurred dimly to the sergeant, but he felt altogether too shattered to put up any resistance. 'Thing is,' said Bill, 'I'm feeling a bit tired and I wouldn't mind giving the drill a miss for today. All that marching about this week has been a bit much for me, and then we've got the night off, of course, and that might be a bit much as well.'

The sergeant peeled himself off the wall. He stepped forward into the sunlight and when he turned to face Bill the sun streamed all over him and shone through his ears, making them look red and inflamed, and his face, which was in a shimmering half-shade, looked pale in an unhealthy, almost obscene way. Give him his potty, thought Bill, but Sergeant Bohman leaned forward over his shoes. 'Yes, it's your night off,' he said, almost inaudibly, then he turned awkwardly and lumbered off towards the sergeants' mess. The sun shone straight down on his little hunched back and the paint from the wall formed bright red patches on his tunic where his shoulderblades stuck out like the bow of an archer; you might have been forgiven for thinking he'd been crucified and the nails had been driven in just there.

Bill strode into the cool darkness of the barrack room. He stomped rather noisily over to his bed, flung down his rifle and his haversack and collapsed on the bed. The windows were closed and vague, primitive aromas were being squeezed out of the fifty-two beds. After a while he fell fast and sweatily asleep and when he woke up he realized from the noise in the barrack room and the buzz of activity outside that dinner was over and it must therefore be just after twelve o'clock.

Then he remembered Irène and the café, and he lay dozing for a while longer, just thinking about her. He drifted off and started dreaming about her, and in the dream Irène and Sergeant Bohman were sitting on a seat by the golf course, and he crept silently up on them, holding a hand-grenade in his hand, ready to throw. He couldn't decide when he was near enough to throw it, though, and while he was crawling around the grenade became burning hot and in the end it started hissing and then blew up in his hand. It didn't hurt, though, but when he looked down he was horrified to see the shrapnel in his hand had turned into wriggling little snakes.

He turned ice-cold but at the same time sweat was pouring off him. He woke up and crawled out of bed. His haversack was lying on the floor. It was ominously quiet inside and he picked it up carefully, as if it were packed full of explosives, and put it in his locker, stood his rifle on top of it and closed the door quickly. Then he heard the duty officer approaching to inspect the barrack room and so he squeezed behind his locker and when the danger was past he crept out quietly and managed to get to the edge of the woods without being seen. Then he ran through the woods along a path covered in pine needles, his heart pounding and his hands clammy with sweat. He suddenly remembered the dream he'd had not long before, and the memory was so intense he looked down at his hands. They were just as normal, however, big and a bit sunburnt and covered in blue veins. He felt rather embarrassed and slowed down and returned to normal. Cold. Calm. When he got to the café he would be absolutely normal, he thought to himself: 'Well, if it isn't Irène,' he'd say, 'sitting here enjoying herself, and waiting for somebody, eh? It couldn't just possibly be me, could it?'

4

The ceiling fan was humming away like a confused bumble-bee. Cool air was being flushed down into the room, watering the burning atmosphere. By the one-armed bandit was a rickety little table with a marble top and a bunch of dead, yellow dahlias in a dirty vase with a giraffe neck; from time to time when the breeze came swooping down from the ceiling the flowers would start jerking about as if in their death throes, and a smell of stale water came seeping out of the wide mouth of the vase.

They were the only ones in the café, apart from the waitress lounging about behind the bar, gazing at her come-dancing ankles in a mirror that was so covered in dust you could have mistaken it for one big lump of reflective fluff. Now and then she put her head on one side and stared through dense eyelashes at the couple by the window, and there was something both indulgent and attentive in the way she held her head; but when she found she couldn't hear one iota of what was being said, she grew a bit annoyed and returned to contemplating her come-dancing legs, as far up as her taut knees by now.

It was dusty on the road outside and when a car roared past the cloud of dust hovered motionless over the road and you could be forgiven for thinking the road itself had just broken wind. He thought of pointing that out to her as he made the cracked cream jug spit out its last thin drops into her mud-like coffee, but then he heard the waitress humming a tune from *Black Fantasy* and he looked right through Irène into the dark depths of the room.

At first what he saw was a hazy version of himself in the fuzzy surface of the mirror, and beside him the back of Irène's bronzed, mobile neck. Suddenly she was wiped away, and instead it was the waitress, who was called Vera and was very interesting to dance with, whose fleshy form superimposed itself in the mirror. She stood on tiptoe and the slight creaking noise reached as far as their table, and her skirt worked its way up above her knees and he thought his eyes had met hers in the mirror and he felt very passionate. He found it somehow uplifting and exciting to be able to sit in front of a girl who maybe liked him, or in any case thought he was a bit of a devil, and at the same time to be undressing another girl with his eyes over her shoulder. Then the telephone screeched angrily in the adjacent room and Vera gave way to Irène in

32

the mirror. She made her way casually behind the bar, and all the time there was a sort of unbroken line linking her eyes and Bill's. She slunk round the door jamb and into the room where the telephone was in such an abandoned and sensuous way that the line wasn't bitten off by the door jamb but stretched itself as far as the telephone and didn't snap until he heard her smoky and somewhat drawling voice say: 'Hi there, Åke!' Then she kicked the door so hard it slammed into its frame with a loud bang and then it was absolutely still and quiet in the big café and Bill and Irène were alone, all alone. Very much alone.

Irène was facing the window and could feel the dull heat of the day creeping in through the opening and filling her limbs with deadening, hollow lassitude, and as she sat there in silence, bouncing her gaze like a ball against the bulky, grey, back wall of the station building on the other side of the road, it suddenly struck her that the whole of her life, or at any rate the whole of this day's life, was just as indescribably grey and miserable and she yearned desperately for something which could sprinkle blood on to the greyness. She crossed her legs, and although she knew he could see nothing through the marble table top, she didn't bother to pull down her dress; she ran her finger along the seam of her stocking and thought really intensely about what it had been like that morning, but the heady feeling didn't come back. It was silent and dead. She closed her eyes and let her hand glide up her leg, over the crest of her knee and up along her trembling thigh, and when she hooked herself on to the thought that it was his hand, things began to get more exciting, but then she opened her eyes and saw him staring over her shoulder and the grey lassitude started pumping into her once more.

She raised her cup of sticky black coffee with little white islands of cream swimming about here and there on the surface, and then she remembered how, in the old days, she always used to deliver cream here in the mornings, and then a little sentimental thought of home sweet home came bubbling up from the depths and deep down in the vaults exquisite little mushrooms of angst began to sprout. She slammed her cup down on the brown-rimmed saucer and decided firmly and definitely: I'm going home today. I couldn't care less about his damned party. I'll pay and leave.

She turned her head to shout for the waitress, but just then the phone rang in the kitchen and she heard the girl shuffling off and thought: I suppose I'd better wait till she comes back. She heard her answer in that unpleasant, rasping voice of hers and she could tell from the caressing tone of voice it was a man and when the door slammed shut she realized it would take some time and she thought: I'm going even so. I couldn't give a toss. She pushed back her chair a little and took a comb out of her handbag, which was hanging by its strap over her shoulder, very fashionable that was, and started combing her hair very energetically. All the time she was looking out of the window and avoiding his eyes, but then she heard him moving a cup on the table and she looked down, by mistake really, and then he thrust his gaze into her and she became hot somewhere inside and she knew straight away it was no use.

Nothing was any use. She gave herself to him, as she was sitting there, with her eyes, and his eyes left her no peace. He fumbled around with the fingers of his broad hand in the breast pocket of his tunic and fished out a crumpled cigarette, which he stuck carelessly into his mouth, and then he stretched out his hand for the matches, but the hand floated past, then shot up and landed just above her plunging neckline and he stroked her breasts with the back of his hand once or twice. She daren't respond, as she thought somebody might be watching, and so she pushed his hand away in slight annoyance and felt a trace of resistance welling up inside her and decided to offer some resistance, a bit of encouraging resistance through her self-effacement.

'Hey,' she said, spreading out her voice like a fan, 'givvus a fag, a whole one,' and she tried to sound very sophisticated and very covetous, although she rarely smoked, in fact. When she'd got it she put it very cheekily in her mouth and when he gave her a light she breathed in until she could almost feel the smoke turning round at the bottom of her lungs and then she blew it out very expertly through the left side of her mouth. He kept the flame burning in front of her face, as if he wanted to illuminate her, and she closed her right eye so that the flame was magnified many times over and so that it scorched away a large heart-shaped part of his face.

'You're playing with me,' he said, and looked very much aroused and he grinned; he grinned so broadly his cigarette fell out of his mouth and into the mud at the bottom of his coffee-cup where it drowned with a hissing sigh. Then they both burst out laughing and she felt almost a little flattered at the fact that he was laughing with her, and she grew warm and gay, almost light-headed, she thought. As she sat there in the silent café with a man she barely knew, smoking in mature and thoughtful fashion, she could feel herself growing hot all over and knew something special was happening. All the greyness and dullness congealed and sank down into the cellar vaults and smothered the mushrooms and she thought, almost triumphantly: something's happening to me. Something's happening to us. She picked up her comb again and combed out a little brown curl over her forehead and she looked out under the curl and through the thickening cigarette smoke and into him and said: 'It'll be great tonight, eh? Is Donald Duck coming as well?' 'Yes, Matsson's coming as well,' he said. 'Huh, that bastard,' she said, gasping a little, and she started to laugh, a throaty laugh in between puffs.

'Now listen,' he said, getting up from his chair and going round the table and coming up close to her and leaning over her and breathing into her hair. Then his lips crept up to her ear and he bit her quite gently on the lobe and said in a half-whisper: 'You know just what you've got to do, OK, with all the things and that, OK?' And she nodded very obediently and nicely and then she turned her face up towards his and let her tongue glide over his lips and thrust out her chest so that her breasts stuck out like little lemons and as she lowered her elbow she felt it land right in her cup. They heard it crack and the bits scattered all over the table and he whispered rather quickly: 'I'll fix that with Vera later,' and then he pressed his body down towards her and her lips were thrust back against her teeth and they kissed until her lips slid up against her gums and their teeth ground against each other.

Then she struggled up from her chair and she felt so weak and so dizzy she couldn't stand up straight and then at the height of her confusion she felt a cool shaft of fear injected into her heat. Vera, she thought to herself anxiously, him and Vera, and she suddenly remembered how cold he'd been before the phone rang. Him and Vera, she thought, but then he came and rinsed that thought away and said: 'Your train'll be here any minute, you'd better go out.' He brought her her suitcase and just as he was going to give it to her, he noticed the marigolds dangling from the handle, and he asked with a little undertone of suspicion: 'Where'd you get the flowers from, then?'

A little devil came climbing up his ladder and she said cheekily, so cheekily it sounded absolutely credible: 'I got them from that sergeant of yours, Bohman's his name I think, this morning.'

He believed her and his face hardened a little and he pressed the case vigorously into her hand: 'Oh, that shitbag,' he said, and she was a bit sorry she'd said it, just a little bit, but it was much too late. They were already on their way to the door, and he had his arm round her shoulders, but as they went out she suddenly realized she was on her own. Bill was still standing in the doorway, and when she turned, slightly surprised, he bowed elaborately, pouted and said: 'We'll be there at seven, OK? Get things sorted out, OK?'

Then, to her disappointment, he was gone, and she crossed the road all by herself, feeling quite miserable, and she came to the little square in front of the station. She could hear the shrill voices of some old women coming from the station building near the lilac hedge around the doctor's garden, and when she looked she saw her mother and the old girl from next door and she realized they were going to catch the train, the same train as she was, and she scampered over the square and just managed to shut the lavatory door behind her as the voices of the old women oozed out over the square.

Inside the café Vera was leaning over the bar, scratching her breasts nonchalantly. 'I thought you were going to run off without paying, sir,' she said, and let the tip of her tongue peer out from its grotto. 'Well, you thought wrong, didn't you?' said Bill, coming to a halt directly in front of her. He leaned over the bar and drummed his fingers on the glass top. There were lots of packets of sweets lying there, looking washed out in the heat. 'Real soldier's hands,' she said, not sounding as if she expected to get paid. He jumped up, then sat down on the bar counter. 'Mind you don't fall down,' she said almost politely, 'that'd really put the cat among the pigeons.' 'You don't say,' he said, creeping a little closer. 'You mark my words,' she said, 'you'd awaken the bloody dead all right.'

He vaulted over the counter and stood beside her. 'You'd better not let the old lady catch you here when she comes,' she said, not sounding all that concerned. 'When will that be?' he asked, not sounding all that concerned either. 'Next train from town,' she said, sounding even less concerned, 'four o'clock.' 'Well, what do you know,' he said, looking at the adjacent room. 'Good news?' he asked, nodding at the telephone. 'Huh,' she said, and she swallowed and seemed almost embarrassed. 'Never mind,' he said, taking hold of her under her chin, and she shuddered and looked out of the window to see if anyone was watching. But the road outside was deserted, and she nestled up to him and he bent down and kissed her lightly. Then he worked himself loose and there was something harsh and abandoned in his voice as he looked down at her and said: 'Let's go in and make a phone call, OK?'

As he kicked at the door and it slid into its frame like a big, pale shadow, he heard the train puffing into the station, its brakes squealing, but he had no idea why he should think about that.

5

Hang on tight, she thought, pulling the door closed by its cool handle. Hot, stuffy air was floating around the carriage, and she stood motionless for ages, staring down into the cup of the spittoon. She kicked it away under a seat and then she heard footsteps shuffling across the wooden platform at the end of the carriage and she felt a flutter in her chest on the left side and she held tightly on to the handle, almost dragging the door over its threshold. The steps had stopped. She stopped breathing and tried not to listen to the little noises streaming in through the open windows and then she sensed someone breathing in through the crack in the door, a foot scraped along the wooden floor and she thought she could hear a hand stroking the outside of the door – she was pressed so tightly against the door that she could almost feel a cool touch on her skin. Hang on tight, she thought intensely – as intensely as possible, given the heat – they mustn't come in, not here, not now.

A door slammed at the other end of the carriage and she looked through the murky glass into the compartment on the other side. A plump face peered round the door like a sweaty orange, then came the rest to complete the picture in the door frame. It was a heated-up youth in military uniform, apparently one of the non-combatants. She didn't recognize him, but it occurred to her that he probably recognized her because there were so few girls in the camp and those that were there no doubt figured in many an indecent dream every night, and it struck her she must look silly standing there as if she were dancing with the door and so she opened it and stepped out.

There was no one on the wooden platform of course and she was able to make fun of herself, although she didn't laugh too loudly. She looked down at the station platform and there was no sign of life apart from the station-master gaping at the clock like an angry bulldog, and the clock was gaping back at him and shifting its minute hand in a series of small, irritating jerks. The train they were waiting for from the direction of town was a goods train and was rarely on time; it whistled shrilly somewhere in the far distance and it occurred to her that if she ran ahead now to the first carriage, she'd be able to see into the café.

She didn't really know why she should want to do that, but she thought for a while, for quite a long while, it was so that she could see Bill and have somebody to wave to. Then she realized, although she didn't let on about it to herself, although she grabbed hold of the lips of the person who wanted to tell her about it, that she wanted to see Bill sitting alone by the window, or Vera alone by the window and Bill on his way out, and although she didn't say anything about that to herself, there was a pinching feeling as if someone were squeezing away at her heart with a small pair of tweezers and she could feel something like angst inside her because she might not be able to see either of them, or both of them together. But she was more curious than afraid and she sailed over the wooden platform and pushed open the door to the next carriage. It was exactly as if she'd opened up a dam, for just as she pushed at the door the shrill voices of the old women came flooding out in a yellow stream and blended with the vitriolic noise of rifle shots spraying over from the woods. The old hags, she thought quickly, and drew back, slamming the door in front of her, maybe too hard, she thought, and she almost decided to open it again and close it more gently so as to demonstrate that she wasn't angry. Just then, however, the goods train came rushing past, the engine snorting down its nose, and their own train started shaking. Then it set off with a jerk and she forgot all about the door and leaned contentedly, although there was nothing to be contented about, against the sign saying 'no smoking' and watched the station building, the station-master, the seats, everything gliding past as if they were on a conveyer belt.

Even though she held a knife to her throat to prevent herself from saying anything, she knew that she'd have to look at the café as they went past and when she did so all she saw was a white curtain flapping outside the window like a white handkerchief. And although she thought as energetically as one bites into a nut: what a pity I couldn't see anything, her throat actually whispered, despite the knife more or less shaving her skin: they weren't there, neither Bill nor Vera, it was empty and they weren't there, they'd gone off together. The pair of them, Bill and Vera.

Then the knife blade cut into her whispering throat and severed her vocal cords and she shrugged somewhat apologetically, although there was nothing to apologize for, and she thought stubbornly: what a pity I couldn't see anything. Then she thought about the curtain flapping away outside the window and she watched it fluttering in a broader and broader arc until she suddenly realized there was a cold breeze and she looked up in some confusion and saw the train had already penetrated the forest. It was shadowy and cool and the sun was bouncing between the trees in restless flashes. When they passed a scorched slope where a forest fire had gobbled up the trees it brightened up, but then the shadows returned. She did a balancing act over the swaying plate linking the two coaches and just as she was about to open the door to her own carriage she noticed that one of the iron gates was swaying in time with the movement of the whole train and unconsciously she linked the swaying gate with the flapping curtain at the café, and when she leaned over the heavy iron gate and slowly closed it she was in fact standing, although she hadn't yet realized it, outside the window and was pushing the tulle curtain back inside the window with her shaking fingers; all the time her grey eyes were gazing restlessly through the tree trunks and she could see the stuffy café, the one-armed bandit, the rickety chairs, the stained tables, the bar counter with its streaky glass surface and the half-open door into the kitchen, and although she could clearly hear the slight whistling sound of the wheels against the curve in the tracks, the faint murmur of passionate voices drifted out through the window and burned into her insides, as if someone had lit a match inside her chest, and she recognized the voices, Vera's a bit shrill and rasping and Bill's booming and dominant.

When she realized that, when the knife blade had withdrawn from her throat and the voice said as clearly as if on the radio: where were Bill and Vera, what were they up to, why weren't they there? she held tightly on to the gate and leaned out over the edge until she could see the faint, well-oiled glow of the rails under the step. A desperate thought forced its way into her brain and started to pound away at the anvil like a sledge-hammer and she leaned way out over the edge of the gate so that her feet lost contact with the floor and her centre of gravity was somewhere aft of her midriff. Sometimes when the rails stretched round a curve she was thrust even further out, so that she could almost see the whirring wheel under the bottom of the carriage, and all the time the impudent, stubborn little thought was hammering away inside her and she remembered, almost as if she were watching it on film, everything that had happened in the café not so very long ago. And the thought was saying so emphatically and regularly and monotonously, like the thud of a horse's hoofs on a pavement: you show him, just you show him, make him regret it, and although she often told herself, as often as she was alone, very emphatically, that she was not in love with him, not at all, jealousy was flaring up inside her like a shooting star now and she felt a wild desire for revenge and it was so easy, so straightforward, just let go with her fingers and slide down headfirst on to the step and then the big bash and then nothing.

The pain in her left side gushed up to her lips and turned into a bitter little goodbye-smile and she felt she was very close to goodbye, but all of a sudden the forest gave way and the sun took over and a very flat, extensive plain with closely cropped grass and thin cows, and then a crossing with its stupid barriers down, and behind them two boys on their bikes gaping vacantly up at the train, chewing away, and there was the girl who was in fact herself standing all of a sudden beside her and pulling her back from the gate and smoothing back her hair, adjusting her belt and trying to rub away the line of soot running across the middle of her coat like a hoop round a barrel. She rubbed away like mad and tried to think about the new coat she would buy when she could afford it and then, as the train slunk up to the two-storey department stores in the miniature metropolis and she could vaguely see people buying and selling through the luxurious shop-windows, these things and the two boys on their bikes helped her to shunt the wagons carrying subconscious freight from the day's activities into the tunnel of her subconscious mind. She stood there nonchalantly for a while, absent-mindedly counting the stations still to go and thinking about what she would do when she got there and then she turned just a little hesitantly and walked slowly arm in arm with the girl who was herself into her carriage.

The young man in military uniform, who was corpulent and looked like a conchie, had taken a seat close to the door and seemed to be looking for company: the moment she walked in he looked up at her with a look that was pretty serious stuff coming from a young man as fat as he was. She was ready to fight him off, though; he had no chance of looking her in the eye and so, oozing desire, his eyes caressed the outline of her body and she was defenceless and it was far from pleasant – she just squirmed about in the doorway and looked desperately for some sheltered place where she could sit down. Although she wasn't looking straight at him, she could see from the corner of her eye that he was gaping open-mouthed at her and baring his teeth and then his legs began to twitch and rather clumsily he got to his feet, but he managed it even so, and then he said, embarrassed and stammering and obviously inexperienced (and now she realized he wasn't dangerous any more): 'Er, hello . . . er, perhaps . . . maybe the lady would . . . sort of . . . like to sit down . . . to sit down here, perhaps?'

That gave her the excuse to spin around, energetically surprised, and look him straight in the eye, or at least as far as she could, because she knew that young men who stare at you like vacuum cleaners and talk in a series of pauses are about as dangerous as grass snakes. Stupid, harmless grass snakes, she thought to herself, totally without deference, and she tickled the young man's eyelashes with her generous looks. 'Thank you,' she said, nodding slightly with her head and neck like they do in films, a sort of bow that starts round about your bum. Then she sighed, a sigh he could interpret however he liked, let's hear it again, however he liked, and slouched down on to the seat and all the time she was looking frankly and not really very politely into the young man's phlegmatic, Lassie-eyes; but as time passd they went out like an extinguished searchlight and an impeccably even blush settled over his face like a deep meat-red handkerchief. Aroused, she continued to look him straight in the eye, until he lifted his hand from his knee and charged his gaze by looking at his watch.

That made her realize he was boring, and when the young man had plucked up enough courage to launch a new attack she'd already turned to the window, displaying her profile decoratively against it and allowing the telegraph poles to waltz past her nonchalant eyes. The train had chugged into the small station in the little metropolis and it soon slowed right down and the fence that had been running alongside for ages let go and a few redundant goods wagons in a siding took over its role in limiting the view. She counted them all as they entered the window-frame, not because she was interested in goods wagons but mainly as an excuse to stop thinking, a very common excuse among passengers. Eventually the wagons came to an end and the train glided as slowly as possible into the shadow of an enormous shed squatting on its left and effectively turning all the windows on the left-hand side into mirrors. The young man seized his chance and plunged his gaze into the mirror and tried to grab her with it and eventually managed it, because she thought it was exciting and because he looked much bolder and much more experienced in the grimy glass. She almost started to regard him as a worthy opponent, one you must defend yourself against, until someone flung open a door in the shed and the mirror cracked. Then she had to look at him to see whether it really was him – and it was, none other than him – and she closed her eyes in disappointment as the train slowly moved away, all the mirrors cracked, and she could feel his hairy gaze struggling over his eyelids.

She then abandoned herself to her daydreams, the little brook of memories from earlier in the day. What's Bill up to? she thought, and then Vera appeared on a lead behind him, of course, because she was so busy shoving the memory of Bill and Vera into the sack of oblivion that she found it hard to think about anything else. Now somebody had suddenly emptied the sack all over the floor and whoops, all the things that ought to have been lying down at the bottom of the pile of memories were now right at the top, roaring with laughter. When she began rummaging through the pile for something more pleasant, the confounded thing rolled out of her fingers, and when she finally tried to run away from the empty sack and its contents and to smash open windows into other worlds, it flew after her like a ball and bounced its way into her head – and then she was beaten once and for all and she decided it would be diplomatic to think it through, Bill and Vera, to think coolly and clearly and see it as it really was, just as it really was.

Then she heard a knocking on her eyelids and she realized it was him knocking and she opened her closed doors ever so slightly but then she flung them wide open because it had suddenly dawned on her that he could help her. She smiled at him in that helpless way she'd learnt in order to make people think she was begging for help rather than flirting, and in the end little becks of sympathy started trickling over towards her. That gave her renewed strength, as if she'd taken a stiff drink, and a little feeling of revenge which shot up like a sunflower took root inside her when she thought about him, the man sitting opposite her, and herself as a pair, and placed Bill in the aisle as a passive observer, a dogged observer standing there like a statue. She thought so intensely about that statue of Bill that she could eventually see him there, with his furious expression and blotches on the top of his head that had nothing to do with pigeons but with jealousy, standing just beside her.

Bill and Vera, the thought came slinking up to her, but it wasn't so red hot, not so hurtful, because she wasn't being faithful herself any more, because she was betraying him. The feeling of jealousy was toned down and gave way to the intoxicating sensation of triumph that almost always follows every time one overcomes jealousy by being unfaithful oneself.

The young man started to read a whole novel or at the very least a short story from the promise in her eyes and his eyes acquired a glow like a newly iced-over lake, and in the end he started speaking, all by himself; he was so keen to tie her down with his words that he missed out all the full stops and commas, but eventually he remembered a question mark and stopped dead to wait for her answer. And she answered him, not because the question interested her but because she convinced herself the relationship became deeper and less innocent that way. She started to tell him about herself a little, but coquettishly, and he told her his name and she was so keen to deepen their relationship and make it more dangerous that she asked him to write his name and number and company on a bit of paper, and he dived down after the opportunity like a pearl fisher and asked her for something to write on. She was evidently a very willing and cooperative pearl: she lifted her fancy bag on to her knee and let the zip open its mouth wide and he was there like a shot with his groping, rather suggestive hands, which went on a little improvised and badly concealed journey of discovery around the bag. The young man was very enthusiastic, indeed, almost dangerously enthusiastic, and she decided to break off his journey of discovery as tactfully as she could and to give him a pen and a piece of paper. She could feel it in her knees that the invitation to give her his address was a bit crude, but she wanted to have the bit of paper as a sort of receipt to prove something had actually happened, a receipt she could take out and show herself, and him as well, when she was feeling like a dose of revenge again. But the young man, whose name was Berndt Claeson and was more of a combatant than one might have imagined, was feeling like Livingstone on his way to the source of the river. And she was so keen to get the receipt written out she was most surprised when a pair of well-filled, high-sided boots supporting a well-darned black funeral coat suddenly and brutally burst into view on her left.

'Good afternoon, Irène,' said Maria Sandström, planting a gigantic exclamation mark in the proceedings. The young man looked as though he'd bitten a stallion and tried to effect a calm and unobtrusive retreat from the compromising situation. His hands seemed to be three-stone weights with flashing lights and the retreat was both clumsy and obvious. Maria Sandström observed the retreating forces with merciless zeal until the young man had managed to withdraw to neutral ground.

Then she slumped down on to the seat beside Irène and Irène's hands slid out of the cool depths of the bag, and she swung her head round slowly like a giant crane and planted her gaze on her mother's face at the base of her bulging forehead. 'Good afternoon,' she said almost nonchalantly, and placed a little question mark like a pair of scissors on the seat between them.

Maria Sandström moved closer, until she was almost pressing Irène into the window-frame with her enormous shadow, and Irène slowly turned as pale as an anemone and tried to tear her eyes loose from her mother's forehead but the glue held and she couldn't get away. Maria Sandström thrust forward her swollen bosom and her yellow, distorted face crept closer to Irène and she opened her mouth to let the words out and a little puff of bad breath drifted into Irène's nose and swelled up inside it. Something nauseous started bubbling up inside her throat and she flopped back against the back-rest in a sort of helpless trance. And all the time she could feel the young man's astonished eyes biting into her skin. He mustn't know, she thought, getting a grip on herself and trying to concentrate, he mustn't know she's mine, yes, mine.

She was so intensely and violently ashamed and it was a double-edged shame aimed at both her mother and him. He mustn't know, the thought kept hammering away, and at the same time she sharpened the dagger of her resistance and placed it between her teeth. When Maria Sandström opened her mouth and the words gushed forth accompanied by poisonous clouds of breath, she was overcome by disgust and that stimulated her resistance, her desire to get rid of her. She let her gaze slide down into her mother's eyes and there was unspoken but harsh frankness in it and she thought: I've nothing to be ashamed of, I've done nothing, there wasn't anything going on, if that's what you're thinking. That's what she thought and she was confident because she knew it was true and so the feeling of shame, of half shame, lost its suffocating grip and a quite new emotion, something more than resistance, hatred, in fact, sat down on the seat beside the half of the shame that was still there.

She's got to go: the thought was red hot and the dagger was trembling between her teeth and the silent hatred slunk out in all directions, and the more she thought about what it had been like beforehand, the hotter she felt inside and the hatred poured forth, because she was ashamed of him and because she

47

was disgusted and because she knew, she knew with transparent clarity, that nothing had happened, that she was innocent, and that she had nothing to set against Bill and Vera. Jealousy came pouring out of the hole in her sack of oblivion and she felt a twinge as it arrived and it was as if she had been forced to face the truth, and when her mother's words were spat out into the compartment like sticky bullets that fastened on to the windows and seats, shining away, she let all the feelings that came pouring out take possession of her and lead her to the narrow frontier where the meadows of reason and reflection give way to the morass of emotions, and she experienced that little feeling of absurd triumph when she crossed over the border and thought: I don't give a damn. She didn't give a damn whether he knew the old bag was her mother or that the sticky bullets of her words were chattering on about her having run away from home, and that she didn't behave like decent people should, that what she needed was a good thrashing, and that she ought to be ashamed of herself. No, she couldn't care less about what was being said, only about who was saying it, and she left the frontier a long way behind her and she became intensely cool and clear-headed and knew how she was going to do it. When the young man awkwardly and timidly wormed his way out of his seat and slipped into the toilet, she knew she was going to do it.

She got to her feet quite slowly, lingering, like a tiger before it makes its leap, and all the time she was holding on to her mother with her gaze, and when she was standing in front of her, quite tall and calm with her hands in her coat pockets, her mother realized for the first time just how wide and impassable the gap was between them, and her words dripped out in fewer and fewer drops until in the end silence flowed down from the ceiling and the only sound to be heard was the monotonous clickety-click protests from the railway lines. Then Irène thrust one foot forward and transferred her weight to it, drew her hands up to her sides, and said clearly and without a trace of nerves: 'Right, madame, time to go!'

48

'Oh, I'm going, am I?' said Maria Sandström, releasing an evil-smelling little puff of air as she got up from her seat. 'So, my own daughter tells me it's time I went, does she?' 'That's right,' said Irène, and there was ice in her voice, 'yes indeed, madame, it's time to go. Do pass on greetings.' The old woman's hands shot up towards Irène's throat but stopped at her coat collar, took hold of it and twisted it violently as she hissed like an angry little burst of steam: 'You'll regret this, my girl, regret, regret. You bitch.' Then she pushed her away so hard that she nearly fell, turned awkwardly and slunk off in silence towards the door.

In the doorway, just as the clatter of the train came gushing over her, she felt a vice-like grip on her arm just above the elbow, and when she half-turned she saw an enemy glaring down at her bitterly. Then she was afraid for the first time and she half-whispered entreatingly: 'Come on, now!' But nobody was listening to her and Irène forced her out on to the wooden platform and slammed the door behind her. Her face was red hot and her voice shrill and excited, as in a hunted animal. 'What was that you said I was, eh?' she said, tightening her grip on her upper arm. 'What am I, eh?'

The train was cutting its way straight through a ridge and there were big piles of golden sand on the right-hand side. Then came the forest, with sunlight glittering between the trunks. She stared vacantly over her mother's shoulder and into the trees and she could feel her grip tightening, without her actually doing anything about it, and then the sun was shining straight into her eyes, forcing her to screw them up. They were crossing a clearing and she could hear a whinnying from a big, black horse grazing there; she watched him set off galloping after the train and looked down at the fence running alongside the track merely because the horse was galloping along it, and then when he couldn't keep up any longer she took back her eyes and she saw something which made her start trembling deep down inside. She looked down at her mother and afterwards she knew it would never have happened if only her mouth, her mother's mouth, which she saw in appalling close-up and which she would never forget – the rubbery skin around her toothless mouth, the elastic bands of her lips, the jelly-like tongue swaying back and forth in its hole – if only it hadn't exposed itself and the word, the word in reply to her question, hadn't been sent on its way by that slimy tongue.

When she heard it, it was as if she had been swept off her feet by a wave and her hands stretched out and her legs and feet banged hard into her mother's so that her mother staggered back against the gate, but when she put her hands behind her to stop her falling against the iron of the gate, there was no gate there and she managed to twist the upper part of her body round in astonished horror before she fell with arms outstretched like a diver towards the gravel of the railway embankment. Her legs, which had hung on doggedly to the platform, turned sluggishly in surprise and followed the upper part of her body and while her body was lowered bit by bit towards the embankment her feet still hung on stubbornly to the step, until they too were flung out from the train as the carriage swung round a curve.

Then the train burst out into a plain and a young man clearing a verge with a scythe put the scythe to one side and waved at her with his colourful, snuff-stained handkerchief. She watched him and she saw the whole plain with its luxuriant, clover-filled meadows and apathetic cows and a red-painted cottage with a glittering glass conservatory and a cracked chimney, and she saw it all with vacant, dead eyes. She suddenly felt sick and she whipped open the door and came back in on shaky, unsteady feet. The young man was sitting with his back towards her and he looked round at her as she came in and she was very grateful for that. She shoved open the toilet door, then pushed home the bolt with trembling fingers. She poured water into the basin and took out a handkerchief, soaked it, and bathed her inflamed face with it. Straight away she felt a little cooler and a little calmer, and she tried looking in the mirror and she said slowly and persuasively to herself: keep calm, calm, calm, and she felt a sort of indifferent, casual calmness take possession of her. She took her powder compact out of her pocket and toned down the shiny parts of her face.

As she put the compact away her hand brushed against the bit of paper on which Bill had written down instructions for her, and she took it out and read it – which bus she should take from the station, where she should get off, where the cottage was, and where to find everything in it. She read it casually and apathetically, glanced at her watch and saw she would soon be there, then she got up and fetched her case and went out on to the platform and all the time she was wondering if she was dreaming. At the station the guard punched her ticket and closed the gate behind her and all the time she was wondering if she was dreaming. Then she walked past the next carriage and saw Agda Morin's flabby face glowering at her through the grimy window and then she knew she wasn't dreaming; all the time as she walked towards the exit she could feel her gaze X-raying her back and she tried to walk steadily and assuredly, even though she knew she wasn't dreaming. When she walked through the waiting room and her heels echoed all around her and the gaze at her back lost its sting, she started to think about something else, intensely and to the exclusion of every other thought. All the time she was walking along the scorching street to the simmering cauldron of a bus that was coughing away at the square, she was thinking of something else. All the time she was thinking about someting else, and all the time she was repeating to herself what she had to do, just like a diver sinking down into the depths.

6

There was a faint humming noise in the room. A cool sigh was rustling through the trees. A fly was drowning in a vase. A bumble-bee was buzzing against a cream jug. The wall clock was wheezing and indicated half past two. The sun streamed in through the lilac bush. The window was open and squeaking against its hook. There was a steeple of clean cups on the kitchen table and a tower of clean saucers. A sponge cake was sliced up on a plate. The coffee-pot was hissing away on the hob.

He stood up and took a few tentative steps towards the closed door, then went over and stood right next to the door jamb. Voices were droning on inside a bit like a tired bumble-bee. Although he tried to stretch his ears and poke them through the crack in the door, all that reached them was a faint buzz which occasionally sharpened into a little point which gave him a prick. He withdrew cautiously. There was a creaking under the lino but in the relative silence it sounded like a Mauser shot. Nobody out there was hit, though. Relieved, he lay down on the sofa and stared up at the ceiling, which bulged in a series of gentle waves.

He traced the cracks in the ceiling paper with his eyes and tried to ignite a smile on his lips. He ought to smile, he wanted to smile next door to danger. The smile came forth shakily with an unsteady flame, and as he stretched himself out as far as the sofa would allow he thought: I'm not afraid. Not a bit. Just come on in. Even so, he knew he was shaking inside, and his fear was dripping down in black beads.

Now it seemed as if the voices were starting to move towards the kitchen door. He tried to stay calm and cool as he lay stretched out, and tried to convince himself he was imagining it all and that Vera would no doubt keep him away. To be on the safe side, though, he sat up and estimated the distance to the window. Now it was all quiet again outside and he assumed Vera had managed to convince Åke, who was an assistant at Larsson's general store, that old Mrs Blomgren was lying on the sofa snoring and in no circumstances must be disturbed. That was actually his idea, for just as Vera was sitting on his knee buttoning up her blouse somebody had come into the café and shouted for her. They could hear, both of them, that it was Åke.

'Don't let the cat out of the bag,' he'd said, 'just make sure he doesn't come in here. Get rid of him. Tell him it's old Mrs Blomgren, tell him what the hell you like.' 'Aha, m'lad,' said Vera, 'you're scared. A big strong boy like you,' she said, tugging at his ear. 'Nearly as strong as Åke.' Then Åke had shouted again, and they heard him drumming on the counter like an eager woodpecker. 'Go on,' he whispered anxiously and a little threateningly, and she'd looked at him as she was fastening the top buttons of her blouse, just as if she were looking straight through him. 'Are you hoarse, eh?' she said, a bit too loudly, he thought, and she slipped away from his sweaty hands and the situation was so familiar to him – he knew he was being left behind by an enemy. Someone who had been conquered but was picking herself up from the pain of defeat and was now putting up some resistance for the first time. He could see that in the muscles of her face, which were slowly tightening, like when you are getting ready to shoot a catapult, after the necessary laxness demanded by passion. He knew it was only fear for her own skin that would prevent this departing enemy from betraying him.

His fear continued to drip and he lay listening to it just as you listen to a dripping tap in the great silence of the night. Needless to say, he didn't have the courage to get up and turn it off. He thought of a convenient way out, which was in fact a cleverly disguised piece of cowardice: it's only imagination, that business of a dripping tap; and his cowardice made him go even further than is usual in cases like that as he thought: no doubt the house doesn't even have running water.

Now somebody was moving out there, now somebody was kicking a chair, somebody coughed, somebody dropped a coin. He lay quite still but tense with fear, his fear had taken over the functioning of his will and appointed itself commander-in-chief of all his powers of resistance. Fear stood there stimulating all his reagents with its field-marshal's baton. You never think as quickly as you do in moments of fear, and so the instant the door handle moved he was at the window and had one foot on the table and the other on the way up, but then everything happened so quickly his fear got out of step, as it were.

'Stop, you bastard!' yelled somebody and his fear was overpowered and he stood there on the table like a statue of Flight captured in mid-movement. While he was still a statue the woman standing behind Åke thought to herself: let's hope he catches it now. I hope Åke'll give him something to remember him by.

She thought she was thinking like that because he was standing on the table-cloth in his muddy marching boots ('What will the old lady say?'), or she persuaded herself that was what she thought, but in fact it was her slighted virtue she wanted avenging. The sensual pleasure at being conquered had vanished now she realized her conqueror was more cowardly than she was, unworthy of conquering her. She felt like an enormous fighter who had succumbed to a momentary weakness and allowed himself to be knocked down by some miserable little turd who only fought as a form of cowardice.

'Get down from that table, you bastard,' yelled Åke. He was shrieking shrilly because he knew he was beaten if he didn't have his voice on his side. He whipped off his cap with a sweeping, heroic gesture and flung it on the sofa while pretending he didn't even know there was a sofa there. That was the kind of thing that made an impression on people. He'd learnt how to make an impression on people in the shop, so it all came to him automatically. Then he took a few little tap-dancing steps sideways on his light rubber soles. 'Shut the door,' he said over his shoulder to Vera, and gave her a cheeky little wink. He'd been practising that on the errand boy. Vera gave him an encouraging nod and the part of his ego that dealt with good impressions gave his fingers the order to start unbuttoning his jacket. A jacket flung aside nonchalantly would complete his heroic attitude.

He started to wriggle out of it, tried to slide out of it like an eel out of a glove. Just for a moment he concentrated exclusively on getting the gesture right, indeed, he devoted himself to this to such a degree that he even forgot why he was doing it. Then Bill saw his opportunity, or rather, his fear, which had become active because it was his flight that needed courage now, used his eyes to observe all his opponent's movements, and just like a stopwatch told him when the right moment had arrived. He had tensed himself for the jump without giving it a thought, and with a sort of surprise mixed with horror he could see his opponent's shiny, light-red apple-face come rushing towards him like the boiler of a railway engine. His fear was controlling his head as one's hand does a fork: he pressed it down and dived blindly, straight into the counter-wallah's belly. The buckle on the fellow's belt bit into his forehead and a delayed echo from the falling table he'd taken with him when he'd jumped slipped through him without taking hold. It reached him in several stages at clearly marked intervals, the pleasant chinking sound of breaking coffee-cups, the angry crash of saucers, and as the battering ram accompanied the collapsing shelves to the floor there was the heavy, corroborative thud of the table as it took its place overlooking the scene of destruction.

His opponent was wriggling underneath him like a worm, from pain and fury. But fear had made his grip so efficient that the body beneath him was emptied of all power to resist and became still. Only the man's arms in the half-cast-off jacket were jumping about like a fish in a net, and his lips were open so wide around his bone-white teeth that they seemed to be stretched round a rectangular wooden frame. Bill raised his knees in calculating fashion then thrust them down like awls into his opponent's groin. Bill could see him screaming inwardly with pain, but the scream got caught behind his tongue, which was standing to attention in his mouth. Then he braced his hands against the floor and lifted himself up and brought the whole of his bodyweight to bear on his knees in order to loosen the scream. He could see his tongue being sort of pressed out of his mouth, stretching out like a neck.

Now, thought Bill, now he'll scream and give in. But then there was a sudden booming noise in his head, which was filled with extreme, dull pain and through the roll of drums he could feel something flowing out of the back of his head. Blood! The shout echoed all through him and he forgot about his grip and tried to stand up with his hands pressed against the back of his head. The drums were still rolling, but the beats were less rapid now. He got up and tried to stand erect under their weight. He managed it, although he had a vague feeling that the back of his head was swelling up like a lead balloon and was trying to turn him over.

Then came a sharp cry which burst the balloon and he suddenly became almost clear-headed. His hands crept out of their hiding place and he stared at them as if they were newly born. They were damp on the inside just like slippery stones. Am I dreaming? he thought. It's not blood. He set the tracking dogs of his nasal organ on them. It was coffee, a faint aroma like the one that hovers over undried marble tables. Damn and blast, he thought, it's only coffee.

Then came the echo of his shout. He turned round slowly and clumsily and he thought it must have been so long ago that he turned into lead, he was surprised when he found he recognized the room. The reel of film must have snagged and the spool had been going round and round in neutral. 'What the . . .?' he said into the silence. Vera was standing by the wall holding the handle and a small piece of the coffee-pot in her hand. There were still a few drops coming out of the pot's spout. Åke was leaning against the bottom of the bed, wriggling his way out of his jacket. And then the film started off again.

Åke ran at him as if he were in a heat for the hundred yards. You didn't scream, you bastard, thought Bill, and understood why Åke was coming at him so fast now. The scream was all over his face, even inside his ears, which were trembling like big petals, and in his eyes, which were nearly bursting because they hadn't been allowed to scream. In the punch as well, which came from down below and up at his chin, as cunning as a torpedo, and it forced its way as sharp as a nail and as straight as an arrow and highly effectively into his head. Not bad, he thought, not bad at all, and he hiccuped as if he'd just taken a whisky that was unexpectedly strong. He didn't fall, though, despite really wanting to. He started defending himself, not because he wanted to fight but for the sake of some short-lived principle. He might just as well have been fighting in a cellar, a dark room, or with his eyes blindfolded. Åke was a gentleman. Here you are, he said with his fists, and jumped into the way of the clumsiest of punches. He pretended to be a stylish boxer and parried, blocked jabs, and drew up plans for hooks and straight rights. He was the perfect salesman in a shop for noble chin-punches.

All of a sudden Bill stopped fighting. He simply let his arms drop by his sides like a pair of wings after the wind has blown away all their feathers and struts. Åke was so involved in his role he thought: ha ha, the customer's tired. He wants to stop now, does he? He's had enough. But he was furious, he felt he'd been insulted like a salesman who thought he had a buyer on the hook but then loses him at the last moment in the currents. There was a singing noise in the ceiling as a car whined past, but it was only the preface to a long chapter of silence.

'You can throw that coffee-pot away,' said Bill eventually. 'You can sling it among the rest of the bloody debris.' He moved forward and picked up the table and kicked at the broken china for a while. Then he looked up at Vera and tried to smile, although he felt as if there were a nail going through his chin and his lower jaw and right up into his nose. 'Did you hear what I said? You can throw that bloody coffee-pot away.' Then he kicked it out of her hand so that there was just a little china ring dangling from her index finger. 'What about this bit, then?' she said. 'Aren't you going to try to smash this as well? Coward, you bloody yellow-liver!'

'You say that to me,' he said calmly, grinding his heel in the bits of china. His boots were covered in white dust. 'You'll be able to open your own chalk factory soon. Who the hell do you think I'm afraid of?' Åke came strolling across the room, moving like a tram with his eyes running along the lines. Why don't I fight him, he thought, I'd soon sort out that bastard. But instead his feet went over to the sofa, his hands picked up his tunic, and his arms and back helped each other to put it on. Leave me out of this, he thought. 'Why don't you let him have it?' asked somebody. Then somebody laughed. Just a minute. He must get a spoon and fish out the answer. It was at the bottom of the big cauldron. Oh dear, it was so deep he needed a long spoon. He must make a very long handle for it.

'No, but you might soon be frightened,' said Vera, going over to the window. The wind was shaking the smell of lilac out of the bushes and it was absolutely silent but then came the sound of bicycle tyres outside on the road. 'Eh?' asked Bill. 'Just think, if you were going to get scared,' she said, 'so

58

scared you had to jump out of the window, you could break your leg.'

Then his fear told him to look out and he turned round more quickly than he knew but it was already too late. All four of them had fixed bayonets and he'd no doubt get impaled if he tried to get out through the door. He took a few paces backwards even though he knew the window was closed. 'You rang, you bastard,' he whispered to her without turning round. The bayonets slunk into the room and the sergeant stepped forward and announced as formally as if he were reading an address from a balcony: 'On account of the absence of the company commander the prisoner will not be interrogated until tomorrow.' Then he fell down from the balcony: 'The rest o' you lot had better turn up at company office tomorrer morning. To the left, quick . . . march.'

Vera opened the window and let in the cry of some summery bird. It hammered a little wedge of pain into the room. The clumping of the patrol's feet died away. The bird hopped down from branch to branch in the dusty lilac bush. Will you cry instead of me? she thought, and it seemed to her as if the summer were lying dead under the scorched lilac leaves.

7

She's on her own now. She's just got off the bus at the deserted crossroads. The roads are covered in scorching, ash-grey asphalt, and on a little roundabout surrounded by kerbstones is a signpost. As tall and stern as a lighthouse or a large cross with four arms, it towers over the flat countryside which the dead-straight black roads make look like a sliced cake. She stands stock still for a moment and sees a pale face with unnaturally big eyes staring at her from the rear window of the bus. The bus shudders away across the plain and gets smaller and smaller, its little trailer stuttering merrily along behind it, until it disappears altogether behind the low, almost unnoticeable hills that take over from the plain to the east.

But those eyes just get bigger and bigger. It's as if they had been removed from their pale face and hung up on invisible threads under a couple of the unlit lamps dangling over the road, and then blown up like balloons. She wipes a damp hand over her own eyes – and when she looks up again there stands the cross with its four threatening arms, burning itself on to her retina. She feels as if she were all alone in the whole of this dreadful plain which has nothing but black roads and flat grey barns that seem scared of being seen by unknown eyes. Terrified, she looks down from the arms of the cross and discovers the little roundabout where grass once grew but which has now been eaten away comprehensively by blazing sun and hot wind.

Burnt grass, she thinks anxiously, where did I see that? She doesn't need to strain herself in order to remember. The steep slope of the embankment with its sparse, scorched-brown mat of sorry-looking grass flickers past her eyes once again, although she does shut them and tries not to see anything.

There, she thinks in horror. Then. She runs panic-stricken down one of the black roads that look from a distance like fat insulation tape somebody's had fun rolling out all over the countryside. She runs along the right side of the road where the asphalt meets the verge and she gets stones in her shoes and they cause pain under her heels. She keeps on running, though, as if trying to unwind the whole of the black band.

Eventually, however, she can't go on any longer. She almost falls headlong, she's so tired, and she has to sit down for a while by the side of the road. The steep ditch by the road is so new, all that's growing there are fat goosefoot plants. She sits down carefully on a little stone and takes off her shoes and empties out the gravel. She does it thoroughly and stretches out her legs over the ditch and tickles the soles of her feet through her thin stockings with the seed-laden goosefoots. The sun is now right in her eyes, and she has to sneeze.

'Atishoo,' she cries loudly and cheerfully, breaking the silence that has been hanging so heavily over the whole plain. Looking straight ahead over the flat ground, she doesn't find the countryside quite so frightening any more, now that she's on the same level as the ground itself. She calmly puts her shoes on again and scrambles across the ditch and crawls under the loose, dangling barbed wire. She gets up on to the wide expanse of brown grass stalks, which are already beginning to take on a nuance of red. Encouraged by the morning dew, a few little pale green stalks have started spiralling their way up among the burnt tufts. She bends down over the ground as one does over a small child and breaks off one of these stalks right down at the bottom, near the rust-like earth. She puts the stalk in her mouth and continues on her way over the pasture land.

The hay still hasn't been taken in although it ought to have dried already under the wing of the harvester. It's piled up in flat, shrunken cocks looking like buns that haven't risen properly. From a distance they look like boils on the surface of the ground. She sinks slowly down into the hay, which is so dry it almost snaps like dry twigs. She lies on her back and squints up at the summery clouds floating across the sky. Between the clouds the sky is so relentlessly blue and the distance so infinite, she feels dizzy and has the liberating feeling she could just disappear into it without feeling any pain.

What's happened? she asks the blue infinity; but there's no one there to answer. Only emptiness. She closes her eyes in relief and knows that if she allows herself to be gobbled up by it, nothing can happen to her. Deep down, though, she knows that hope is deceptive. It is the cowardly tightrope walker who thinks he's cured of his poor head for heights merely because he closes his eyes. Deep down inside her in fact is an animal gnawing away with its pointed teeth, and she has it shut away in a little box; but already she can see its fang through the fragile wall. So she quickly puts the box inside a slightly larger one, but the little animal keeps gnawing away and so she goes and fetches a carton and then a bigger one and then a bigger one still, and every time she has the same childish feeling of happiness and the same sensation of staring into an abyss when fear rubs up against her.

In the end she has to leave the haycock when it suddenly becomes clear the store of cardboard boxes is about to run out. She brushes off the strands of hay clinging to her clothes and takes a mirror out of her bag, but the little animal is nearly out and she puts it back again without having dared to look at herself. Instead she raises her eyes and looks up into the clouds, which have now acquired black, jagged edges and are moving towards the sun. Then one of them, the darkest and most threatening, suddenly sticks its fist into the sun's face and it grows so dark she thinks it's raining.

She starts half-running over the soft, springy ground towards the road. I must get under a roof, she thinks rapidly and feels a great sense of relief at having made up her mind. But she doesn't have to run many yards before she knows she's fooled herself again. The animal is there, gnawing away. It's chewed its way through the whole lot of boxes and cartons, and its tail is whirring around in the extended space it now has. It's not raining either.

When she's almost got to the barbed wire she notices a cyclist on the road. He's coming towards her, swinging backwards and forwards over the road like one does when one has a lot of time, or is drunk. A desperate hope gets the better of her and she falls to her knees and crawls quickly under the barbed wire. She slithers down into the ditch and sees that the cyclist is an errand boy. He's tall and thin and has a blue striped apron round his hips. He's whistling shrilly something unfinished, and at regular intervals tosses his head to displace the fair lock of hair that rolls down over his forehead like a wave. He's already seen her and he's now staring straight at her while the bicycle continues to zigzag all over the road, sometimes making it looks as though he and the bike are going in different directions. The box lying loose on his luggage carrier is sliding about as he does his risky manoeuvres, but he always puts it back in place with his foot a split second before it tips over. He is disciplined tomfoolery personified.

She climbs out of the ditch and deftly tosses a sturdy box over the little animal that's still gnawing away. He hasn't quite reached her yet and she stands waiting at the roadside with her back towards the ditch, as if she were at a bus stop. He breaks off whistling like a bird that's been shot in the middle of a cry. In an elegant gesture he puts his foot down on the road as if it were a pedal and comes to a stop right in front of her. He turns the handlebars towards her so that the whole bicycle is staring at her like a bull with lowered horns.

When she looks up at him, though, he looks so different from what she'd expected that she's a bit confused at first. She may even start blushing, she thinks quickly. The boy's so young, and the only reason he looks so tall is that he has the saddle of his bicycle screwed down so far. He must be much younger than me, that lad, it strikes her.

Then the boy says, 'Hello,' and screws up his eyes to look at her, even though he's standing in her shadow. He fumbles around frantically in his pockets for his cigarettes and matches, in order to cover his embarrassment and a blush that's spreading over his thin face like raspberry juice on a table-cloth. He tries the most unlikely pockets in his apron and jacket in an attempt to gain time. By Jove, he's really sweet when he blushes, she thinks to herself, forcing out the clichés, and her fingers are itching to stroke back the quiff that's fallen down over one eye. She feels for him in his embarrassment, like a sympathetic mother. Without even having to clear her throat, she says: 'I was wondering if you could tell me how to get to May Road.'

He eventually manages to find a crumpled cigarette in his left trouser pocket. It's taken him quite a while because he knew that was where it was, and so he kept that pocket till last. In the end he also produces a battered matchbox, and he tries to twist his face into a malicious grimace as he shields the cigarette with his hands and lights up.

'May Road,' he says thoughtfully, aiming a puff of smoke up at the sun and tapping away on his rusty bell with his empty hand. 'May Road must be down that way,' and he nods his head in the direction she's just come from. He stares down at the tarmac road that seems to be taking time out in the sun, which has now dragged itself to its feet again after the knockout punch and is standing in the ring burning away just as before. She can see the signpost pointing around absent-mindedly on its island in the sea of tarmac. She can't believe how small it is; it's like a dream between then and now.

'I'm going that way misself,' he says with his mouth full of smoke slowly oozing out between his teeth. 'Maybe we could go together.' He straightens himself up in the saddle and modestly pulls down his apron over his knees. She notices how the apron is covered in dark, nearly black bloodstains at such regular intervals it almost looks like a pattern. 'Maybe we could go together as far as May Road,' he says again, almost insisting on it, and she can tell he's only doing it so that he can say 'we'. He dwells on it for as long as the sentence will stand it. She thinks it's touching, thinks that in a motherly sort of way, and she's so keen to humour him, she says: 'Let's do that, then.'

She almost has to run in order to keep up. It's as if he's faced up to his responsibilities once he gets on his bike. He's put on a more or less sullen expression, and he raises his upper lip to reveal his teeth, just like a horse, and you can see him biting on his cigarette. She notices this as she trots along beside him, and she's almost impressed by how incredibly clumsy he is.

He glances down at her for one more split second of doubt, then he drags the cigarette from his mouth, puts it out by squeezing it between his thumb and his index finger and lets the butt slide down into his apron pocket. Then he speaks out into the air, as if he were sitting talking into a microphone, expressionless and in a surly, almost furious tone of voice: 'This is a bloody job and a half, this is. Gorra go dashing the length and breadth of Enskede with this bloody box of tricks. Sometimes you've gorra go toddling off as far as Erstavik. Yesterday this silly old bitch out at Stuvsta rings up and asks for some pork chops – anybody'd think they didn't have any pigs in Stuvsta. Mind you, with a long trip like that you can take it easy, have a swim and muck about on the way there and back. It's all bloody go, day in, day out. Still, before long they'll let me stay in and see to the slaughtering mask.'

Now the road sets off at the double and his bicycle gets more enthusiastic and she nearly has to run properly to keep up with him. He's been talking all in one go, like a trumpeter who has to keep blowing in case he runs out of breath, but he says the last bit with such enthusiasm, she realizes he's boasting about it.

If only he'd go on talking, she thinks eagerly, a bit out of breath, then I wouldn't be on my own, and the animal is shut inside such thick walls she can hardly hear the hollow echo of its teeth gnawing away. 'Slaughtering mask?' she says, a bit hesitantly on purpose.

He reacts straight away, like a group of gymnasts to a whistle, and he even puts one foot on the pedal and backpedals to brake and let her catch up properly.

'Yeah, one of them thingumajigs you finish off pigs with. Bulls and cows as well, come to that.' His voice is tense and just a little bit excited. He does a little mime with his free hand. He puts his index finger to his forehead like the barrel of a revolver, then lets his head flop down like a dead flower to show what happens when it goes off.

'But,' she says, looking up with her innocent eyes into his tense, serious face, 'isn't it horrible, killing animals?' 'Gerraway,' he says, slowing down even more and moving closer to her, 'they don't feel a bloody thing. You just put the thingy to their heads and it's all over and done with.' He drops his head and shrugs his shoulders and looks as if he had a hole in his forehead. He's like an affected actor doing a repeat run of an effective scene he's just been applauded for.

'You bet your bloody life them pig bastards don't feel a bloody thing – it's all over before you can even blink,' he says at the top of his voice, his words throbbing with the idealism of youth. 'It's almost worse for the poor butcher, who risks getting the pig bastard's teeth into him at any minute.' He jumps off his bike so that he can expand on his theme in more detail for her. He walks by her side, red-faced and eager, his quiff halfway down over his forehead. He's a bit shorter than she is, and she can look at him right between his red-hot ears that stick out in such a young-boyish way she's almost moved again.

'Then, when you're going to cut 'em up, that's just about the worst part, of course. You get the knife and . . .' He turns his face towards her, his expression serious and just a little excited, and he puts his index finger under his upturned chin and she can see the down on it swaying like marsh grass in the breeze and she has an almost uncontrollable urge to pull it up by the roots. 'And you stick it into the flesh' – and he runs his index finger down, over the tightly stretched skin of his throat, over his chest and stomach and down to his crotch – 'and you cut 'em open like this. They haven't let me do that part yet, though,' he says with a successful attempt at appearing nonchalant as he spits over his bike.

She feels like a benevolent old aunt listening to a little boy's account of what he's been doing at school, and then she says, sounding very interested, as she may well be or at least has to be because of the animal: 'Oh, so you're thinking of becoming a butcher now, are you?'

They've got back to the crossroads by now and she glances absent-mindedly at the signpost. It says Dalarö and Stockholm and Älvsjö and Nynäshamn on the pointers and one of them is hanging down despondently as if it had grown tired of standing to attention. It's not big at all, in fact it's pretty puny when you think it's as near to town as this, she thinks vindictively.

'Yeah, but first you've gorra run a few errands,' he says, jumping back on his bicycle as if he'd suddenly remembered his duties. They come to a little incline and she has to more or less run in order to keep up when he stands on the pedals and gets up to speed to cope. The flat terrain, criss-crossed with cornfields and pasture land, gradually gives way to a narrow belt of wild meadows and a slightly broader belt of lush, deciduous woodland and then turns into a real evergreen forest, looking for all the world like the north of Sweden. Hidden away in the belt of woodland is a well-camouflaged cluster of holiday cottages which gradually turns into a little estate of detached houses as you get closer to the conifer forest.

The only indications from the road that there are houses nearby are a few roughly constructed wooden bridges over the roadside ditch, covered with gravel, and the occasional rubbish bin leaning idly against some tree trunk or other. Out of breath and sweaty, she gets as far as the brow of the hill. The boy is a bit in front of her, his expression just as intensely morose and sullen as it had been before the slaughter.

All of a sudden he slams on his brakes with an angry-sounding little squeal and he jumps off his bike with a little jerk of his legs and thighs. 'This is May Road,' he says, with as little emotion as a signpost, pointing nonchalantly with his free arm to a narrow, stony, root-covered lane that disappears altogether into the dense conifers.

She suddenly feels very frightened, scared out of her wits by the silence following his words, which falls over her like a sack and is drawn tight round her throat. She's afraid of being suffocated, of not getting enough air to her voice before he goes away. The fir trees would stoop down over her and suffocate her under their skirts if she were left alone now. The little animal will soon have broken out and she can hear its teeth gnawing away at the last of the planks blocking its way. The boy has already mounted his bike. He's sitting astride it with both feet planted firmly on the road. Even so, he doesn't give the impression of wanting to leave. His hands are groping around nervously in his pockets, looking for cigarettes and matches – and all at once it dawns on her with an intoxicating rush of wild joy that he's sitting there waiting for her to say it. The words stumble out of her, there's a commotion inside her like people in an agitated queue: 'Do you think, you might actually know . . . I'm supposed to go to Borg's . . . to Borg's house . . . it's supposed to be here on May Road somewhere . . . maybe you know where it is . . . you . . .'

'Oh, Borg's,' he says, sticking a new cigarette in his mouth with trembling fingers. 'I sometimes have to take stuff out to them – they're only out here on Saturdays, it seems. Nice old bloke. I sometimes play badminton with his lad in the garden. So, they're coming out today, are they?'

'No,' she said, pleased to be able to talk without having to think, 'but you see we're going to have a little party out here tonight, just a few of us, and I've come out in advance to get things ready, do a bit of cleaning and that kind of thing.'

'I see, so there's nobody in their place just now, then?' he says, and his hand is shaking as he lifts up his match and lights up. She's too excited to notice, though, and without the slightest hesitation she says quickly: 'How about coming with me and showing me where to go?' 'Yeah, it's bloody hard to find your way around these parts when you haven't been here before,' he says, jumping smartly off his bike again and leading it by the horns straight across the road, keeping ahead of her all the time. 'Gorra take this little bugger with me all over Enskede,' he says, almost caressing his bicycle when it bumps up and down on the stony lane.

She walks behind him, eyeing his slender back and thin neck under his bushy hair. The knot in his apron is dangling down and is clumsily tied over his backside, which obligingly fills the seat of a pair of faded and excessively short blue trousers.

He must have tied it himself, she thinks, smiling slightly and feeling strangely moved once again.

Now they are walking through the dense belt of fir trees where it is silent and half-dark and littered with gleaming tin cans, egg-shells and torn paper bags. But soon the firs come to an end and the lane broadens out unexpectedly and suddenly there are fences on each side of it. It's almost a real road covered in coarse gravel, with just a few stubborn tree roots here and there that they've allowed to remain as souvenirs. Behind the fences on both sides are cottages or the beginnings of little houses separated from each other by more fences brightly painted in a variety of colours. It's only where they face the forest that the gardens are open, perhaps so you don't have to bother about opening a gate when you're rushing to the privy. Sure enough, in a more or less straight line, like soldiers on parade, is a row of privies carefully built and decorated with all kinds of fancy wood-carving, one for every house, just where the gardens peter out and the forest takes over. It's as if each house owner had invested the whole of his fortune in order to make these essential little buildings as splendid and worthy as possible.

She's walking by his side and he's still pushing his bicycle, and from time to time she glances down at his severe and somewhat sullen face. His cigarette is sending out a thin blue strand of smoke rising straight up from its tip. His lips are clamped firmly round it, and it's only with the greatest reluctance that they let any smoke leak out. She thinks it's the same sullen boyishness he displayed back on the main road, and in order to disperse it she suddenly says: 'You know, my grandad used to work for a butcher for a while – but he couldn't stand it. My dad says he used to have to go out and be sick every time he saw a lump of meat on the table.'

The boy's eyes light up, but she misunderstands his eagerness and he says in a voice that's almost shrill: 'Yeah, it can be pretty bloody like that at first, until you get used to it. Once you've got used to it, though, you can lie down and kip inside a split-open pig and not think twice about it. The worst thing, though, is when some bloody old boar bites you, they're right buggers they are.'

He holds his bicycle upright with one hand and suddenly and without warning he grabs hold of her hand with the other. It's the first time he's touched her. She can feel his sweaty hand pressing against her knuckles and in fact she has to glance down to make sure it isn't covered in blood. 'The other day, for instance,' he says, and his voice breaks in his excitement, 'one of the lads got bit straight across here,' and he strokes her knuckles to show where he means, 'and his knuckles cracked like porcelain when that bastard of a boar dug his teeth in,' and he presses her knuckles hard so that she gets an idea of what it was like when the boar bit him.

He lets go, and she wipes her hand discreetly on the sleeve of her dress. He crosses the road and leans his bike against a fence with green railings and white cross-pieces. 'This is where the Borgs live,' he says, tossing his head so that his quiff falls down over his forehead. It's the last house on May Road, which comes to an end just as inauspiciously as it started, shrivelling up and petering out among the fir trees again.

The house looks like something that was intended from the start to be a real house, but due to a misunderstanding on the part of the builder or a shortage of money or lack of interest, it was stunted in its growth. There's just one storey, and at the gable end is a splendid glass conservatory that matches the rest of the house like a sou'wester suits a terrier.

She intends asking him in, partly because that's the logical thing to do when he's gone to so much trouble, and partly also because of the animal that needs bigger and bigger boxes. But he's into the garden before she is. 'Just look, the bastard's forgotten to take down the badminton net!' he yells so loudly they must have heard him all over the village, but it doesn't matter because they haven't seen a soul anywhere in the whole of May Road.

She gropes around in her handbag for the key and

eventually finds the right one. She unlocks the veranda door and they go in. The air inside is thick with stale tobacco that has been standing still for so long it's got stuck. 'Let's leave the door open,' she says. The veranda table is full of empty beer bottles. An empty vodka bottle towers over the crowd. The door to the right leads into the kitchen where there's a little cooker squeezed in a corner. Then there's a big room with a made-up bed-settee with a portable gramophone on it, a tall corner cupboard, a rickety table and a few wooden chairs. The walls are covered with pinned-up covers of old *Picture Post* magazines. The other room has a rusty stove, a sideboard and a few chairs. Two beds are fixed to one of the walls. The lower bunk contains some puffy bolsters, but the upper one just has a bare steel frame.

When she gets back from her tour of inspection he's sitting on the bench on the veranda with his hands on his knees. He looks even younger when he's indoors like this, she thinks, and she feels sorry for him, sitting there shyly and staring at the forest of empty beer bottles. 'They must have had a real booze-up here,' she says cheerfully. No response. She starts picking up the bottles from the table, hoping he'll give her a hand; but he just sits there, fiddling with his apron.

'I wonder where they hide the cool store in this here place,' she asks herself, half-aloud. She knows the answer because she's learnt everything on the bit of paper off by heart, but he takes the bait. He gets down on his knees on the veranda floor and lifts up a trapdoor. 'It's down here,' he says sulkily. She looks down at the back of his slender young neck and his red ears that look from above as if they're sticking out almost at right-angles. She can hear him groping about among the bottles and cans down in the hole, and she can't resist the temptation to give a little tug at the knot in his apron. 'Christ, there's enough here to keep a whole regiment going,' he says, and starts lifting out bottles and tins and bags and what have you. 'Course, I've given 'em a hand to fetch some of this stuff,' he says, and it echoes as in a church.

A whole forest of bottles and cans starts growing up around the trapdoor. There are a lot of beer bottles, a few bottles of vodka, a very strange-looking bottle with 'whisky' written on it, some bottles of lemonade, and tins of all sorts with various labels. Soon there are none left, and he puts the lid back and starts transferring the whole lot to the table, having first wiped it down with his apron. There's a bag of potatoes as well, and she says, with genuine female cunning, half-aloud to herself: 'I wonder where they hide the well in this here place.' Whereupon he takes the bucket from the kitchen cupboard and goes out for some water.

Meanwhile, she's found a clean cloth in the corner cupboard. She puts it on the table and starts opening the tins, which she then puts on plates. When he comes back with the water, surly and miserable, she washes the potatoes in a basin, tips them into a pan and lights the primus stove. All these little chores give her rhythm a fixed tempo and build up considerable barriers round the little animal who has thicker and thicker material to get his teeth into.

She goes out on to the veranda again. He's sitting on the bench eagerly opening tins. 'These are some of our firm's,' he says, displaying just a glimpse of pride in his work. 'I'm a dab hand at opening them.' I don't really need him any more now, she thinks sensibly, and there's no sign of life from the little animal; but she wants to let him know she's grateful to him for accompanying her all the way here and so she says, 'Can I offer you a dram, perhaps?' (It would look mean if she didn't, seeing as the whole table is covered in bottles.) 'I bet you butchers knock it back like old sailors,' she says, to help him over the barrier.

'Too bloody right we do,' he says, and actually smiles. 'You should see what goes on at the abattoir on Saturday afternoons! The lads have bottles of beer and the odd bottle of vodka hidden away in pigs' carcasses or in the salt drums. One Saturday one of the hanging carcasses were taken off for delivery by mistake, and one of the lads had a half-bottle of vodka hidden in it. He nearly had a heart attack when he saw the carcass had gone. "Some bastard's gonna get my half-bottle in his pea soup, damn him." He were going on and on about it all the next week.'

They both laugh. The boy's eyes light up, but she mis-understands that as well. She thinks he's enjoying retelling the story. She fetches six spirits glasses from the kitchen cupboard, and while she's at it brings six plates as well, which she places at intervals round the table. She takes a half-bottle of vodka, puts it between her knees and twists out the cork. It sounds good as she fills the boy's glass. She pours out half a glass for herself as well.

'Cheers!' she says, tipping it enthusiastically but in fact only sipping the drink, which makes her feel as if there's a furnace blazing inside her. But the boy empties his glass more or less at one go. He pulls a face but when he looks at her his eyes are bright and strangely fixed. Like jelly, she thinks, and puts it down to the drink.

She goes into the kitchen and fetches a collection of knives, forks and spoons from the cupboard and some tumblers from the shelf. When she comes back, her glass is empty as well. She pretends not to notice, but sets out the cutlery and glasses. 'Would you like another glass?' she asks, pouring it out as she speaks. She puts a drop in her own glass as well, but doesn't drink anything herself.

Then she goes into the kitchen and feels with a fork that the potatoes are done, and turns off the primus stove. She puts a towel over the pan so that the potatoes will still be hot when the others arrive. She takes a few saucers out on to the veranda with her, for the potato peelings. Both glasses are empty. She puts the cork back in the bottle and stows all the unnecessary bottles under the bench.

The boy's eyes are gleaming more brightly than ever and she thinks it's due to the spirits. His quiff has fallen down and is almost covering his eye. She feels a mad urge to stroke it up and away from his shiny face, and this time she actually does so. He sits absolutely still, and his face turns deep red all over. It must be the booze, she thinks once again, and she feels worried in a motherly sort of way that she's led him astray. But he's so sweet, she thinks, and forgives him. She goes and fetches some chairs and places them carefully around the table.

Then she remembers the unmade beds in the inner room and goes in, led on by her expansive drive to keep doing things. On the way she thinks about the boy, and how it would be better if he'd gone by the time the others get there. She begins to regret having dragged him along with her, but she forgives herself for that as well when she realizes she had to. I'll stroke his hair and send him home, she thinks, like a mum who's been entertaining one of her own children's friends when it's starting to get late.

That's why, that's exactly why she is overcome by such deep-seated and indescribable astonishment when he suddenly thrusts himself upon her and flings her down by the beds like an overturned chair. His eyes are glinting like a wild animal's, but even so she's not scared at first. For one long second she's shocked by what has happened, without being really sure what it implies. She can't defend herself at first, because what has happened is so unheard of, it exceeds her ability to comprehend it. But the heavy body on top of her and the smell of the blood-soaked apron are starting to choke her, and she starts resisting.

'Gerraway, you beast!' she shrieks, punching away with her fists at his flushed face with its eyes shining like neon lights. She opens her fist and grabs at his long hair and pulls and pulls. He fights like a madman to break loose. He pulls away and raises himself to his knees and that's when she manages to evade his grasp, and gets to her feet. Then they fight, like puppies fight, clumsily, awkwardly, without hurting each other, but obstinately, and in the end he overcomes her fury and her nails and her fierce teeth.

She hits her shoulderblade against the hard floor. If only

he'd laid me on the bed, she thinks, feeling strangely weary and strangely remote from reality, and, as if through a shop window, she watches him unbutton his trousers. And the sight she has always known would be like this fills her with disgust and horror, but she's so weary after her defeat that when he comes down on her she can only manage to whisper: 'Take off your apron at least.'

He rips it off so roughly that the tape breaks and he flings it away over the floor. She feels so remote from everything and so ready to sink that he doesn't even have to go to the trouble of forcing her legs apart. With her eyes closed and his breath swilling around the corners of her eyes and his raw young body pressed tightly against her own, she waits for it to happen. For it to happen, and be over with as soon as possible.

But nothing happens. The pressure of the boy's body is constant, and after a long moment when she's switched off all her senses she comes back into focus and can perceive things again and she can feel his hot, clammy hands feeling around inside her clothes as if that's where the secret is hidden. She slowly and reluctantly opens her eyes and with a sort of shocked surprise notices that his young face is twitching nervously and that the relaxation of his facial muscles brought on by sexual desire has given way to a spasmodic tension. His eyes are rolling and his expression is being taken over by fear and, grotesquely enlarged, she sees a drop of sweat trembling in his drooping hair like dew on a blade of grass.

What is it she feels? Is it pity? No. And it ought not to be disappointment when she'd been fighting so hard to avoid it, but even so – she suddenly sees or perhaps feels one of his hands leave her body and then she watches it waving around helplessly in the air as if it had suddenly gone blind. Is it on its way to caress her? No, it's creeping along the floor and when she turns her head slightly she can see his arm wrapping itself round the leg of the bed that's just to one side of her. She watches the blind arm embrace the leg of the bed as if it were the arm's lover, and then all of a sudden, without her being able to help it or bothering to stop it, laughter comes bursting out of her throat. The bitter laughter of a frustrated female at an incompetent lover.

She lies there stock still and listens to her own laughter gushing forth shrilly and hysterically as if from the mouth of a bird. While she's busy listening to herself, she notices the body on top of her stiffen and become as rigid as a pole. Her laughter keeps on pouring out into the room, drowning everything else. Nothing is pressing against her any more. The boy has left her and is standing on the floor, trying helplessly to fasten his apron. His face is twitching. His muscles have become uncontrollable and are acting independently; it's as if they are doing their best to make up for what they've missed when they were controlled by his will.

She's lying on the floor with her legs open wide and her clothes in disarray, just roaring with laughter, and the laughter keeps on cascading from her mouth as she slowly and shakily and full of listening gets to her feet. Still laughing away, she sees how every muscle in his young, terror-stricken face breaks down and all the tension dissolves in a flash as he starts crying – a wild, blind, ruthless crying which is a substitute for a scream. Still laughing, loudly and triumphantly, she sees him coming rushing towards her. And now they're fighting, him like a mad, wild tomcat, purposefully, crudely and ruthlessly, with tears rolling down his face, and she laughing all the time, defending herself with the ineffectual gestures of a drunk.

When the laughter still doesn't stop spurting from her mouth, though, despite the blood pouring down each side, he gives up and, his abandoned weeping turned into a hiccuping sob, he just flings her down on the bed. Still laughing, she hears him rush through the room, across the courtyard, through the gate and out into the road. She hears the rattling as he starts cycling away, then just the rasping of the bicycle wheels on the gravel road, like the sound made by folding up a large sheet of paper.

Then she turns over on to her stomach and the laughter gradually subsides into a spasmodic hiccup which is the start of spasmodic sobbing, but the transition is so gradual it's some time before she realizes she's lying there crying. She cries as she knows she's never cried before in her life, because she's never had any reason to, and the bolster grows wet and cool beneath her. She cries, and cools down. And behind the weeping she never ceases to be surprised that she can cry so much over having lost something she's never possessed.

She's still crying when she hears shrill female voices and muffled male voices intermingling outside on May Road. She gets furtively to her feet and, still sniffing, throws the damp and bloody bolster on to the upper bunk. She goes to the kitchen and fills a bowl with water and tries to rinse away everything that's happened. She looks through the veranda window and sees them coming down the lane and wonders almost indifferently if the lads will gape in disbelief when they notice they're a half-bottle of vodka short.

8

The room is small and as hot as a boiler room, even though it doesn't face south. It's three long strides by three, although the third stride always hits the wall. Moreover it's locked from the outside, so that the prisoner doesn't get it into his head to leave. As the room serves one day a week as an office where the company chief clerk receives complaints, there is a niche in the wall, behind which is concealed the communal telephone, shared by everybody in the block.

When soldiers have been arrested it's called the cell, and the niche has a little lock on the door so that the prisoner can't call the fire brigade and claim he's been locked up in a blazing building. The easiest way of turning the office into a cell is by carrying out the typewriter, a lopsided Continental that clatters away like a machine-gun the moment you put your finger on the space bar, and by closing the window, which is normally left open on warm summer days. By these simple procedures you ensure not only that the prisoner cannot type letters to his nearest and dearest and set them off getting him out of there, but also that the prisoner is not subjected to the unnecessary temptation of using the window as an escape route if he happens to have some business to attend to outside.

On the other hand, the chief clerk's cabinet where he keeps all his forms is left unlocked, and nobody bothers to carry it out, partly because it's heavy, perhaps, and partly because it's assumed the prisoner will make lots of good resolutions during the period of his arrest, such as getting married, for instance, and in such circumstances he would need all the good advice he can get regarding the family allowances described on the forms in the cabinet. There is a calendar on one wall, but the prisoner won't get much help from that. What he needs is not so much to count the days, but rather the hours until the moment when some reliable sergeant unlocks the door and escorts him to the CO's office, where the prisoner is tried in the presence of witnesses, high-ranking military officers and a clerk who notes down extremely meticulously the whole of the important exchange. It's especially important that the prisoner has a watch so that he can give precise information about the exact time of his actions on the day of the crime. If the prisoner was drunk, he will also have to say how many doubles of whisky, gin, vodka and brandy he partook of before committing the crime. Such things give order and precision to the records which are then placed in a large folder in the company office and can be read there by the prisoner once he's been set free and is feeling bored.

The guard-room window is directly opposite the gable of one of the barrack rooms, and since the doors are open at both ends of the block Bill can see straight through to the entrance of his own block; he works out that if he wanted to escape, it would be like running through a tunnel nearly all the way and then via the last of the billets straight out into the depths of the dense forest. Then he'd make a big detour round the camp until he got as far as the railway line where it's crossed by a bridge. The whole operation would take no more than a quarter of an hour, provided he wasn't spotted by the guards and chased, in which case it would be a bit quicker. When he got to the bridge he would dive into the bushes on the slope and slither down to the railway line. Then he'd run the short stretch to the siding and creep into a goods wagon and hide there until the train came.

He's sitting at the table which, in common with office furniture in general, suffers from lameness, and he's making plans. Mainly to make the time pass. The whole escape procedure is too easy for him to need to think it over more than once. It doesn't need any rope ladders, master keys or chloroformed guards in order to be carried out successfully. It doesn't even need a bit of courage. Courage won't be needed until later, when he has to come back again, but, like all cowards faced with a bold decision, he convinces himself that the action will put a full stop to the passage of time, that eternity will dawn the moment he's done it, that time will come to a standstill and never move again, a bit like a gramophone record that gets stuck in a groove.

In order not to be carried away by irrelevant thoughts, though, he takes the clerk's indelible pencil and draws a sketch of the camp on the back of an envelope. He makes several versions of it, each more accurate than the previous one. Bit by bit he extends it to become a map of the whole village, and he racks his memory to reproduce the location of every little lane and every outhouse. He has the idea of marking in defensive bases round the outskirts of the village, and locates bunkers and anti-tank barriers. He draws in enemy tanks in the woods, and finally establishes a war cemetery in the MO's garden. He thereby confirms the general opinion of the MO's achievements.

He also draws the café. He doesn't pay any special attention to that particular building. Objectively and accurately he supplies it with a forecourt, arbour, hedges and cycle stand. Coldly and methodically he fills in the road that swishes past the café, jumps over the railway line and, in passing, as it were, tosses out a side-lane as far as the camp. He draws that road so calmly you'd never believe it was only an hour ago he was walking down it with a rifle in his back.

As he was walking along the dusty, sun-burned road like a prominent criminal surrounded by the patrol, he worked out how to deal with the person who'd brought this upon him, quickly and efficiently and with as little hesitation as a surgeon about to make his incision. He made up his mind so quickly and so thoroughly that it was all over and done with by the time they traipsed past the guard post and the guard came to attention for the sergeant's sake. The guard had stared at them with eyes as fixed as butterflies on pins. Then he'd started whistling, purely for the pleasure of seeing them start to flutter. The sergeant had run up abreast of him and yelled out a shrill 'Shurrup', but it had run off him like water off a duck's back.

He makes a few more refinements to his plan of the village, sketching in the market garden, part of which forms a little wedge between the butcher's and the bank. He makes beds for cucumbers and celery, and draws in the narrow strip of strawberry plants alongside the beck, which is dried out and cracked during the summer, but that's just as well so you don't get your feet wet when you go raiding it on your way back from a day's pass.

Now he can hear doors opening and slamming again so violently that the windows rattle and the corridor outside the guard room is filled with good-natured banter bouncing back and forth between the walls. He realizes it's the secretaries packing up for the day and going back to their barrack rooms.

Five o'clock, then. He takes a family allowance form from the cabinet and methodically fills in all the yawning gaps. He reckons it takes five minutes. Then he fills in another at exactly the same rate as before, and then he gets up from his chair and tiptoes over the creaking floorboards to the door and listens with his ear pressed to the crack.

But there's nothing to be heard apart from the stubborn, irregular thudding of a typewriter being used by somebody who's not used to it. Reassured, he goes over to the far wall and puts his ear to the door of the telephone niche. All that penetrates through from the guard room is a grey murmur of subdued voices.

Reassured, he walks over to the window, opens it quickly, leans out and has a good look around. He carefully lifts up the table and swings it round and away from the window. Then suddenly a shrill noise spurts into the room like a hot beam and he drops the table and hurls himself over the window-ledge like a hurdler; the sounds go into overdrive and catch up with him as he's in mid-air: the thump from the dropped table and the shrill peep from the telephone.

The rows of beds in barrack room number one fly past him, he stumbles into the stirrup-pump used by lazy cleaners to clean the billet floor and curses as it falls over. 'What the hell's going on?' shrieks a voice behind him but he doesn't dare turn round and find out if it's the cleaner or one of the guards. He slams the door behind him and darts into his own billet. He fumbles about blindly among the cupboards lined up on parade at the bed ends. He does a body search on all of them until he finds his own. He rips off the lock, drops it on the floor, let's it stay there, and grabs hold of his haversack. His rifle tumbles down to the floor. He flings his haversack over his shoulder, stuffs the rifle back into the cupboard and races down the corridor. He stumbles out into the open air and lands like a parachutist.

Into the next barrack room. Suddenly the open door in front of him is filled by a hunched back belonging to someone who's backing into the room while chatting enthusiastically to somebody standing outside. A dog-lead is hanging down his back like an iron mounting. Without slowing down he hurls himself into the partitioned-off washroom, slips on the wet floor, and bangs his knee on a tile so hard it feels as if an incredibly long pair of scissors has been stuck through his thigh. Dragging his pain with him, he makes an ungainly leap through the open window.

He falls flat and lies stretched out panting on the ground, which exudes a pungent cloud of dust from underneath the mat of pine needles. His haversack is pressing against the back of his neck and as he lies there letting the pain roll through him in waves, he sees the situation spread out before him on a sharp, ice-cold razor blade. He sees the window he forgot to close, the cap he didn't take with him in his panic, the pump he knocked over, the cupboard he didn't lock and the sparse woodland before him through which he has to pass unobserved.

The pain goes over into long, sucking billows and he gets up on to his knees and his haversack slides down his back. A feeling of terror shoots quickly through him when he hears the animal slide down like a lump of wood to the bottom of the haversack. Then he risks it and runs straight into the pine forest, which is uncluttered and clear and has a carpet as smooth as a dance floor. He crosses over the well-worn path to the latrines and hears a door squeaking from over there. Then suddenly he hears the sound of a marching squad rolling towards him from diagonally in front – it sounds like when you're grinding corn in a hand-mill. He has to change direction and run parallel with the barracks, which refuse to sink back into the woods behind him but stare at him with their stubborn, bull-like eyes.

He passes within a stone's throw of the latrines and is startled when somebody suddenly starts whistling. He flings himself to the ground behind a tree trunk and gets his hands full of dry earth and prickly pine needles. He peers out cautiously from behind the knotty roots. Then he gets to his feet, reassured and angry with himself for being so startled. It's only the latrine emptiers who have taken a little break before the official end of their working day and are playing cards to see who pays for the beer tonight.

Then he comes into the dense, suffocating spruce forest, where clusters of berries have been ripped out of the ground, which seems to be bleeding with deep black wounds. This is where they do their camouflage training. It looks as if a mad dog has raged through, or a wild boar grubbing away at the earth. He can walk slowly here because he's hidden, and anyway he doesn't want to get to the station too soon as there's bound to be a patrol posted there all evening, at any rate whenever a train is due to leave. Here and there in the forest are enormous ex-fir trees that are now no more than a resiny flag-pole. He grins broadly and kicks at one of them so that it dances down towards the normal fir trees.

These fir flag-poles are not the result of distorted growth, but rather the camp's patented method of collecting fir branches to put on the barrack stairs and tent floors. Instead of relying on the regulation but impractical method of taking out a few twigs here and there from healthy trees, you simply get an axe, chop into the trunk of a suitable fir tree without being heard from very far away, but only so far so that the tree can still remain upright. Then you take hold of the branches and the trunk and bend it down into a horizontal position and strip it bare of all its branches with the axe. Then all you have to do is to lift up again; you all join together to raise it using the same technique as you do for maypoles, and in the end there it is, an interesting natural phenomenon to be viewed by visiting officers.

Now the commands start to echo through the forest and the sound of tramping feet grows into a little hurricane. He continues nonchalantly. After a while the earth gets darker and he comes to a stretch which is swampy at wet times of the year. Just now the only sign of dampness is the blacker colour of the soil. The fir forest gives way to an ancient, degenerated pine forest with trees spreading their grey umbrellas over the ground and light coming through as in a church.

The ground gives way in unpleasant fashion after each step, and you get the feeling there are big black birds perched in the trees, ready to sink their beaks into your neck. His mouth goes dry with suppressed tension. He walks hesitantly, looking both upwards and downwards into the darkness under a giant umbrella. Then he suddenly hears a shrill squeaking noise to one side, and he starts before standing still, ready to defend himself. As slowly as a searchlight he turns his gaze, and his body is as stiff as a pole until his safety is established.

It's a little mouse running round and round the open patch under the umbrella. It's running in a tight circle a bit like a toy train on its rails, and when he creeps towards it, it just moves the lines back.

You little bastard, he thinks, looking down at the small ball of grey fur dancing around in the gloom. He jumps forward and it squeals under his boot. The animal is lying on its back with its legs in the air, as if somebody had shouted 'Hands up!' at it. He takes off his haversack and with all his senses on the alert he unfastens the strap. It's totally silent at the bottom. He doesn't dare to look inside. He just takes the mouse by one leg and drops it in. But the haversack is half-folded so that it gets caught halfway down. He fastens the strap just as fast as he can and shakes the sack until the little bulge in the side slides down.

Then he slings it on his back and flees over the loose, treacherously springy earth. Why am I running? he thinks, as the branches swipe him in the face and it gradually gets light ahead of him. When it's completely light he feels calmer and he can run because he's in a hurry. The forest is still dense enough for it to be a waste of time admiring the view, and so it's only when the sound of broken twigs and subdued shouts registers with him that he realizes he is caught up in a squad of soldiers going back home, practising the art of advancing into battle under fire.

He flings himself to the ground with his chin pressed against a tuft of grass and his body pointing in the direction of the advance so as not to arouse suspicion. In the distance he can see grey figures trudging past. A few blank shots ring out and bodies slump down into the bushes round about him. He wriggles over to a bushy pine tree and peers cautiously through the branches. He can see Matsson crouching in the clearing and he shouts softly to him three or four times before he hears.

'Yeah, what the hell do you want?' says Matsson impatiently without raising his head.

'It's Bill. Come over here!' he shouts from behind the pine tree. Matsson looks round cautiously before wriggling over to him. They talk to each other as if they were separated by prison bars. 'I've done a bunk. Don't tell no bugger you've seen me.' 'Done a bunk?' 'Yeah, dammit, got mixed up with Vera's bloke at the café and the bitch put them on to me.' 'The little shit!' 'Yeah, but don't worry, I'll fix her. Come down to the train and bring an extra bottle. I forgot my little bugger. You are coming, aren't you?' 'Hell, yes! Shh, here comes the bloody sarge, making sure we're doing it properly. Clear off, for hell's sake. The train goes in half an hour, right?'

There's a rustling in the woods behind them and Bill runs smartly and silently past grey figures crouching in the heather and then turns off towards the road. He runs towards it at right-angles. For the last bit up to the road the forest has been burnt down and there's a crackling noise underfoot when he steps on piles of charred wood scattered at all angles over the pitch-black earth the fire has eaten through and down to the rocks.

He gets to the road and runs over it like a hare. He can see down as far as the railway line stretching itself languorously across the valley. A broad strip of woodland has burnt down as far away as that. It's the trains that set fire to it; when it's

85

dark thesparks glisten in the smoke like fireworks. Just a few isolated, blackened trunks point skywards. Apart from that the ground is like a running track. He runs along in the deep ditch by the side of the road until the forest starts again. Only the tops of the trees have been burnt here; the crowns of the pines are charred and the trees look like houses with their attics burnt out and the blackened traces of flames that have been licking the walls.

He walks through the woodland as far as the railway bridge. At this point the line turns in towards the village and cuts its way through the rock. The walls are too steep for him to be able to climb down and he follows the line until he comes to a cleft where he can get a foothold and get down that way.

The coarse gravel sounds like salt under his boots and the sun is as hot as a blowlamp in the gorge. He rounds the bend and the bridge arches its bow over the steep slope before him. Suddenly the knife-sharp silhouette of a little procession comes into view above the parapet. All he can see is four heads in a row. They bob up and down as if being tossed by waves, and cast grotesque, enormously enlarged shadows on the side of the cliff. The barrels of their rifles are sticking up out of their heads like index fingers that have grown on to their ears.

The patrol! The realization rushes through him and he leaps towards the cliff wall and presses himself close to it. He peers through the shrivelled leaves of a little birch tree clinging stubbornly to the side of a crevice, watching the row of heads bobbing up and down comically before being swallowed up by the cliff. Then he moves away from the rocks and runs straight down the middle of the track so that he can go all the more quickly. He realizes the patrol is on its way to meet the evening train so that they can look for him among all the soldiers with legitimate passes. He comes to a halt directly under the bridge and stands in the shadow of the abutment. He squeezes a cigarette out of his breast pocket and sticks it in his mouth in order to entice his nerves out of their state of shock, but he doesn't light it.

He starts creeping cautiously along the side of the cutting which suddenly slopes down so sharply he has to crouch so as not to be seen from the road. Now and then he sticks up his head like a periscope and observes the patrol striding along the side of the road like a funeral procession in a hurry. When they waddle over the road in order to cross the railway line near the station building he makes a dash and covers the few yards to the goods train standing in the siding. There's plenty of time yet, so there isn't a soul on the platform. One of the covered wagons in the middle of the row is open and he jumps inside and as he slides the door closed he can hear the clunking of the patrol's heels on the platform.

He leaves a narrow opening and through it he can hear the patrol commander yelling into his loudspeaker and informing the whole station and any thugs wishing to hear what his orders are. Rifle butts thud down on to the platform and then a series of footsteps comes thumping into his ears. He pulls back from the opening and holds his breath as the heavy steps approach. Having started off energetically and purposefully, however, they are now slow and hesitant and he gathers the spring isn't as tightly wound as it was any more.

He crouches down behind a big crate in one corner of the goods wagon and listens as the soldier passes by so close he thinks he can almost hear him breathing. He sinks back against the wall and closes his eyes and that's when he feels it, first against his back: it's as if a tap had suddenly been turned on and he is covered in sweat as his haversack suddenly comes to life. There's a scraping against his back like the hand of a child. He stretches out his legs and, simply because he has his eyes closed and can't avoid it, he sees the wide open mouth of the snake slowly wrap itself around the mouse. He stretches out on the floor and gazes up at the little beam of sunlight dancing about just under the ceiling.

A murmuring sound starts to swell outside on the platform

and he lies on his back listening to its white billows being crushed and then the breakers smashing down like houses as the train approaches. He gets up and goes over to the door. Through the crack he can see the open platform at the end of one of the carriages, and slowly and carefully he slides open the door with his fingertips. The guard's 'All aboard!' crashes over the station platform like the crack of a whip, and slowly the side of a coach glides into view. He lets that one pass, and the next, and then he leaps out and jumps on to the step and up on to the wooden platform. Now the train is getting up speed and the smoke from the engine is pressed down by the bridge. He leans out and through the white haze he can see the patrol with the index fingers on their backs wandering about among the goods wagons.

Then he enters the carriage, nonchalantly and full of triumph. A group of bombardiers are playing cards on a suitcase. A girl is sitting with her back towards him, thumbing through a magazine. He walks slowly and quietly towards her seat, and as she doesn't notice him he stands right behind her, bends down and speaks quite loudly and pointedly in her ear: 'Well, now, the lady's out and about, is she?'

Then, quickly and as sharply as a razor blade, he bites Vera's ear.

9

Dusk falls like a timid thunder-shower. It extinguishes the little lamps of the apple blossom and the white knobs on the fence. It silences the grass and the light-green grasshoppers. She's standing by the water butt, which has cracked from an excess of sunshine, and gapes hungrily at the downpipe. In the silent grass, filled with the ash of twilight, she sees a stone. It has stopped gleaming with the departure of the day, and when she leans forwards over the water butt she thinks it's a dog that has been lying quietly in the grass all day long, but now as dusk falls it's slowly waking up and stretching.

She just has to stroke that dog, so she lets go of the leaky water butt she's been leaning against until she felt a bit better, and she walks a few paces through the grass, which rubs itself lazily against her ankles. Then the little dog gets to its feet and disappears, its tail wagging provocatively, and she orders her legs to run, but only one of them wants to and hence she falls flat in the grass. Once she's lying down she doesn't bother to try to get up again, not even for fun. She just turns over on her back so that the whole of the crowded firmament with its painful pinpricks for stars is suddenly slung over her. As she watches a star with a blood-red mouth being impaled on a blade of grass arching over her eye, she thinks to herself: ah, so this is what it's like to be drunk.

It's a light, summery thought that rises up from inside her like a balloon and she lets go a whole bunch of such balloons and in the end she thinks she's full of an intoxicating gas and she grows so airy that she floats up into space sitting on the back of the little dog. But all the time, and this is what is remarkable about it, she knows with a cold, enlightening sense of unease that she's really lying flat in the grass with her helpless legs stretched out, her face glowing, and her shining eyes like misted-over mirrors.

As she feels her breast being filled with that jolly gas she can hear the shrill voices coming from the house and the equally shrill music from the gramophone on the window-ledge. 'Sweetheart,' shrieks a voice and it sounds as if it's splitting open, and then a girl laughs loudly and crazily and a door slams behind the laughter. Then the music stops, not abruptly but slowly dying away like an air-raid warning, and she can hear the shuffling of feet still moving mechanically even after the music has stopped.

'Some bugger wind up that gramophone!' says an aggressive

voice and she realizes it belongs to Eric, who's been looking for trouble ever since his third glass. She slowly turns her head so that one of her red-hot cheeks is dipped into the coolness of the grass. It feels as if her whole face is on fire, and she thinks it must be glowing so intensely they'll see her from the house. But they don't, of course. Otherwise the bastards would come out and offer me a drink and a sandwich, she thinks, and is sure she's floating in mid-air.

Now two heads appear in the window-frame and that gas bubbles up through her throat and into her head, which becomes so light it seems to be floating of its own accord, and when she strains her eyes to look up at the house she can see the two heads as if in a painting. The sharp light from inside the room spins a halo round the curly one and cuts through a blood-red ear on the other one. 'The Queen of Light and Laurence Oliver,' she says in a half-whisper and yawns and tries to kick a star with her right foot, but just then Uncle God jerks his yoyo and she notices that all the stars are yoyos bobbing up and down in space above her and she has to close her eyes before they hit her on the forehead. Then she suddenly gets a yoyo in her throat and she turns aside and vomits quietly into the grass.

When she comes round it's so dark she thinks at first she's in bed in her barrack room and has kicked off her blanket, which is why she feels cold. But then, after having fumbled for the blanket in vain, when she looks up at the ceiling and see stars poking through here and there her memory gradually tells her where she is, drop by drop. She wants to get up and walk, but her head feels so heavy she hasn't the strength to lift it up and so she just lies there helplessly. Then she looks up in desperation at the sky where the moon is shining like a lantern under a sheet. She slowly turns her head and the balloon has burst and all that's left is a nagging pain. The window is a sharply outlined, mercilessly yellow square of light in the darkness and looks threatening, and the whole house is completely silent, as if it had suddenly been struck dumb.

What's happening? she wonders and tries to get up, but then she hears a muffled, castrated murmur coming from inside, sounding like glass and giggling. Then somebody pulls back the sheet from over the moon and she thinks it's as if she is lying inside a green bottle. There's a creaking noise from near the outhouses and at first she thinks it's a bird, but when she looks that way she sees a door is standing wide open and somebody giggling loud and long comes out into the moon-light. Then she sees there are two of them. There's a boy in plus-fours, which means it's Eric, and pressed up close to him, so close that she seems to be glued on, is the giggling girl. They make their way across the garden meticulously and unsteadily as if they had only just learnt how to walk, the grass squelching at their ankles, and all the time the giggles come spurting out of the girl for all the world as if they were as necessary as breathing.

Irène is still lying inside the green bottle and as they get closer she sees that Eric is holding the girl up with his arm and that otherwise she'd fall down in the grass. She's taller than he is and so thin she looks like the stalk of a sunflower that has acquired a bigger bloom than it can cope with. Since Irène is still inside the green bottle, Eric catches sight of her and stops with his sunflower and although she can't hear anything apart from her own giggles he says to her, slurring his words: 'Look, it's that bird Bill brought with him. What the hell's he want with two birds, eh? Is he that desperate for it, eh? Ha ha! By God but she were away almost before she'd started, that bit o' skirt.'

The sunflower responds with a shrill giggle and with a blind man's gestures tries to stroke back the hair that's hanging down over one half of her face. 'Teehee, teeheeheee,' she giggles and opens her mouth wide as if she wants to say something, but nothing comes apart from a few hiccups hopping out like frogs. Then Eric gets annoyed and drags her back towards the house and from inside her green bottle Irène can see that her hair, her neck, her back and her legs are glowing ghostly white from the sawdust clinging to them.

'Two birds.' A little hammer is hammering away at the theme while her eyes are watching the sunflower tripping over the steps. 'Gerrup, you bitch. Gerrup, Ing-Lis,' yells a rough voice and helps Irène to avoid the little hammer. Why can't I be like her, she thinks, and remembers what Eric had said when the lads and *the others* as well, come to that, had started to get going: 'I'd like you to meet Ing-Lis and her sister Inga, good stuff; you know, these two are on intimate terms with the inside of every bush from the dance hall to the railway station.'

Then they'd all roared with laughter and thought it was very funny and Ing-Lis and Inga had laughed loudest, in fact Ing-Lis had laughed so much her drink went down the wrong way and they'd had to thump her on the back to stop her choking. But Irène had just blushed and didn't know where to look, and Matsson had noticed and shouted to the others: 'Hey, look at little Irène, Miss Goodie Two-shoes, she's gone all shy!' And he stroked her cheek ever so nicely and then she'd grown angry and thought: right, now I'll be just like the rest of them.

She wanted to be like the others, you see. She wanted them to like her, after all. She didn't want anybody to think she was odd or stuck-up, and most of all she wanted Bill to like her, although she'd nearly burst out crying at first when they arrived and she saw he'd brought Vera with him. That's why, to make everybody like her and not think she was sulking, she'd forced herself to drink more than the other girls. In fact she'd even led the way with a drinking song she'd heard the officers sing when she'd been serving in the mess at one of their parties. The others had joined in, and the boys had looked admiringly at her, or so she thought. Inspired by this success she'd run in and started the gramophone and thought the lads would be fighting each other to dance with her, but once the music had started the pairs waltzed in through the doorway and there were three pairs – and who'd noticed her! Then she'd slipped out on to the veranda and poured vodka or whatever it was into the biggest glass she could find and she'd drunk and drunk until she couldn't drink any more.

Then she'd gone outside and seen the dog and the balloons, had been happy and drunk and floating on air, but now she's lying in the grass, full of ashes, looking up with dead eyes at the house which has started talking again and is echoing with shouts and merry laughter. What's the matter with me, she thinks, why doesn't anybody dance with me, why doesn't anybody take me to the woodshed? Then her memory whispers something about that Colgate advert she'd seen in the newspaper with the girl nobody wanted to dance with because of her bad breath.

Then she starts hiccuping with laughter but too late she realizes her memory only wanted to trick her into crying and, racked with sobs, she turns over on to her stomach and kicks her feet in the grass. She feels she now has the strength to get up and go over to the others and say: 'Here I am, does anybody want to dance with me?' But what would be the point? And so she just lies there, sinking deeper into the grass, right down as far as the dry soil.

In the middle of her crying the little hammer comes back to her and bangs and bangs away. Two birds, think her thoughts, quoting Eric. Why had he brought her with him? Just think how marvellous it would have been otherwise. Then I wouldn't have been the odd one out. She scratches at the grass and claws at the earth like a cat at a tree. The sobs just come pouring out of her, without her being able to do anything about it.

Suddenly the veranda door rattles and somebody comes out on to the steps and stands there trying to kick the snow off his boots. Then feet tramp down the steps and she can hear there are two of them. It feels as if someone has gagged her and she's absolutely silent as she turns over on to her back. It's grown dark, there's a thick curtain hanging in front of the moon and she thinks she's lying in the blue bottle of the night. Somebody's singing, one of the girls, in the room with the gramophone, and it's a little chick-chick-chick-chick-chicken that's been badly knocked about and hops out into the silence and does a couple of somersaults before somebody drops a bottle on it and swears loudly and enthusiastically.

But the pair at the bottom of the steps are just standing in the blue bottle of the night without saying a word and it looks as though they are talking to each other through the glow of their cigarettes, which are jumping around in the darkness, first getting closer and then separating with a jolly little jump. There's no need for anyone to tell her who they are. She knows full well, just as if it were a green bottle she was lying in. Now the cigarette sparks fly through the darkness like little glow-worms and land in the grass in front of her, and a little evening breeze wafts a faint whiff of cigarette smoke into her nostrils.

The pair at the bottom of the steps start walking through the grass. It rustles a little against their legs and they're coming straight towards her and she tries to make herself as flat as possible so that they won't notice her. But they're so taken up with each other, they don't see her, even though they pass by only a couple of paces from her feet. Vera's legs seem almost luminous in the darkness. Bill has his arm round her shoulder, and to Irène lying on the ground it feels like a gigantic fish hook poking into her chest.

Now the only thing to be heard in the whole wide world is their footsteps and she tries to open her mouth and scream in order to force her way into them, but she can't. Instead she hears Vera saying, softly and enthusiastically, and it is clearly audible because it's the only sound in the world: 'Where are we going, then?' And Bill says, and he also speaks quite softly but to her lying on the ground it sounds as if it's coming through a megaphone: 'Ah, you'll see a minute!'

Vera laughs and it sounds like cooing and the fish hook twists inside the woman on the ground. She raises herself on one elbow and sees the woodshed door standing open and inviting. 'Not that,' she wants to scream, as if she'd only just realized what's going on, 'not that!' But she doesn't shout because the world isn't made for her screams, and in any case they don't go to the woodshed. They stop at the well, which is not much more than a round hole in the ground with a lid on. Standing on the lid is a bucket with a rope attached and you lower it into the well when you want to get water.

'Can't we just lie down in the grass, eh?' says Vera hoarsely, softly and urgently, and it's the only thing being said in the whole wide world just now. This time, though, Bill doesn't answer. Vera sits down in the grass, which is especially tall round the well, and only her legs are shining in the darkness. Now Bill lifts up the lid and lights a match to look down inside. Then it falls like a star and drowns in the bottom of the well.

What's going on? wonders Irène and sits up inside the blue bottle. Bill looks round and she darts down rapidly and silently into the grass. When she dares to look over the top of the grass stalks again, Bill is standing at Vera's side and in a voice that's the only one in existence he says: 'Come on, then, I know a good place.' He says it curtly and brutally, almost like an order. 'Oh, won't this do here?' she says tenderly, purring like a cat and trying to pull him down over her long legs.

Then he grabs her by the shoulders and lifts her up so that she squeals and tries to wriggle out of his grip. 'Come on then, darling,' he says, holding her steady. Then she laughs, gently and willingly, and the fish hook digs right into the woman on the ground. They take a couple of paces backwards just for fun, caressing each other all the while, and suddenly there is a scream inside her and she wants to shout out to the couple over there that they should be careful because the lid of the well isn't on, but as she doesn't have a voice in this world, she can't.

Then what she knows is going to happen happens. Vera suddenly disappears and there's a muffled plop from the bottom of the well and a scream carves its way out of it as if it had suddenly acquired a voice of its own. No doubt she can hang on until she sees if they can pull her out, she thinks, very soberly, but then the scream is cut short as if by a pair of scissors. She doesn't really gather what's happening at first but then she sees him standing there in the blue bottle, stamping on the lid of the well before striding off through the grass and getting caught in the badminton net like a fish. Before the penny has really dropped she hears him cursing, tearing himself free of the net and running away into the blue.

He put the lid on, she thinks at last; he knocked her into the well meaning her to stay there. At first she's blissfully happy because she hasn't yet really understood what's happened, but then thin little strands of scream penetrate the lid of the well and she feels scared. Then somebody lays the moon bare and she runs through the green bottle in a panic, through the swaying grass to the well. She might die, the thought flashes through her mind and she pulls off the lid and draws the cork out of the scream barrel. 'Shut up,' she yells down the well shaft, 'shut up or he'll hear you.' The scream subsides into a series of shuddering sobs and the face looking up from the bottom of the well is as green as a tree frog in the moonlight.

She's standing up to her knees in the water and her arms are upstretched as if she's in a hold-up, but Irène can't reach them even when she lies on her stomach and stretches way down into the shaft of the well. 'You'd better try to climb up the wall,' she says firmly into the echoing space, and she's efficient and clear-thinking because she's happy. The walls of the well shaft are covered in timber that has rotted away and some of it has fallen down to the bottom. There are gaps between the boards that could serve as the rungs of a ladder.

Vera is petrified at the bottom of the well, though, and can only sob and rattle her teeth with fear. Good God, is my face as green as hers? wonders Irène with a quick smile but without losing an ounce of her efficiency. 'You'd better grab hold of the bucket, then. I'm letting it down now.'

She lowers the bucket down into the well and Vera splashes her way over to the wall and Irène starts pulling at the rope.

She puts all her weight behind it but then there is a snapping noise and the rope breaks and she falls backwards into the green bottle. The bucket clatters down to the bottom, but Vera is silent. As long as she doesn't start screaming again, thinks Irène in businesslike fashion and leans over the edge. 'Now you'll just have to climb. If you can manage just a little bit, I'll try to pull you up.'

Vera stares up out of the shadows in the well and her face is blue with black edges. The whites of her eyes are shining like torches, and she starts climbing. Her shoe gets caught after the first step and she has to pull her foot out of it in order to make any progress. 'Take your shoes off and throw 'em up to me,' says Irène, and Vera does as she's told and takes one shoe off and twists the other one loose from the woodwork and hurls them up so hard they land yards away on the lawn. Then she clings on to the wall of the well shaft and starts edging her way up.

When she's got far enough up for Irène to reach her, Irène stretches her hands down and braces herself against the edge of the well and starts pulling. Vera is heavier than she is, and sometimes it seems as if she's going to be pulled down as well; but she's filled with the strength happiness brings and thus she hauls Vera up inch by inch out of the shaft. Her face, still tainted by fear in every pore, is shining green with white eyes. Surely I can't be as green as that, thinks Irène. Gradually her long neck glides up over the edge, then her white blouse black with soil and rotten timber, her skirt, ripped by nails, and her knees, grazed and bleeding, and her soaking-wet legs with the torn silk stockings.

She gets unsteadily to her feet and Irène hastens to put the lid back on to make sure she doesn't fall down again, and she stands there, shivering and dumbstruck, in the green bottle. Irène runs to fetch her shoes and puts them on for her. 'Now you'd better get the hell out of here,' she says softly, quickly and businesslike, 'before he gets hold of you again.' She daren't think what might happen if he does, and therefore she tries to give the impression of being as concerned about the other woman's welfare as possible. She tries not to think that Bill might be only too glad to find that Vera had been rescued, without him having to do it.

She says threateningly and quite close to the other girl's green ear: 'You never know what he might do if he sees you after this. Come on, I'll show you the way out.' She walks hastily over the grass towards the edge of the woods, and she doesn't need to look round to see if she's being followed. Vera's wet shoes make a slapping sound and Irène can't help giving a little smile. She walks past the whole row of houses with Vera following her like a faithful dog. No sugar lumps needed in this case, thinks Irène, and doesn't turn round once until they get to the main road. 'You go down there,' she says, pointing to the road which is sliding wearily down the slope in the moonlight. They're standing facing each other in the middle of the road and the moonlight is shining straight into Vera's face and playing magic tricks with the whites of her eyes; Irène notes she herself is slightly taller. She looks the other woman straight in the eye without a trace of animosity, and Vera's face is totally expressionless apart from a slight reflection of the surprise one might well feel at having suddenly been pushed down a well.

But she doesn't say anything and her lips, which are grotesquely enlarged by her lipstick that's started to run, don't even move. All there is is a sudden squelch and she's on her way to the crossroads, swaying like a tightrope walker. Irène goes into the woods and finds the path she took earlier with the boy, and this time she runs along it and runs herself into a state of wild, mad euphoria.

The house is silent, balancing its square of light. She goes in by the veranda door where it's dark, but she sees him even so, sitting on the bench in the corner with his head in his hands. 'You don't need to sit there like that,' she wants to yell at him, 'now you can be as happy as I am.' But she doesn't shout, although she now has a voice in the real world. Instead she puts the light on and moves the table away so that she can creep up to him. Then she realizes he's sitting there asleep and she's a bit disappointed, but she puts her arm round him and blows into his face.

That wakes him up, in a series of spasms, his eyes last. He peers at the light in annoyance and when he sees her he just mutters: 'Where the hell have you been all night? I've been running around looking for you all over the bloody place.' She thinks she detects just a little trace of suspicion in his voice, and so she points towards the road, where the well isn't: 'I've been having a little lie-down in the grass.' 'Bloody hell, have you been spud-picking?' he says, looking at her black hands. 'Oh, that,' she says, 'I felt a bit drunk and I fell down.'

He's properly awake by now and he laughs and pulls her up on to his knee. 'But now you wouldn't mind another little drink, eh?' he says, fondling her knees. She nods and reaches out for the last of the bottles with anything left in it. Do whatever you want with me now, she thinks, her head in a whirl; I want to be like the others now, so that you'll like me as much as you do Ing-Lis and Inga and Vera.

Her throat is burning when she swallows, but she smiles bravely through her tears and responds when he bites her mouth. He's lying heavily on top of her on the veranda bench but she doesn't draw back as she would have done before. Then somebody moves in the next room and they both start and sit up. 'Come on,' he says, winking at her, 'you and me haven't had a dance yet tonight, have we?' They go into the room where the ceiling light is pouring forth floods of merciless white light. Ing-Lis is lying on the sofa by the window on her elbows and knees like a four-footed animal, fast asleep. Eric is hanging out of the window, smoking.

'It's a bugger,' he says as they enter, and he speaks straight out into the night as if there were somebody out there listening. 'It's a right bugger! I could swear I heard somebody screaming out here not long ago. Have you heard anything?'

She looks up at Bill's face and it's ashen and his skin is so tight it looks as though it might burst. 'All right, love,' she'd like to say to him, 'take no notice of what he says, he's no idea what he's talking about.' Eric turns his white, porky face towards them and stares through a cloud of cigarette smoke. 'Yer what?' yells Bill, squeezing her shoulder so hard she could scream. 'You'll be seeing bloody pink elephants next. Heard anything? We're not that far gone we wouldn't hear if there were some bugger screaming. Wake the lasses up and we'll have a bit of fun, eh? We haven't come here to sleep, for hell's sake.'

He lets go of her so suddenly she almost falls down and he goes over to the sofa and slaps the sunflower's bottom so hard it sounds like a sail in the wind. Then he puts a record on, winds up the gramophone and lowers the needle and he's back with her by the time the first notes of saxophone solo come galloping into the room. They glide around and she pushes the well far, far away from her and everything else as well and then the whole room starts spinning, slowly at first like a gramophone record, then quicker and quicker. It's as if a knot has suddenly been untied somewhere inside her and a wave flings into her oblivion. When the window buzzes past she can see that it's a blue bottle outside. I want to do it now, she thinks in a frenzy, and she pulls him closer to her and bites his red ear as it hurls itself at her eyes.

All of a sudden the music stops and they stand still and she's flung back into the room again and the unseen hand puts everything back in its rightful place: the window, the lamp, the sofa, the cupboard. 'You're a right frisky little beast, aren't you, eh?' he whispers in her ear. If only he says it now, she thinks, looking out into the blue bottle, why can't we go out right now?

Then somebody just behind them starts screeching like a mouse that's been stood on, and it's Ing-Lis. Eric had lifted her up and stood her on her feet, but even so she didn't want to wake up, so he's stuck the end of his cigarette into the back of her knee. 'Why can't you let a poor bastard sleep?' she asks morosely, and pouts. She's still just as flaccid as before, but a bit more sober. 'Why can't you let anybody get some sleep?' she asks cantankerously. 'You can wake our lass and her bloke as well, then.' She takes a shoe off and belts away at the door. 'Hey, out you come!' she screeches and pulls the door open.

Why can't I ever do something like that? thinks Irène. Why don't I ever take my shoes off and belt on a door with them? Why don't I ever do something mad so that the others can't say I'm always the old sourpuss? She's standing all alone as the cold light streams down on her, and she feels dejected again. Bill has left her, and is over by the window winding up the gramophone. Suddenly, there's some sort of disturbance by the bedroom door. 'What the hell's going on here?' somebody yells, and she sees it's Matsson. He has to lean on the door jamb for support and is dressed only in his regulation underpants. All of a sudden an enormous mop of hair round a bright red face appears in the doorway, and Inga's voice cuts through the noise like a circular-saw blade. Then she runs out into the middle of the room and takes guard like a boxer.

Irène looks round the room at everybody's face, but she can't see the slightest sign of surprise or indignation and she feels bewildered and thinks helplessly to herself: Why can't I be like the others? Would it make any difference if I were to run in stark naked, wanting to start a fight?

'Come on, come on, anybody who dares to wake *me* up in the middle of the night!' wails the circular saw, and the sunflower points limply towards the window: 'There he is, if you wanna fight him.' The clarinettist starts his trill and Bill strolls over to the middle of the room where the circular saw is standing expectantly and silently, and he says: 'Huh, so you wanna fight, do you, baby?' But she's changed her mind by now and she doesn't resist when he sidles up close and they start dancing.

Now the fish hook has come back and it's a new one with a sharp point and crueller than ever. The hand twisting it round and round inside her is well used to it. Why, she thinks, why isn't that me? Why don't I strip naked and laugh and look for a fight and do something so the others can see I can be daring?

Now she knows it's hopeless, more hopeless than she'd thought, because she has nothing to look forward to, because everything is behind her and because what she was waiting for, what was going to happen to her, had come and yet not come at the same time. That's why it's so easy for the little animal inside her to get to work. It digs its teeth into delicate things. A wave of blood-red despair flushes through her and, without anyone sticking knives into her, she knows that all is lost when her dead eyes reflect the naked girl who is so superior to her because she can live life to the full without having to strain herself.

Then something happens to rescue her, at least for the moment. Matsson is still leaning against the door jamb but suddenly he starts shouting, full of triumph as only a drunken man can be when he thinks he's discovered something the sober people have overlooked, despite their saint-like expressions. 'Was it Vera who screamed?' he bellows, leaning forward like a drawn bow. Then he flops back against the door-post and grins, pleased as punch with his intervention. 'Yeah, where the hell's Vera?' roars Eric, stamping on the floor to drown the music.

Then Bill flings the naked girl away and she falls down and he races over to the gramophone and slams his fist down on the record so that the clarinettist dies in the middle of his final solo. 'I don't give a shit for your mad fantasies,' he screams right out into the blue bottle. 'I'll show you something that'll make all of you say bollocks to your fantasies. Come on.'

He rushes past Irène and his skin is as tight as a drum over his cheekbones. 'Have you the guts to come and look, eh?' They gather in the door opening and watch him dashing about the veranda. He gathers up all the beer bottles and all the rest of the bottles and stands them all over the table. Then he rummages under the bench and pulls out his haversack.

'Now then,' he yells, 'have you the guts to come over here,

eh? Have you the guts to stand round this table?' They wander in, all five of them, and the naked girl is yawning and shivering and Irène stands next to her and notices that her shoulders are all black and blue. She looks at Irène with her piercing eyes and says the only thing she's said to her all night: 'Yeah, it's all right you staring. That's what I got from the old man when I came home a bit merry last Saturday. Neither Ing-Lis nor me has been home since then.' Irène goes cold.

'Well, now, ladies and gentlemen,' says Bill, a bit like the compère at the variety theatre, 'turn your backs on the table and close your eyes till I give you the word.' They all do as they're told because they're too tired to offer resistance, or too drunk to be able to concentrate on anything. They hear something fall on to the table, then they hear a glass fall over, several in fact.

'Right, ladies and gentlemen,' he says, and his voice is on ice and they all turn round and the first ones to scream are Inga and Ing-Lis. 'Help!' they shriek, their eyes ridiculously wide open, and it sounds as if their voices are hanging from the same thread. 'I'm buggered if I'm staying in this house one second more,' squeaks the circular saw shrilly, her eyes nailed to the table as she shuffles slowly backwards, tender step by tender step. But Ing-Lis isn't shouting any more, and she isn't running away either. She's petrified and gaping as if ready to swallow every scream that might be given vent to. The lads aren't screaming either. They're staring at the table and look more sober now that they're white in the face. Irène stays put at the end of the table. She doesn't want to scream. She doesn't want to run. But she can feel something happening to her, something worse than the fish hook.

Once the naked girl has disappeared, nothing in the room moves, apart from the snake. It's looking wide-awake and lively. It looks as though there's a little torch shining behind its cruel eyes. It slowly threads its way through the little copse formed by the vodka glasses and plates. There's an ominous rattling noise when its body scrapes against the glasses and they all think it raises its flat head to scout around as it approaches the forest of beer bottles.

Now all five of them are standing round the table, feeling like they did when they were little, standing with their playmates around the tubs of washing down by the river, watching the fire burning away underneath and then suddenly sticking out a tongue of flame straight at one of them, and that one was out and dropped out of the game. That's what Irène thinks, at least, and now everyone realizes the snake is making its way towards her. It knocks over a few glasses with its long strip of a body and now Irène knows she's done for.

It's her terror whipping around inside her with its little barbed whip and she stands naked before her terror and knows it's true. And she knows it's been true all the time and that everything she's done and everything she's said had only one aim and that was to keep her terror at bay. Her terror is the little animal that nothing can keep shut in any longer. All of a sudden she screams, in fact it's the little animal that screams, as she herself has no will left any more, and the scream bubbles up through her like the carbon dioxide in a bottle of pop. Then her scream turns into words and she's scared of them and starts running: 'It's true,' she hears herself scream, 'it's true. She's dead.'

She's already outside on the veranda steps and she dives straight into the blue bottle. She stumbles and falls headlong into the grass, but she's soon on her feet again. She's already racing past the houses that are fast asleep, their eyes blind in the night. Now the pine branches are slapping her face like the hard wings of birds, but the path comes to an end and flings her on to the main road. She stands there, uncertain about which direction to run in. Then she hears footsteps coming from the forest, rapid steps, and she wants to run away from them, but just then the sheet gives way and the moon dives down out of the sky and she knows she'll never be able to get away in the green bottle.

10

Just think what it's like when daylight returns after the brief summer night. Someone's put hydrochloric acid on a broom and sweeps away the stars from the vault of the sky, which is as bright and firm as a steel lid. Somebody throws some small drops of red ink into space, and they spread out as if they've hit a piece of blotting paper high up there. The daylight arrives and it's as if a layer of spiders' webs has been taken away from the night, thick black spiders' webs that are easily caught, but the thin grey ones are still hanging there stubbornly over the earth, and that's why the man walking through the woods from north to south thinks it's still night until he sees the heather in front of him start to sparkle. It happens so suddenly and so quickly that at first he might well think it's a butterfly flapping away in the glade with its yellow wings, and he might run through the wet heather in order to try to catch it. Then he realizes his mistake and when he turns round the sky behind him from the edge of the forest and for miles and miles right up into the heavens is glowing so intensely with the deepest red colour, you'd think the sky would collapse in the heat. Instead, though, it's cold, it's the coldest hour of the day, and its clearest hour as well, when the last web of the night is brushed away by the steel brushes of the morning.

They stand still for a moment, until they start freezing, on the little crest thrusting itself up cheekily from the ocean of the forest, and watch the sunrise. They both light a cigarette, and the match goes out in the wet grass with a sizzling noise. Then they turn their backs on the sun and clamber down the wave and wander into the deciduous woods where the trees are standing newly washed and shivering in the morning breeze. They stick obstinately to the same direction they've been following all night, the one that'll take them to the railway.

What has happened is this.

He catches up with her on the main road and walks beside her in the green moonlight without saying a word. He's walking faster than she is and she has to make an effort to keep up, even though he's the one who's joined up with her. They go past the crossroads and keep going straight ahead, and the silence does a balancing act between them on a little thread. Then he says abruptly, and she realizes he's needed all this distance in order to get it out: 'What do you know about it?'

Then it dawns on her what he's thinking and she starts crying and he takes her arm and leads her into the woods. They lie down in the heather where the warmth from the previous evening still lingers. She curls up like a caterpillar and he tickles the back of her neck underneath her hair with a piece of heather. She can feel the coarse heather against her lips and without raising her head she tells him about everything that's happened to her. But she doesn't say a word about Vera because she's forgotten all about it, now that she's been touched by terror.

He lies on his back, smoking and gazing up at the moon, listening to what she has to say, and then when she's finished he says: 'You must have been dreaming it all, eh?' He doesn't say that to console her, or to be nice. She thinks he's saying it in order to forget about the well. He thinks that if what's happened to her turns out to be a dream, then what's happened to him must also be a dream, according to the useful law of compensation. That secures for himself two emergency exits. The other one is: of course they're bound to hear her in the end and fish her out and anyway nobody dies of having stood in a well for a bit.

That's why he tells her everything's just a dream, but she doesn't believe him as she lies there on her stomach, gazing down into the forest of heather. But the more animatedly she insists everything she says must be true, the more insidious his arguments become. He tells her about the strange things that can happen to people when they're a bit drunk and fall asleep in a garden, and in the end he tells her the tale of Big Jimmy, who came round one morning and thought he'd killed one of his mates. There's blood on the neck of a bottle. His skull is pounding as he wanders around the room searching for the dead body. He turns the wardrobe inside out and lifts up the bed and looks behind the stove. In the end it strikes him he must have carried him down to the cellar in order to conceal the murder, and his knees are knocking as he staggers down the stairs. He thinks he can see a dollop of dried blood on one of the handrails and that morning-after-the-night-before feeling stirs things up inside his guts. A bit further down the stairs he meets the caretaker's wife and thinks she's staring at him most oddly and giving him as wide a berth as possible. Then he creeps down the steps to the cellar and he goes more and more slowly as he thinks about the horrible sight that's in store for him down there. The moment he gets down he comes upon him slumped across the entrance and he almost curses aloud at his carelessness in leaving him in a place where anybody at all could bump into him. He lifts up his mate and takes hold of him under his arms so that he can drag him over to the office in the corner of the cellar. Then his friend starts moving and cursing and shouting at Big Jimmy for waking him up in the middle of the night. He starts waving his fists about and Big Jimmy sees his mate has a big wound in the palm of his hand, and then he remembers how he'd cut himself on a tin during the party. Then his friend tells him how he'd been thrown out of his digs that very same day and he'd only remembered that as he was standing in the entrance hall on his way home, and he'd been too drunk to go back up the stairs again and so the others had helped him down into the cellar.

While he's telling the story she starts to feel cold and her teeth are chattering and she creeps up close to him with her head inside his unbuttoned tunic. The moon sails away out of the sky and leaves behind a little hole that's soon filled by light clouds. It's like lying in a little, grey, transparent medicine bottle. She knows it's true but even so she starts playing the arduous game with the cartons and starts shutting in her little animal. There might be a way, she thinks into the prickly heather, watching the sky grow lighter through his button-holes.

'D'you think,' she says, creeping out and snapping after his cigarette with her mouth, 'd'you think we could go and look?' 'Go where?' he says absent-mindedly, pushing her down on the ground beside him. The glow from his cigarette casts a shimmering shadow in the corners of her eyes, and her eyes glisten a little in the red lighthouse beam. 'Can't we do what that other bloke did?' 'What other bloke?' he says, kneeling astride her. 'That bloke you were talking about, because till we do I won't believe it,' she says, trying to get up; but he pushes her down into the heather again with his hard hands.

Then he lies down beside her but she wriggles out of his grasp and gets giddily to her feet. A stainless-steel padlock is glittering on the catch and inside the cage the little animal is struggling impotently to escape. A feeling of mad joy at having made the decision takes possession of her. It's so easy, after all, she thinks. All we've got to do is go and look. It's as easy as that, dammit, as easy as that.

'Are you coming with me?' she asks, smartening up her hair around her ears. He's set fire to a heather twig which burns, quiet and dignified, like a candle in the fading night. He lights a cigarette with it and blows it out. Then he walks at her side in the cold light of dawn which chases away every puff of heat over the turf.

They've been walking all night but he hasn't asked her how she can know the precise spot where it happened, and she hasn't asked herself that either. But he thinks of the emergency exit: if it isn't true for her, how can it be true for me?

Shortly after sunrise they're walking through a narrow strip of deciduous forest when they suddenly find their way blocked by a broad ditch eating its way heartily through oat fields and pastures. It looks as if a slight breeze is blowing through the oats, rippling the surface, but after a while they realize it's the sun that can't raise the strength for anything more just yet.

When they've jumped over the ditch and are wondering which way to go on the other side, she sees a red cottage shining like a patch of wild strawberries straight across the fields. The sun is breathing on the veranda's eyes in little puffs, and it looks as if it were blinking at the coming morning. The chimney is hanging over the house, dead drunk. A black crack runs over it like an earthworm. There's a scraping noise as an outhouse door opens and somebody who hasn't really woken up yet walks through the glittering dew back to the house.

Slowly her memory dredges through the Imperial Canal. She bites her lower lip and shouts something out into the clear crystal air. Then they run side by side through the oat fields, and the heavy panicles, white with dew, slap against their thighs. They're out of breath when they reach the railway line, where the tracks are tossing and turning as they wake up.

'Now I know,' she says. Her breasts are heaving violently and he clasps her to him, tenderly. She looks up into his face and she is serious and pale and as tense as a violin string. They start walking along the oily gravel. The forest closes in on the railway line like a mouth.

'Just here,' she says, walking slowly now. They leave the railway line and walk side by side, slowly and reverently as if they were in a funeral procession. They pause and take a deep breath before every patch of shrubbery, but nothing other than the light of morning is lying in wait behind them. In the end the forest is thrust brutally aside and inlets of grassland reach the rails. They stand at the edge of the forest and see the railway line cutting its way into a gravelly ridge like a ruler. A grey footpath gambols its way over the field and comes to a sudden stop at a little hut raised on little stilts beside the track. The sun spits on its windows and then dries them with its dusty towel.

'I was dreaming,' she says perplexedly, out loud but to no one in particular. She yells it out loud and throws herself into his arms. Then it can't be true in my case either, he thinks, and tries to feel pleased. But then a muscle in his chest gives a twinge, and he notices that it won't work. He feels as though he's been walking all night and his trouser legs are soaking wet and his face is slashed to pieces and all that's happened is that he's found an emergency exit barred. It's not fair, it's a right bugger, he thinks to himself, turning cold.

She's hugging him tight, though, and doesn't notice anything. Then she feels his haversack on his back and just for a moment the lock rattles and the cage door shakes. 'Set it free now,' she whispers over his shoulder, and feels a lovely feeling of tiredness flowing through her veins like wine. He disentangles himself from her and strides away angrily towards the station. She sits down in confusion on a stone, and rolls down her wet stockings.

He returns after a short while, and she's surprised to see how fast he's running. Something must have happened, she thinks, and feels a little scared. As he gets nearer she can see his agitation is burning in two small, bright lamps, one on each of his cheeks. As he gets nearer still, she can see his eyes blazing as well, and they're strangely wooden and expressionless.

He comes to a stop directly in front of her and stares down at her sitting on the stone, even though she knows he can't see her. But she's surprised he is so remarkably controlled when he starts talking to her.

'You often travel this way, don't you, eh?'

'Yes.'

'You know every little station on the line, of course.'

'Yes.'

'You don't know there's one called Långtorp, though, do you?'

'Er, no.'

'That little halt down there's so tiny, you won't have noticed it before, right?'

'Yes.'

'What would you say if you knew it was called Långtorp, though?'

She shouts out in desperation, piercing the silence: 'What are you getting at? I don't follow.'

Then he says quite calmly, bending down and rolling up his wet trouser legs: 'What I'm getting at is, I don't reckon there's much point in running about looking for old woman on the Nynäs line if they've fallen off a train on the Södertälje line. I'm just saying you'd better pay a bit more attention to your geography another time. It's too bad you don't know the railway splits into two branches a bit further up, isn't it? That's what I'm getting at, you see.'

Then he slaps her face so hard she falls off the stone whimpering and lands headfirst in the grass wet with the morning dew. When she dares to raise her scorching face she sees him racing along the track at break-neck speed, his haversack bobbing up and down on his back. All the time laughter is spewing forth from his mouth like water from a spring, and when the forest cups its hands around the railway line the laughter is compressed to form a thin thread of a scream that hangs over her all the morning like a whiplash in the clear blue air. The sun climbs higher and higher in the sky and dries all the grass except for the spot where her body is resting. She's not crying, she's not thinking either, and she's not dreaming. She's just lying still in the grass under the alder tree and at first she is sprinkled by weak sunshine and then bathed by stronger sunshine and then the mature sunshine comes along and burns her helplessly outstretched legs, her body, stiff beneath her heavy clothes, and her trembling neck, burning as if through a magnifying glass with a mother-of-pearl handle.

Yes, just imagine what it's like when daylight returns after the brief summer night.

We Can't Sleep

We Can't Sleep

No, we can't sleep. There's eight of us in bed in a billet far too big for us: it's meant for twenty, but the rest are away on manoeuvres. It's not the size of the billet that prevents us from sleeping, though. It's not the light either, standing guard between the barrack rooms and showering us with beams. Nor is it the echo of the lights-out bugle bouncing from barrack wall to the barrack wall when it gets to ten o'clock. And it's not the big lorries that sometimes come rumbling past our windows at night, keeping us awake. No, it's not even the thought that tomorrow we might be summoned by the major to explain why the corridor hasn't been properly cleaned.

It's none of these things that stops us from getting to sleep. It's just that when the duty corporal puts the ceiling light out after inspection and we curl up under our thick, dusty blankets, every one of us suddenly grows aware of the faint, suffocating smell of fear oozing up from between the floorboards. We try to protect ourselves from it. Maybe we pull the blankets over our heads and cover our ears with our hands, which are icy cold after our visit to the washroom. After a while, though, we have to give up. You can't lie all night long with a thick army blanket over your head. You'd suffocate.

Then we stretch out with a sigh and breathe in the raw barrack-room air, which never seems to change but is the same intake after intake: a bit of sweat, a portion of boot polish, a dollop of floor polish, a whiff of the stables left over from the calvary days, and the rest dust. It feels as if there's always been somebody sweeping and stirring up the dust in barrack rooms, corridors and offices. We're lying in bed and breathing the air from 1909, as the billet joker said in the days when we could still sleep.

That wasn't as long ago as we thought when night falls and we nestle down under the sheets and look at our watches. We don't need to, because we can hear every time St Oscar's church clock chimes. But sometimes it's so long between chimes we think we must have dropped off and overslept, but then when we look at our watches we find it's only ten minutes since the last time we checked.

It was funny how everybody thought at first, every one of us, that it was just him who couldn't get to sleep, and nobody dared tell the others the first few mornings that he hadn't slept a wink until the brief moments between the red gleam of the sun shining through the top windows in the barrack room and reveille. Everybody tried to look as cheerful and rested as possible at morning parade, and tried to be as cheeky as they dared to the duty officer.

But at the lunch hour that first day we were all a bit surprised and embarrassed when we unexpectedly bumped into each other near the benches in the park – we'd all made our individual way there in order to have a nap. When exactly the same thing happened next day, the surprise and irritation were even greater, especially as most of the benches were taken that day.

'Good God, but you look sleepy!' we all said to each other, yawning. 'I should bloody well think so, when a man can't get a wink of sleep at night,' came the response. And then the bubble burst. We felt as if a heavy burden of secrecy had been lifted from our shoulders, and started gaping at each other. It was the same feeling of relief the whole company shared that time we all got diarrhoea after eating the veal, and had the runs all night long.

When the lights-out sounded the next night it didn't seem so bad any longer. After the lights were switched off and the door closed, we all started talking, even though we knew it was strictly forbidden. Nothing makes a man so desperate as lack of sleep, though. You get at least as desperate as you do after a shortage of food, and so it wasn't long before there were peals of laughter at some risky joke from the comedian among us. It would be wrong to think we laughed so loudly because we thought the jokes were funny. It's just that the laughter helped us to hold our fear's head under water and the effect was like a loudspeaker.

That's why it was no surprise when, after a while, the duty officer whipped open the door, turned the light on and shouted: 'Come on, then, who was it that was talking, eh?' Needless to say none of us said a word and we turned over on our sides and tried to get to sleep, and he couldn't get a sound out of us, even though he came up to every bed and shook us by the shoulder. He soon got tired of that and muttered away and turned the light out and left. We just lay as still as mice until we could hear he was no longer standing outside the door, listening.

Then we started again, but we tried to arrange it so that we wouldn't be interrupted, as we thought we'd go mad if we had to lie still and just breathe in that slightly pungent smell of fear for one more night. So that it couldn't be heard outside, we agreed we'd take it in turns to tell a story and nobody would laugh no matter how funny the stories were. We only managed three stories that night, not because the stories were all that long or because they were told in such detail, but because we simply fell asleep one after another, for the simple reason that the three stories – and in fact some of us didn't manage to hear all three or even two but just the first one – made us forget all about that smell of fear. The stories may not have been that remarkable, but they had to be told in such a low voice that we had to strain our ears so as not to miss the point which we knew would come at the end of each one.

The first person to speak wasn't the company comic, even though his mouth was always moving, even when he wasn't saying anything. We used to pull his leg and suggest his mouth must have been greased with grade-one leather polish in order to resist temptations. The bloke smelled of leather polish from head to toe, in fact. That was because he worked in the stores, where leather polish and rifle oil were the primary smells. Maybe that's why he didn't smell the suffocating aroma of fear quite as acutely as the rest of us, because the next day he claimed when we went on parade that he hadn't even heard the end of Joker's story, and even the sleepiest of us had done that.

Joker was the first one to speak, then, and we were a bit surprised because we'd normally have expected him to be the last to open his mouth. In fact not many of us had heard Joker say a single word since he joined the company a month previously. That's why we didn't know much about him. Apart from the fact that he was called up in 1919 and was the oldest of all of us in the barrack room, and that the registration book said he was a general labourer, born in Örebro. Oh, and we all knew, of course, and so did the rest of the company come to that, that he'd lost sixty crowns at poker even before he'd drawn his uniform the very first day.

It was Cheerful Charlie, our humorist in the stores, who used to get hold of the new recruits who looked as though they might be ready for it and take them into the barrack room, shuffle and deal behind one of the beds and put the stakes in a boot, and as often as not they got fleeced. That's what happened to Joker; mind you, he wasn't called that at first, but after twelve minutes, which was as long as Cheerful Charlie dared to be away from the stores sergeant's gaze, there were five folded-up ten-crown notes, a tattered five-crown note, four crown coins and a collection of silver and copper adding up to another crown in Charlie's marching boot.

Actually, that was the occasion when they were standing behind Cheerful Charlie's bed and the sergeant major came in and caught them red-handed. It was as if he'd been able to smell Charlie, or so the lads said afterwards, because he'd gone past all the doors the length of the corridor and then burst straight into Cheerful Charlie's room. 'Hmm,' he said, like the little fox he was, 'a man might well ask what you two are up to in here, eh?' But both of them were well practised in the art of furtive card-playing, and they shoved the cards up the sleeves of their tunics. 'Ha ha,' said Charlie, holding up his boot, 'I'm just showing this new lad how to polish a pair of marching boots. I reckon he needs to know,' he added, and sounded as if anybody who tried to get in the way of such a noble activity ought to know better.

When he'd gone, Joker, who wasn't called Joker yet, said, and it was the first thing he'd been heard to say: 'Good job there weren't any small change in the boot.' But there was before long, five minutes later in fact, whereupon Cheerful Charlie and the boot containing sixty crowns and a pack of cards made their way on his short, bowed legs back to the stores, which were at the far end of the corridor. Before he got there, though, he heard a thunderous voice roar out behind him: 'You bastard, you didn't have a joker, did you?' Charlie darted into the stores cubby-hole like a frightened rabbit, and Warrant Officer Boll, who was checking the locks on the corridor lockers and wasn't the quickest man there's ever been on the uptake, didn't grasp what was going on until a quarter of an hour later, and by then Charlie had thought up an explanation that was so complicated and sharp-witted he had to learn it off by heart in order to remember it. Or so he maintained afterwards.

That's how Joker got his name, although he ought really to have been called Gobless, because the one who'd had that nickname before, a pale, toothless character who was a butcher, though you'd never have thought it, had just been demobbed. Nobody had ever heard Joker say anything since the day he'd been called up and Cheerful Charlie had fleeced him of sixty crowns in twelve minutes, and that's why we were all rather perplexed when he suddenly started gabbing like normal people do. It was a good story, too, we all agreed on that – we were all on the same wavelength that night, even though we normally had such different interests, and that wavelength was just right for his story. There was something in his voice that got to you as well. It sounded as though it had been on ice for ages and now for the first time it had thawed out and could be used for what it was meant to be used for. Of course, he started so hesitantly and awkwardly that at first we were afraid he might not make it and leave us all disappointed and alone with our fear. But there was no risk of that because then, as I said, he got right on everybody's wavelength.

'I've been working all over the country, I have,' he said. 'The furthest south I've been was some little dump near Kristianstad, I reckon. We were going to blast out a well for this rich farmer, but anyway one of the lads got killed down the bottom of the shaft, and next day the old bloke comes yelling and screaming and saying he weren't going to have no cadaverous poisoning in his well, that he weren't. So we tell him to go to hell and we get his best horse and cart and we drive in to town the whole lot of us, with the old bloke tied to the back and yelling and screaming for help. We go to the square and we tie the horse to the pump and then we go to the pub for a spot of refuelling before we take the train back up north. Now none of you had better think we'd forgotten our mate just because we'd gone for a drink and a laugh and a bit of fun. It's just that when you've got a job like ours and nobody knows what the hell's going to happen when a shot goes off – if the fuse is going to go out or if you're going to be drilling down an old borehole and all of a sudden you drill right through some old bloke, like it said in the paper the other day – then you miss them that have snuffed it in a different sort of way. You don't bawl your eyes out and make a big show, but when you're sitting in the hut after your shift, or on a pile of sleepers on some embankment and eating your sandwiches, one of the lads sometimes says: "I wonder what that old bugger Olle would've said when the engineer went arse over elbow over that trolley and started whining like a lost dog because no bugger went and lit a match so as he could see and didn't spoil his best suit on a shitty old railway trolley." Then maybe somebody remembers how Olle carried the chief engineer himself up the ladder and out of that turbine shaft when they were building the power station in 1915, and brushed him down over his knee and put him down a couple of feet from the edge and then went down the shaft again, as calm as custard, no shouting nor yelling. Then the lads all laugh and remember their dead mate and think how it was when the cement got tipped all over him in that well shaft at Kristianstad.

'Anyway, when we come out of the pub the old bloke's shouting has attracted half the town and he's standing in front of the cart with the local bobby with his fingers stuck in his belt and his legs wide apart like the local bull. "Here come the murderers," yells the old bloke, pointing at us. And the bobby scowls and mutters and fingers his truncheon. And folks are staring and waiting for something to happen. Then Uppsala-Pete, who's the tallest and strongest of us all, walks as cool as a cucumber over the square towards the bobby. There isn't a sound, as if the whole of Kristianstad had been struck dumb. Cool as a cucumber, Uppsala-Pete wraps his arms round the fat bobby's belly and sticks him under his arm and carries him over to the pump in Kristianstad square. And the bobby's cursing and kicking with his podgy pins, but that doesn't do him any good. Uppsala-Pete takes the bobby's helmet off and hangs it up on the pump and then he holds the bobby so that his head is right under the pipe and then he starts pumping. He doesn't need many goes and when he's finished he puts his helmet back on and carries him carefully back to the horse and cart. Water's pouring down the poor bobby's face and his hair's hanging down like a sweeping brush. But still as cool as a cucumber, Uppsala-Pete lifts the fatty up and sits him astride the horse and ties his legs with the reins so that he won't fall off. In passing he grabs hold of the terrified old bloke and sits him behind and then he gives the horse a slap so that the two of them go rattling away over Kristianstad square. And then all the folks start laughing and cheering and it never occurs to any of them to rescue the poor old bobby.

'No fear, they all come rushing towards us and give three cheers and then, to make sure nothing happens to us, we get a big escort down to the station.

'Yours truly was only a lad then, but I was so full of admiration and respect for Uppsala-Pete, I never left him for more than five minutes or so for the next five years. We travelled round from site to site, and if there were problems at any of them, Uppsala-Pete never gave up till he'd sorted them out and got some changes made.

'We were over in Norway for a bit and that was where Uppsala-Pete lost his eye. They were building a railway and the track was going to go straight over a mountain. It was awful. All the boreholes froze up as soon as you'd drilled them and the huts where we lived were so draughty that snow drifted in through the cracks, and when you were eating, your beard would go all white before you knew what was happening. Of course, we all wanted to get away as soon as we could. That's why the bosses weren't all that keen for us to go down to the village, because loads of folk disappeared that way; but one Saturday they were having a party down there and all the gang were going to go down and join in. Somebody had to stay behind up the mountain to look after all the stuff and make sure the dynamite didn't walk, and Uppsala-Pete volunteered. He'd gone so quiet that year we were in Norway, and I didn't know what was wrong with him. Anyway, I thought it'd be a dead loss without him, so I stayed behind as well to keep him company.

'We'd been sitting in the hut for a bit and keeping warm in front of the fire and gossiping when one of the lads appears. He must have been the youngest of all of us, only nineteen, and he was Norwegian. Even though he was so young, he'd been going around the sites just like we had for some years, and he looked a lot older than nineteen. Maybe that's because he'd lost all his teeth – you soon do after a few years of nothing but coffee and sugar. Anyway, this lad had a girl-friend down in the village and he used to nip down to her in the evening when the bosses weren't looking. But that was all over since the previous week, and the lad was walking about as miserable as sin; he reckoned it was due to his teeth. Of course we all thought it was a bit of a bugger if a girl couldn't put up with a good bloke just because he didn't have any teeth. Anyway, this lad comes in moping and his face is as white as a sheet. "Aren't you going down to the village with the other lads?" says Uppsala-Pete, but there's no answer. The lad goes out again and disappears up the mountain. Then after a bit Uppsala-Pete gets up to go out and check the stores, as it's getting dark. He looks at the wall where the keys are kept and suddenly he sees the key to the dynamite shed's gone. He curses and races out, with me after him. It's dead quiet on the mountain and you can't even hear the seagulls that generally come up from the sea to go fishing in the rubbish dumps. Then we see a wisp of smoke coming up from the snow, just at the edge of the mountain where it starts swishing down to the fiord that looks like a blue shadow down below. Uppsala-Pete's more experienced than me and so he sees straight away what the smoke means, and he starts running through the snow. He hasn't quite got there when the bang comes – it sounds like it does when you drop a flower pot from the top of a five-storey house – and he falls headfirst in the snow and lies there moaning. I run up as quickly as my legs'll carry me and I lift him up and there's blood spurting out from between his fingers as he presses his hands to his eyes. I think it looks as if he's sweating blood and I turn him on to his back and run over to the trolley that's standing on the track. There's nothing I can do for him. So I pull him on the trolley all the way down to the village and they take him by boat and car to the nearest hospital. When he comes out again all we want is to shake the dust of that country from off our feet. I find myself a nice girl in Sweden and marry her and her dad gets me a steady job and I can stop working on the railway, where I've been working all these years alongside Uppsala-Pete. And it's one of them last days when it happens. You might think that's odd, when we've been together every single day for as good as five years. Anyway, we're taking the line through a cutting and the rocks we're blasting are pretty loose. It's the last shift on the Saturday before Easter week and I'm finishing at Easter. We're going to do just one more blast, even though it's pretty late on Saturday morning, and the clearing up will have to wait until Monday morning. Still, everything's ready for firing and the blaster, that's Uppsala-Pete, is standing and plucking at the fuse before he lights it. He strikes the special match and all of us lying under cover in the woods can see the blue smoke floating up into the sky. When he's lit it he starts jogging away like he usually does, but then all of a sudden, and we're all dead scared, he turns round and starts running back again and we know the blast'll go off any second but we can't do anything to help him. Afterwards nobody can understand what got into him. And it goes off and we could see how he was smacked down to the ground by all the rocks and as quick as a flash there's a big pile on top of him. We ran over as quick as we could but there was nothing we could do. It was all loose rock and these big blocks of stone had piled up like a pyramid and they were swaying on top of each other and somebody ran up with a crowbar and tried to shift some at the bottom. But it was obvious that wouldn't work and so we ran after a ladder so we could climb to the top of the pyramid. And then one of the lads shouted: "Look, he's still alive!" As I said, all the stones were quite loose and there were gaps between them and one of the lads had just happened to look down and there right at the bottom of the pyramid was Uppsala-Pete's eye staring up at him. There was nothing more to be seen of him, just that horrible living eye with a black sheet over everything else, and everybody was all excited and wanted to have a look. And afterwards lots of them were ashamed and felt sick when they realized they'd been acting like folk at the monkey cage in a zoo. The engineer, who's gone all white and is looking down at the ground, shouts: "Stop buggering about. Put a hanky over the hole." And he slings his own hanky up to me where I'm standing on the ladder. But then comes Uppsala-Pete's voice from the bottom of the pyramid and the funny thing is, it sounds more or less like normal: "Bugger this for a lark! Get me a drop of water instead, I'm so thirsty." So I fling the engineer's hanky away and I jump down from the ladder and knock him over as I land and I run like a greyhound to the hut where the bucket of drinking water is. I fill a scoop and run back to the pyramid but it's too late. When I get there our mate's dead, they tell me, and somebody's laid his hanky double thick over the peephole. I just drop the scoop and think it's a shame that I couldn't even give him a drop of water before he died when we'd been travelling around together and working together for five years. We spend all Saturday afternoon taking the pyramid to pieces and when we get to him, there's none of us can understand how he could manage to live for one second with the injuries he had. When we'd finished, and we had to work by lamplight the last hour, one of the lads says: "There's not many gentlemen that get a monument for themselves when they're dead as big as the one Uppsala-Pete built for himself."'

We lay still and quiet in our beds when Joker had finished, and from that moment on all of us acquired a very special kind of respect for Joker. Most of us, or maybe all of us, had never experienced anything remarkable, anything that was so special it deserved to be told like this. We lay there trying to remember our own little adventures, our work places, and tried to conjure up somebody we knew who'd been as great as Uppsala-Pete, but, strange though it might sound, we couldn't think of anybody. Of course, you might say it was the mood and the liberating feeling of being able to forget our nagging fears, which blew up what we'd heard out of all proportion, but even in more normal circumstances we could hardly have failed to be impressed.

Several of us also lay there feeling a bit jealous of somebody who could tell a tale so well, and it was probably pure jealousy that made Cheerful Charlie, for instance, maintain afterwards that he'd fallen asleep in the middle of the story about Uppsala-Pete, because it's often the ones who are wittiest and always ready to chime in with a comment in all circumstances who actually find it rather hard to tell a serious story with a meaning.

It was probably jealousy that drove Sörenson, the ex-sailor with the angular profile, to volunteer. Everything about him was angular, in fact, from his forehead, which looks as if it could stab you, to his pointed nose, and his chin that stuck out almost like a goat's beard. He was a little fellow, slightly built, and his shoulders and knees and elbows were as sharp as javelins. But the most angular thing about Sörenson was his voice. It was shrill and screechy like an old woman's, yet there was something about it that prevented you from making fun of it. There was something about the man that inspired respect, despite his wretched appearance. Inspiring respect may not be the right phrase, but one sort of drew back when he came and said something or wanted something. Maybe it was just having been a sailor that gave him a certain aura, although you could hardly say he boasted about it. Perhaps he did indirectly, but in any case it didn't annoy anybody.

When Sörenson started talking, several of us probably thought he was quite the wrong person to follow Joker, and generally speaking we didn't really expect much of Sörenson as a story-teller. The problem was his voice, which wasn't exactly full of charm. It could be effective when he wanted to frighten somebody or to make a point, but to be forced to lie listening to a long story told by a voice like that was a bit like going to the cinema and having to sit on a bed of nails. That's what we thought, at least, but we were a bit wide of the mark as it turned out, because his voice wasn't quite as bad as we'd thought, and although he told his story quite badly, with long pauses and a few fits of coughing, we got rather a lot out of it; we were frightened by it and, although we were reluctant to admit it, of course, quite impressed by it as well, in quite an idiotic way, in fact.

'It were during the last war, one of the last years,' he started off, and at first we were a bit put off by his piercing tone of voice, 'when I were doing my national service in the navy. I want to forget as much about it as I can, and I had actually forgotten most of it when I went out to sea after it were all over, but it were real hellish, much more hellish than this one. If any of you in this room's been in a town with a naval station, you'll know how bloody it can be. You're being watched all the time from all sides, by the locals and by the officers, and if you don't behave like a bloody Sunday-school teacher when you're out in the streets, you can be bloody sure some bugger'll come and run you in. And you know what the girls are like in a dump like that. What they want is blokes with something on their sleeves, otherwise you can bet your bottom bloody dollar they won't even look at you.'

Oh my God, we thought, now he's going to start moaning again.

'There were only one place in the whole of town, in fact, where an ordinary rating could go, and that was a café called the Green Cottage. The message was passed on in a whisper from man to man in every new intake, and the ratings would hang around in groups at the tables and try to work out some reasonably fair way of dividing up the girls there. They were sort of common property, and nothing for a boy who wanted a steady girl-friend. There were a story attached to one of the girls as well. Every new intake heard it and everybody who told it swore blind it were one of them true stories that get passed on from class to class. Anyway, they reckoned that some of the boys had managed to smuggle a bit of skirt past the guards one Sunday night. They say one of them had pretended to be drunk and lured the guard away from his post and the rest of them had taken the opportunity of slipping past. Then they'd all had their fun with her in the barrack room all night long, and when the reveille sounded, the poor girl were so exhausted she could hardly stand on her feet. Anyway, one of the boys were missing from parade that morning. He'd been painting the town red and hadn't managed to get back in before lights-out, and so to save him at parade time some bright spark hit upon the idea of letting the girl take his place in the squad. They put a pair of uniform trousers on her, pulled a tunic over her head and stuck a sailor's hat on top. Then they led her out on to the barrack square and stood her in the right place. She were quite well hidden and the boys managed to fix it so that she turned more or less the right way when the commands were called. No doubt it would have gone OK if it had been the usual half-blind warrant officer, but as luck would have it a lieutenant by the name of Wester, a new boy, were taking the parade that morning. He suddenly got it into his head the boys weren't wide enough awake and so he gave the command to go running at the double, and it had never happened before that they'd been made to do anything like that before breakfast. Anyway, when the boys started running around the poor girl was frightened to death and didn't know what to do with herself. Then the lieutenant comes rushing up to her and gives her a poke in the chest and she falls over: "Can't run at the double, eh?" he yells, but then it occurs to him that it was unusually soft where his fist had landed and so he picks her up by the shoulders, knocks her cap off and discovers she's a girl.

'Nobody knows what happened next, but there's some as maintain the whole story were made up by Lieutenant Wester just to make himself popular. That would have been just like him, because Lieutenant Wester were incredibly cunning, but the fact is, it wouldn't have helped him much because there weren't another officer everybody hated as much as him. You heard about him as soon as you came to the camp: "Watch out for Lieutenant Wester. You're in trouble if he gets his hands on you." It was amazing how scared everybody was of that Lieutenant Wester. They reckoned that even his superiors were very careful how they handled him.

'It was a long time before I really understood why the boys were so frightened of him, and the first time I met him I thought he were the nicest officer in the whole navy. But then I met loads of boys who said that's exactly what they'd thought the first time they'd seen him, and that first time were generally when they'd done something wrong, like climbing over the barrack gate or forgetting to salute or some other misdemeanour. Then he'd been nice to them and helped them, and they'd been grateful to him for a whole week, until somebody came and told them they were on jankers with Lieutenant Wester.

'Well, it wasn't clear what that meant, so I didn't pay much attention to what they said. Anyway, one day, or one evening rather, I were out walking in the country all by myself. There can't be anywhere where as much sexual desire builds up in concentrated form as in a garrison town, and as the city girls were so unapproachable, the sailors used to go prospecting in the villages round about and try to flush out a few bits of skirt. Some people thought it were best to go hunting alone, of course. Anyway, there I were strolling down this country lane all by myself when this girl comes cycling up behind me. I wait till she catches up with me and then I grab her handlebars and ask her if we can't keep each other company for a bit. She can't very well do anything else but get off her bike and so we walk along and lark about and prattle away. When I reckon we've walked far enough, I ask her if it wouldn't be a good idea to put the bike down and sit on the verge for a while. Anyway, things went the way they usually go and it was pretty good all round and when we've finished, we hear there were somebody walking towards us along the road. It's a feller dresser in civvies, short and fat, swinging a cane in one hand and puffing away at a cigar. "Shh, there's somebody coming!" I whisper to the girl, and we try to make ourselves invisible. At first I think the feller's going to walk straight past, but then I can hear from his footsteps that he's stopped right in front of us. "Oh," says the girl, "it's Lieutenant Wester." "That can't be no lieutenant," I whisper in an attempt to calm myself down. But then the feller on the road says, and he sounds so friendly and understanding: "Isn't it a bit wet to be lying in the grass?" Then I believe her after all and I try to sound cheeky and unaffected: "No, Lieutenant, it's OK." Then he takes his cigar out of his mouth and he gives us a friendly nod and he smiles and he takes the girl's bike and he puts it down beside the ditch so it won't get in the way of the traffic. Then he continues on his way, swinging his cane just as contentedly as he were before.

'That were a decent feller, I think to myself as I brush the girl down. But I don't get a chance to say a word before she's up on her bike and pedalling away as if the devil himself were behind her. Then I realize she's been scared the whole time, and that she's only done it because she were scared. Well, that were the biggest disappointment I've ever had in all my life in that line.

'A few days go by and I forget all about it and because of my bad luck I manage to get myself quite a cushy number. There's a boat that usually plies the islands off Stockholm that the navy's requisitioned, and it needs repainting. But then I hear I'm going to be on jankers for Lieutenant Wester. Only too true. That afternoon the friendly gentleman in question comes down to the old tub. He's in uniform now, though, but he's still puffing away at a cigar and his face is still just as puffy, but he's not quite so friendly any more. "You'll report here tomorrow, Saturday, at three o'clock," he says. "You know why." Then he goes and I think, that's a stroke of bad luck. On a free day and all that.

'In any case, there I am standing on the quay and I see I'm not the only one. There are three more standing there, gazing glumly down into the oily water. On the stroke of three

Lieutenant Wester comes out on to the bridge and invites us on board. He doesn't shout at us when he meets us on the foredeck. It sounds as though he wants to take us for a little cruise. He calls us "gentlemen" and he's so nice we think the others must have got it wrong. We're going to start with a bit of PT and we'll have that down in the engine room because it's so nice and cool down there. We reckon that sounds great and we're only too pleased to take off our boots and socks when he asks us to. It's not as cool as we thought in the engine room, though, because the furnaces are all burning and the doors are wide open and we're sweating away in our thick uniforms even before we start moving. Then the PT starts and we realize why we had to go barefoot. He's scattered a layer of coal all over the floor and we have to jump on the spot and rise up on our toes and then fall forwards and do press-ups on the sharp pieces. At first, before we start going quick, we can manage to avoid putting our feet on the sharpest bits, but when the pace hots up it's impossible to manage anything at all and after a quarter of an hour of PT both our hands and our feet are bleeding and we reckon it couldn't be more hellish even in hell. Still, after half an hour the bleeding's stopped and we think how strange it is that you can get used to anything, because we can't feel a thing, in fact, and coal dust has got into the wounds so that they've stopped bleeding, but there's coal dust in our mouths as well and we're so thirsty we'd give anything for a mug of water. After three quarters of an hour we feel no pain at all and we're not thirsty either, actually. We're just so bloody tired it'd be bliss if we could just fling ourselves down on the coal and drop off to sleep. But we can't, because a PT class lasts for an hour, and when that hour's up we're robots and we think it's a pity we have to stop now that we've just got into the swing of it. It's only when we start climbing up the ladder we feel that our feet and hands are nothing but big wounds and then we see red and we'd love to wring the neck of the person that's done that to us, but only for a short while, because then we feel so exhausted again we'd give three cheers for our tormentor. I think that's what all four of us were feeling as we tried to find our boots and socks up on deck. There were no point in trying to put them on because it would be some time before our feet would go into a pair of normal boots, and we noticed how bloody hard it was to walk on a floor that didn't have bits of coal scattered all over it.

'If that had been that, then you can be sure nothing would have happened, because we'd got to the stage where we were quite harmless. It goes in shifts. The first half-hour you're raving mad, the second you're apathetic, but then comes a time when you're hopping mad again. When the lieutenant gathered us round him on the foredeck, pointed to the foremast and said he'd like to take a picture of us standing up there holding a block and tackle on the yard-arm, all four of us knew without looking at each other what were going to happen. First we went on our tender feet to fetch a long ladder that were lying on the quayside, and, in spite of the hellish agony we were going through, we raised it and leant it against the foremast. Then we went to fetch the block that were also lying on the quayside. It were a massive iron block and we could barely manage to lift it, even though there were four of us. When we'd got it on board we had a little rest and the four of us stood in a bunch staring at the yard-arm that were such a ridiculously long way up, we were all so shattered, you see.

'Then Wester appeared with his camera and yelled at us, "Haven't you got the block up yet?" and it were remarkable how light we suddenly thought it were when we lifted it up and started climbing up the ladder. It were so broad we could climb two abreast with the block between us. We edged our way up step by step, and we were frightened the ladder would slip and take us with it, but it were leaning at a good angle and it didn't look as if there were a risk. Finally, when we'd nearly got to the top, Lieutenant Wester appeared and stood next to the ladder directly underneath us, looking straight up at the yard-arm. We lean over the edge of the ladder and, although we haven't even looked at each other, we all know exactly what's going to happen. We look down and scrutinize the bone-white forehead which looks like a white ribbon from up above. The rest of his face is sunburnt, but his forehead is shiny white, as if he'd put some ointment or other on it. We look around but there's no sign of a soul in the whole harbour area. Oh yes, I remember seeing a black cat jumping out of the control cabin of a crane just at that moment, and then the iron block started slipping out of my hands and I don't know who let go first or if we all let go at the same time but we looked down at that white forehead just once more before the block crashed into it.

'Anyway, there were an enquiry and everybody thought it were a regrettable accident. Here's the remarkable bit, though: there weren't a single one of us four who'd dropped the block on his head who said or even thought anything except that it were an accident. Indeed, if any one of us had said to one of the others: we killed him, you know, we'd have stared at him and said he must be mad. That's why we slept easy at night. We never met, we barely said hello to each other, and then we lost contact when we were posted. It were at least a year before I actually started dreaming about it. I would wake up covered in sweat in the middle of the night and be convinced he were somewhere in the room with his head split open, and after a week of that I were forced to move. I found some new lodgings and hoped I'd be able to sleep better, but it were hopeless. In the end I had to go to sea in order to get away from it all, and I managed to forget about it when I were together with all my mates on board. It took time, though. But when we got to Lisbon a Swede signed on and before many days had passed, we recognized each other. I think both of us had been hoping against hope we weren't who we thought we were, but it weren't until we got to Malaga that we dared to ask and by that time we'd been looking askance at each other and sleeping badly all the way from Lisbon. The other bloke went ashore in Malaga and never came back again, and nobody could understand why – except me. But I didn't say anything and I haven't ever said anything till now.'

When Sörensen had finished it was so quiet in the barrack room that even the soft chiming of the clock at St Oscar's sounded like a bugle call. There was nothing anyone could say about his story, nothing to ask. There was something unresolved about it, it wasn't quite finished somehow or other, or so we thought, and we actually lay there thinking we were somehow participants in it. It was just as if we had been one of the four who had brought about the death of that lieutenant one hot, sunny afternoon. Of course, we gradually came to realize it was probably what had been happening to us that made us feel this mysterious sense of solidarity in the face of something horrific. At the same time, though, we no doubt thought about the situation with regard to Sörenson's and the others' guilt, and wondered whether it really was a murder. We probably reached different conclusions in that respect. Perhaps the more advanced of us, whoever they might be, started thinking about the borderline between a crime and what looks like an accident. But it's dangerous to start thinking about such matters, especially at night, when you're scared and haven't been able to sleep for ages because of that fear.

That's probably why we felt pleased and relieved when the silence was finally broken. It was as if someone had bound us together again, and that gloomy mood that had been oppressing us had been dispersed. The best thing was probably that the one who started talking was so soothing and confidence-inspiring, we knew he wouldn't scare us with his story. He was chubby in both his face and his body, without being podgy and flabby. There was something steady about his voice as well, come to that. He very rarely said anything, nothing lengthy at least, but what we'd heard from him in the past made us expect we were going to hear a story that would sort of smooth things over – well, maybe that's not the right phrase – something that would round off the edges of what Joker and Sörenson had said, and was now lying inside us, chafing away.

That's why we were a bit startled at first when he started talking in his calm, steady voice and announced that he was going to tell us about something that happened to him when he was in Spain in 1938, 'doing a bit of shooting', as he put it in his dispassionate, rounded way. There were two reasons why we were startled when Edmund said those introductory words, no matter how round, steady and confidence-inspiring his very name sounded. Firstly, and in view of the mood we were in this was the most important reason, we thought we were going to hear something shattering and we were far from sure we'd be able to cope with it on top of all the rest; and secondly, we were extremely surprised to hear Edmund had been down there in Spain, fighting. It seemed to us so incredible because it was so difficult to associate the chubby, unflappable Edmund with anything to do with fighting, such as killing somebody. It seemed strange for another reason as well, namely that a few of the more alert amongst us hadn't really begun to grasp the significance of the civil war in Spain for world peace until now, when the real war had been going on for several years. We were surprised that Edmund had caught on to that idea so soon. In fact, some of us were even a bit jealous.

Still, once Edmund got going and started telling his tale, we soon realized all our misgivings had been unnecessary. It was typical of Edmund, in fact, that he didn't tell us about what had happened during a bayonet attack or about hand-to-hand fighting among the cypresses at the edge of some little Spanish dump. It was typical of him that instead he told us the following story.

'We were retreating somewhere near the Spanish Mediterranean coast in the east. It's a bit hard to name names, partly because we'd only just got to Spain and it was difficult coping with the names of places in Spanish, and partly because you tend not to remember the names of places when you're retreating. It's very different when you're advancing. In that case you have your eyes skinned for every little road sign you pass, but when you're retreating it's as if you just stare down at the ground and you've no idea where you are. Still, there was no question of a chaotic retreat, because it was before we'd realized the situation was hopeless and we weren't miserable or depressed. It was just as if we were taking a few days' holiday, and we'd be back at work again before long. It was quite a different story when the other side were retreating. The first few days after I got there we'd launched an offensive – well, not a real offensive, I suppose, but just a quick little raid – and we'd managed to take a few prisoners. They were shaking like a leaf when we rounded them up in a little ravine – they'd thrown away their rifles so they could run faster. They were mostly Italians shouting and yelling at each other, and in fact we had to threaten to shoot them in order to shut them up. Anyway, that episode led us to underestimate the enemy, or at least the newcomers amongst us did. When the reinforcements arrived and we were forced to withdraw, we were optimistic enough to think, as I said, that it was just a question of a couple of days' holiday. But, as I said, no matter how voluntary a retreat might be, you still stare down at the ground, and we marched or drove through village after village, little town after little town, without really noticing what they were called. Another factor, no doubt, was that they all looked so similar. All the villages, whether they were huddled in the forest or sparkling away on the hillside proud as peacocks, shared one common factor with the towns we came to: they were all deserted and burnt down. Village after village, town after town, they were all comp-rehensively bombed by the enemy air force, which was naturally at our heels all the time we were retreating. During the last days of the retreat, they hit our supplies back-up, and we were as starved as rabbits by the time we eventually met

up with our reinforcements and could point ourselves south-
wards again.

'Anybody who's seen what a burnt-out house looks like can
imagine what it's like to see more or less nothing else for days
on end. Actually, there were surprisingly few ruins in the
places we passed through, but the houses had gaping holes
where windows had been, and smoke-blackened walls, staring
at us as we approached. They looked like dead bodies standing
there, empty and abandoned. It's amazing how the outline of a
house changes as soon as it's empty, and the curtains and
flowers have disappeared from the windows, the panes have
been blown out, the doors ripped off, and flames have been
licking the outer walls. They look so threatening that you're
actually frightened of them, and you hardly dare go inside. It
was so quiet when we came to the villages that the only sound
we could hear was our own footsteps. There wasn't a human
being to be seen, and in fact it seemed sometimes as if we
were the only people left on the whole globe. At times like
that it could even feel good when the enemy aeroplanes
swooped out of the wispy clouds and started circling round
our column. Without realizing it, we actually walked more
quietly and lowered our voices as we walked through the
burnt-out, abandoned villages, as if we were frightened of
waking somebody up. In any case, we were forced to find
quarters for the night – or rather somewhere to have a rest,
because we were in such a hurry there wasn't time for a
whole night's stay in one of those terrifying houses – and
during the last few days of the retreat when the supplies
back-up had been bombed we even went sifting through them
to see if there was any food left that we could take. There
wasn't, of course. Just the rats running away as we blustered
through the rooms; it's funny how quickly rats take over a
deserted village. If all humans were blasted off the face of the
earth, it wouldn't be long before the world was run by rats.

'Anyway, one evening after an unusually hot day we came
to a deserted village that looked just like all the others we'd

passed through, and it was agreed we'd stop there and have a rest before continuing in the middle of the night. The whole of that day there'd been one aeroplane circling over us and we'd felt a sort of muted surprise at the fact that it hadn't attacked us until we realized it was one of ours. It was such an unusual sight that we felt more encouraged by it than we'd have felt if confronted by a whole squadron of our tanks, and as a result the mood had improved in that irrational way that happens if, for instance, you think you're ruined and you suddenly find a tanner in your trouser pocket. We were in one of those desperately jolly moods when we got to the outskirts of this village that afternoon just as it was getting dusk.

'We weren't expecting anything special, sad to say; we just made the usual tour to see whether some careless farmer had left behind a calf or an ox for us, but no chance, as usual. The patrol I'm in gets to the other side of the village without having found anything out of the ordinary. But then, behind a thicket, we see something that makes us jump and put our rifles at the ready. There's a house, burnt out like all the rest; but this one has blankets hanging in the windows, and the chimney's still there and there's smoke coming out of it. We edge cautiously towards the magic house, ready for any kind of surprise. Nothing happens, though, and we creep up to the front door that's actually undamaged and still on its hinges.

'One of us kicks the door open and then flings himself to one side so as not to be shot in the chest if there's a booby trap laid. But there isn't a sound to be heard at first, and we start getting a sort of creepy sensation – but then it comes. Somebody inside the house starts cursing in pure, unadulterated Spanish, and the Spaniards among us giggle silently, their teeth flashing white. Then they shout something into the house, and we can tell by the tone of it that it's something quite rude, and the next moment a little wizened old man appears in the doorway, the strangest little man I've ever seen in my life. When he sees us he jumps up and down like a football and shouts and makes wild gestures at his throat. But the Spaniards slap the old man on the shoulder, and he shuts up immediately.

'A friend who can speak Spanish whispers to me that the old man thought we were Franco's troops arriving, but the Spaniards had reassured him. I look closely at the old man, but he just stands there quietly in front of his house. He looks like a piece of dried meat that's been hanging a bit too long. He has the usual Spanish sandals on his feet, *albagatas*, but otherwise he looks almost like a cowboy, with his wide, fringed leather trousers hanging round his skinny body from two bits of string. He's wearing nothing on the upper part of his body but a thin white vest, and on his head is an enormously wide-brimmed straw hat and his white hair is hanging out in tufts underneath it. Mind you, he's not silent for long. His eyes flash and he starts spitting out Spanish sounds like the fastest of our machine-guns spit out bullets, and my mate who knows a bit of rudimentary Spanish has no chance of keeping up. The Spaniards just laugh, showing their teeth, and follow the old man over the courtyard to a little wooden shed that looks as though it's about to fall down from old age.

'The old man lifts the latch and opens the door of the little shed: straight away there is a cackling which really hurts our ears – they have been resting for some days after all. In the shed is a big crate with a thick sheet of cardboard over it. There are big stones on all four corners of the sheet, and the old man has cut out sizeable round holes. We go up to the crate one by one and look through the holes, and once we've got used to the dim light we can there's lots of geese lying down inside. It's impossible to count them because the whole thing is a writhing mass of necks and beaks, and the Spaniards are smiling again as they look in, but we others think it's a shame for the poor birds and the colleague who knows a bit of Spanish asks the old man why he can't set them free and let them go and feed on the hillside.

'Then the old man tips a torrent of words over him but one

of our Spaniards explains quietly and precisely that the old man has been keeping his geese in that crate in that shed ever since the war started, and he intends to keep them there until the war is over; he's been occupied once already by the Franco troops (so that's why all the houses are burnt out, we think), and the old man in all his simplicity did a great favour to the Republic; the old man doesn't want to lose any of his geese at any price, but, the Spaniard adds softly, giving us a sly wink, he's probably going to lose the odd one even so.

'We're invited to stay in the old man's house, and we accept with pleasure. He even gives us a bite to eat, and we're full when we lie down to rest that evening, the first time for several days. We roll ourselves up in our overcoats with our rifles in our hands. We've grown so used to sleeping with our rifles, we probably wouldn't be able to sleep if we didn't have them by us. It feels as though we've had our eyes closed for five minutes at most when we're suddenly woken up by an irritating humming noise that's getting louder. It's just as if we had a bumble-bee in our ears, humming away.

'We take our rifles with us and assemble in the clear, silver-white moonlight in front of the house and watch the enemy squadron emerge from the disc of the moon as if by some macabre miracle. Then we clench our teeth and curse our naïvety and optimisim which led us to think the plane circling around us all the previous day had been one of ours. Now we realize it had been one of their observers. The plane had in fact been the same type as one of our commonest aircraft, if you can talk of one type being commonest in the ragbag of an air force our side could muster, and we agreed the other side must have captured it during a snap attack on one of our airfields.

'Anyway, there we were in the courtyard watching three waves of bombers rolling towards us, and I'd be lying if I didn't admit we were scared. We were. You have to be if you're in a little village crammed into a narrow valley. It couldn't have been easier for them if they'd been ordered to drop a bomb in the middle of the Mediterranean while they were flying over it. We felt as if we were stuck to the bull on a target just before a shooting competition starts when we went back into the house and closed the door firmly behind us, as if that would make any difference. Then we sat down in a row along one wall, and just waited.

'And we didn't have to wait long. We'd been in air raids before, both in cities and out in the open, but never before in a rat trap. In the cities you sit listening to the distant booms and wish they would start dropping bombs a bit closer so you didn't need to hear the waves gradually creeping up on you. Then you hear a bang in the next block or so, and you feel you're safe this time at least. It's probably worst out in the open. You lay pressed down in the grass, but know that won't help one iota. You get the feeling the earth is as bright as a bullet, and offers just as little chance of finding a hole to creep into. You think you're exposed to the heavens, and might just as well be bobbing around in the air like a barrage balloon, as a target for their machine-gun salvoes. Then you lie counting when the bombs start whistling. It's the only thing that helps, and when the explosion comes and the air is like a tornado above you but you haven't been hit, then you get this mad feeling of joy. And this crazy feeling takes hold of you while the explosions are thundering all around you, and you've escaped for the time being.

'But this was something very special, more cruel, more relentless. I don't think we bothered to count when the whistling started. The whole house shook in the explosion, although we thought we could locate it on the outer edge of the village. Then the whistling was drowned by all the explosions, and we felt as if we were in a boat in heavy seas. We fell headfirst on to the floor, and could hear through the noise the sound of machine-gun bullets. We realized that part of the column must have run out into the open and been seen. That was certainly what saved those of us who stayed in the house.

'We lay face down on the floor and pressed our heads down

as hard as we could, waiting for the next wave of the attack. But there was nothing, the thick blanket of noise faded away and only the rattle of machine-gun fire was left. Then came a noise we hadn't noticed before and it shut out all the others and we looked at each other in surprise as we slowly got to our feet and ascertained that we were uninjured. Then one of us caught on to the fact that the noise was coming from inside the room, and we realized it was the old man snoring.

'We couldn't help laughing eventually, and we tiptoed over to him as he lay in a corner, wrapped in a heavy blanket. A few individual bombs started dropping a good away from us, and in the clear moonlight that filled the room after the blankets had been blown out of the windows we could see that his lips were moving and he was mumbling something. He was tossing and turning restlessly and he threw off the blanket. We were quick to wrap him up in it again, so that he wouldn't wake up. With the explosions rumbling away in the forest quite a long way behind us, we stood around the sleeping old man and thought about nothing else but his slumbers. It was as if at that moment the only significance the war had was whether or not the old man could get a bit of sleep, and if he woke up the war would have been lost as far as we were concerned.

'But then, after a few minutes of silence, it suddenly starts whistling like a whole orchestra of whistles above us, and the next second comes the explosion. It's so near we feel as if the air's been sucked from inside us and our lungs want to follow and when the bang comes it feels as though our heads have blown up. We fall all over each other and in the middle of the roar we think we can hear some cackling, but maybe that's just our imagination, and then things come flying in through the windows and crash into the walls and on to the floor. We thank God we weren't standing directly in front of a window and just as the noise dies down we hear the old man moaning away and we bend anxiously over him. His eyelids twitch but he doesn't open his eyes, he just tosses and turns restlessly. He mutters half-aloud, and we gather he's partly awake at least. Then one of the Spaniards leans over his face and whispers something, quietly and gently, and we see how the old man relaxes again and sinks back into slumber and starts snoring. Then we sidle up to the window and see it's the old man's shed that's been hit.

'We pick up all the bits of plank and stuff that've flown in through the windows and fling them out again. Then we hear the hum of the engines getting fainter and fainter and when we go out into the courtyard we see the aeroplanes flying into the moon like small silver flies. It's all over, and we go out to look for our comrades. They make their various ways back into the village and we soon see that our losses have been slight, thanks to the fact that most of them had guards posted outside and were more observant than we were and managed to get away into the woods before the first wave of bombs fell. Apart from that, the main part of the village is now lying in ruins and five of our comrades were caught by the machine-gun fire and are lying in the village street. We buried them in a field just outside the village, and placed their rifles over the spot.

'We strolled about the village till dawn, when we were due to continue, and examined the damage. Never in my whole life had I seen anything so comprehensively bombed out as that village, and it was a miracle the old man's house hadn't been hit as well. Some of the houses had collapsed into the street, and up in the top of a cypress tree hung a three-legged table. There were big craters in the road here and there, and one of the bombs must have fallen directly on a natural spring because one of the craters was full of water despite the fact that the summer had been remorselessly dry.

'Eventually we got back to the old man's house, and by then the sun had already started to rise and it was quite light. We stood looking at the house and the devastation that had taken place when suddenly there was a creaking noise from the door, which, remarkably enough, had managed to remain unscathed despite the blast. Seconds later the old man appears in the doorway, wearing the same trousers, shirt, hat and sandals. He has a basket over his arm, and we crane our necks and see it contains food for the geese. The old man stands for a while, blinking in the light, and then we see him walking towards the crater where the shed had stood before the raid. Then we see there's a well-trodden path through the grass from the door of the house, straight as an arrow to the shed. When we see him carefully placing his feet on the path just as if they were made of china, we realize he can't see anything yet, but is so used to walking along that path, he can do it in his sleep. Sometimes he stumbles over a piece of plank, but he can't have realized what its significance is because he just lifts his foot patiently over it and continues on his way. It's then we suddenly realize what's going to happen, and we daren't even breathe.

'The old man keeps on walking till he reaches the spot where the path stops and the crater starts. He puts his basket down on the ground, adjusts his hat in order to be really smart when he serves the geese with their morning meal, and then he reaches out his hand to lift the hatch. We watch his skinny hand fumbling about in mid-air, and then he raises his eyes in extreme surprise, blinks, and then at last sees. We watch him go stiff, and we're afraid the surprise will give him a heart attack. But his paralysis loosens. He rips off his hat, flings it on the ground in fury and starts jumping up and down on it. All the time he's shrieking Spanish curses in the morning air. "My geese, my geese," he yells, still jumping up and down, and he doesn't see us at all, despite the fact that we're standing in the street watching him, barely a stone's throw away.

'It's amazing how touched we are, how ashamed we feel. It's as if the whole of the tragedy of war was concentrated in that little old man at the edge of the crater, bewailing the loss of his geese in the clear morning air. We slink away like criminals, with his desperate cries ringing in our ears. Then we continued our retreat and joined up with the main army and acquired reinforcements and managed to win back all we'd lost before the big defeat. It so happened that I passed through that devastated village as we were attacking again, and during a short rest period me and a comrade who'd also been there went looking for the old man's house in order to sympathize with him. The house was deserted now, though; there were no blankets in the windows, and we could tell from the smell that there hadn't been anybody living there for ages. We wandered about the vicinity for a while, then suddenly my mate gave a shout. He'd been nosying around at the gable end next to the woods, and had nearly walked straight into him. He was hanging from a thick, low branch and beneath him were his leather trousers, because he'd cut the cord that kept them up and used it to hang himself. We stepped to one side and lit a cigarette each, and then we cut him down with our bayonets. He'd already started to smell, and it was important to get him buried as quickly as possible. We carried him between us to the crater, trying to breathe in as much smoke as possible, and it was easy to shovel some earth over him there. Then the engines started thundering – we had tanks with us this time – and we had to run so as not to get left behind in the dead village.'

That was Edmund's story. It made us feel just as bad as the other two, but there was something special about this one as well, something special which relieved our angst. You could probably say we lay there feeling a bit sentimental, and it was probably that which made us fall asleep quite quickly afterwards. There was just one of us who didn't drop off, or so he claimed later, and you could well imagine he'd be unable to sleep no matter what kind of pills he took. That was Gideon, and he was really the oddest of us all, and it was hard not to make fun of him because he was so odd. Anyway, he maintained he couldn't sleep afterwards either, and the rest of us thought we wouldn't be the slightest bit surprised if one of these fine days something happened to him which made us open our eyes wide and pinch ourselves on the arm and ask how on earth it was possible. But we kept our thoughts to ourselves.

Still, as I say, all those who hadn't really gone to sleep gradually dozed off after Edmund's story, all except Gideon, if you can believe what he says, and we didn't wake up until the duty corporal came barging in shouting for the second time that it was time to get up. Then we woke up and experienced that special waking-up routine that had become usual for the last few mornings. First we lay under our dusty blankets, stretching, feeling heavy-headed after too little sleep, and then we'd blink once or twice and turn to our neighbours hoping they would get up first. But when nobody showed any sign of getting up, we'd raise ourselves on our elbows and look down at the floor, peer under the bed, but find nothing apart from the barrack-room dust lying there in thick clumps. Then we'd draw up our knees, fling back the blankets and jump down on the floor, glancing in fear to all sides and waiting for somebody to shout: 'Here! Here it is!'

But the fear floating around the sweaty barrack room in tiny puffs of dawn vapours was not relieved that morning, no more than it had been the previous mornings. Then the boldest of us ran out naked into the washroom, which is the coldest in the whole camp, with its asphalt floor and wooden laths, slippery with soap, to stand on while getting washed in ice-cold cascades of water from the brass taps over the long sinks that looked like troughs in a piggery. The shower hangs down from the ceiling and it's good to have a shower if you want to free yourself from the memories of the night. The ice-cold torrent rinses away everything sticking to you after the night, and that's no doubt why taking cold showers suddenly became such a popular pastime among us. Even a delicate soul like Cheerful Charlie, who normally got washed very sparingly, would join in, albeit on the periphery, and received a few splashes.

It was Gideon, of course it was Gideon, who was the exception, and that morning Sörenson had the idea that we should have a bit of fun with Gideon. Some of us agreed, but

Joker and Edmund thought it wasn't really fair on the lad; on the other hand there were those who reckoned that Gideon wasn't all that fair with the rest of us either. Well, fair might not be quite the right word in this context. He hadn't told tales, for instance, the time we'd sat in the company office with him one Saturday evening when he was on telephone duty and we'd brought with us a half-bottle of vodka. He hadn't touched a drop. 'I'm teetotal, boys,' he said in that voice of his which wasn't nasty but was so very annoying somehow. We later decided it was because he was so terribly nice and well-meaning, and there is a limit to the amount of that sort of thing you can put up with.

No, he wasn't stupid in that sense. But he was so unlike the rest of us that it disturbed the harmony that existed among us. Lads as different as Edmund and Sörenson had at least something in common with us, but Gideon was something different again. That's why he annoyed us so much and hence it was natural that we should play along that morning when Sörenson had the idea we ought to tease Gideon a bit because he was the only one who didn't go into the shower. He was always a bit slower on the uptake than the rest of us, because he had to think through all kinds of things that had been obvious to us for so long we'd forgotten completely that there'd ever been a problem there for us. One of us who was rumoured to be a writer or something of that sort and hence was called Scriber, after the typewriter of that name – he was the tallest of the lot of us, thin, with a deep, dark, almost booming voice that didn't seem to fit him at all – used to say that Gideon hadn't really started living until now when he'd been conscripted into the army for his national service.

When it came to getting washed, Gideon was so slow because he wouldn't dream of going naked in the corridor. That was more than a bit namby-pamby, because the female secretaries didn't arrive until some hours later, if that's what he was worrying about; there were some of the lads, Cheerful Charlie, for instance, who even used to run about in the raw when they were getting washed and dressed for afternoon passes when the secretaries were still working and were running around like headless chickens, taking papers from one office to another.

Gideon had to find his gym shorts first, which were properly marked with GK, Gideon Karlsson, before he could come and join us in the washroom. Not much imagination was needed for the joke we were going to play on him. There was a long hose-pipe with a nozzle on the floor of the washroom, used for hosing down the floor. While some of us chatted away to Gideon, who had his own towel, with his name on it, of course, over his arm and a bright shiny soap box in one hand and his toothbrush in the other, we lured him into one corner of the room. Sörenson attached the hose-pipe to a tap and walked slowly over to the corner. When he was close enough, he signalled towards the door and Erik Jansson, who was known as Dandy because of his long hair, which he stubbornly refused to have cut, turned it on.

That powerful, ice-cold jet must have come as a shock to Gideon when it hit him right in the small of his back. He looked quite pitiful standing there by the window, letting a thin trickle of water fall into his cupped hands. Would he start fighting, or shouting perhaps, or simply rush away with tears in his eyes? That was what he generally did, grown-up man though he was, whenever anybody was more than usually brusque with him. But Gideon didn't do any of the things we expected of him. He just turned round helplessly, and we could see he was very close to tears.

'No, no!' he yelled. 'Stop that! Stop it, I say!' He didn't shout in a way that suggested he was seriously upset. It sounded rather as though he was giving us instructions in how to behave, admonishing, and if anybody's being beaten up and wants more of that medicine, then he ought to behave just like Gideon. Dandy turned the tap on full, and we could all see how much he enjoyed being the one in charge for a change. He always wanted that, but he was the youngest in the barrack room and every time he tried to shoot his mouth off, somebody would laugh out loud or put a tender arm round his shoulder so that he was thrown off his stride before he'd even got started, and an angry flush would spread all over his grinning face. He had a marvellous quirky grin: he always looked as though he was screwing up his eyes to look at the sun, and it certainly attracted the women, because never a Monday went by without Dandy having some story to tell about what he'd been up to in the grass near the city's dance halls and night-clubs.

Now he was standing there grinning and turning the tap on full and the water was rushing out of the hose like a little waterfall and Sörenson pursed his lips and looked even more angular than usual and directed the jet of water at poor Gideon's chest and throat and eyes and stomach and crotch. He'd dropped his towel, which was lying on the floor like a wet rag, and he was trying in vain to protect himself with his hands, but that didn't help much.

In the end, however, somebody thought things were getting out of hand. The rest of us were very surprised to see it was Dandy's pal, known as Happy-Go-Lucky, because he took all life threw at him with the same unvarying bad humour. We'd never seen such a miserable beggar before in the whole of our lives. The excuses he thought up for his bad moods were amazing in their inventiveness. There wasn't a single uplifting incident Happy-Go-Lucky couldn't find a dark side to. Apart from that, we all thought he was a good lad, and in terms of age he counterbalanced Dandy. Happy-Go-Lucky had been a junior boxer once upon a time, and if you didn't believe him, he'd fumble around in his mop of hair and drag out an ear to demonstrate how misshapen it was. He was on very good terms with Dandy on that account, because the only thing in the world the latter was impressed by was boxers, especially if they'd been knocked about a bit.

That's why he didn't start shouting and screaming as usual when Happy-Go-Lucky bundled him away from the tap, turned the water off and pulled away the hose-pipe. He just grinned as usual, and it was a nasty grin because you never knew what it meant, if he was annoyed or pleased or neither. Then he slunk away and Sörenson was left standing all alone in the middle of the washroom with the dripping nozzle in his hand, and his aggressive angularity disappeared when he saw us all standing at the troughs just staring at him. Even so, there was no risk of him losing face, and he was no doubt aware of that; he just turned his back disdainfully on Gideon, who didn't look as though he'd realized it was all over yet, and started to roll up the hose.

There was probably none of us standing there who felt anything but pity for Gideon, and no doubt we'd all have helped him if only we weren't so damned lazy. In any case, it's no exaggeration to say we were most sympathetic as we watched him wringing out his sodden towel in the sink. He was trembling after his shower, and it was cold anyway in the washroom, which faced north, and so we all started feeling a bit cold and got ready to return to the barrack room. It was really a bit odd and unnecessary for us to stand staring at Gideon, even though it would never occur to any of us to walk over to him, slap him on the shoulder and say: 'That was bloody silly. But we'll get that bastard Sörenson before long, you'll see.'

The sun was peeping in round the door and playing on the metal mirrors, and we just stood there; in the end we started feeling bloody stupid. But at that point Gideon turns to us and says, with his mouth full of toothpaste: 'We're still mates, aren't we? Why not shake hands and promise me this won't happen again, eh?'

It was his tone of voice that did it, that irritating, whining tone of voice. Nothing makes you so furious as somebody begging for mercy. We were all glad that interruption had occurred, because once he'd said that, we didn't think we were duty bound to feel sorry for him any longer, and so we went away and left him on his own. What can you do with a bloke like that?

We walked slowly in a bunch through the deserted corridor, which is always so dusty and dark, and the floorboards are so worn by four generations of iron-shod heels you get the feeling that one of these days the crossbeams underneath will take it into their heads to jump up through the floor. The corridor's pretty long even when you only need to walk along it; when you're cleaning it, you start to think there isn't another corridor in the whole wide world longer than this one. All of us are general-duties men, apart from Gideon and Scriber, who sit in the personnel office and just fill in time all day long. Although Gideon works, no doubt. Everybody who sees him working away in the office laughs and asks him if he thinks he's in line for a permanent job before long, the way he's working. There are brass bowls of dried flowers every five yards along the corridor – presented to the company by some society or other devoted to furthering the well-being of soldiers, so you can't really say people have forgotten about our existence.

When we got back to our barrack room we were struck by that very faint but suffocating smell of fear. During the day it's so faint you hardly notice it, but we noticed it because we're always on the alert for it when we enter the room nowadays. Nothing had happened, though, and we put on our working outfits. It doesn't much matter what you look like when all you do is sweep out the corridors, and Cheerful Charlie's the only one who looks smart; but then he does have access to the stores sometimes.

Then we went out into the corridor again, because we didn't feel comfortable in the barrack room any more, not since we started to notice that smell, and we stood smoking by the windows. It was the end of summer, and we no longer had those dewy fresh mornings. The day started off with a rush now, brusque and with no time to waste. We blew smoke into the leafy trees that lined the grass verge outside the barrack wall and nearly reached up to our windows on the first floor. The parade ground stretched out before us like an ocean, and looked boundlessly vast when there were hardly any people on it. It was slightly convex, sloping down just a little towards each of the four barrack walls enclosing it. They looked as though they'd been painted with watered-down raspberry juice at this time in the morning, but once the sun had got up properly, they became almost blood-red. On the raised area in the middle of the square was a concrete bunker with slits like a Chinaman's eyes looking out in all directions. The enormous pointer on the clock hanging on the mess wall trembled like a nervous finger as it jerked its way over the clock face. It would soon be time for inspection.

It was at inspection that morning we got the big shock. Generally speaking, inspections are rather boring and dull affairs, with the duty corporal calling the roll. There's only one day a week, when gymnastics are prescribed, when things can get a bit exciting, because everybody tries on all the cunning tricks they can think of in order to be excused. The expert, of course, is Cheerful Charlie. One week he has sores that are so bad he can only hop along on one foot; the next week his knee is so swollen he can barely pull down his trouser leg; but the record holder without a doubt is a lad in billet number three called Fixer. The performance he puts on for the duty warrant officer has to be seen to be believed.

But there was no PT on the programme that morning. Just the usual half-hearted roll call, and nobody could understand why we needed to line up in two columns just for that. It has to be said, unfortunately, that there wasn't much discipline on such parades. In fact, there are few things so demoralizing and so calculated to undermine one's idea of discipline as the military concept of discipline. Everywhere else in life discipline is straightforward and automatic, as it were, but in the army it has to be spelled out and armed with paragraphs and sub-paragraphs and it all seems so stupid that you simply can't help but make fun of it. That's why even those of us who were normally most prudent and careful were slowly but surely transformed into scruffs and layabouts, hanging about like washing on a line, sometimes brushing dirt under lockers and making rag-bags of beds simply because there were detailed instructions, stencilled in three hundred copies, explaining in great detail what you should do when making one of His Majesty's iron beds.

This demoralization with regard to discipline naturally spreads in the end, if you're in barracks, that is (it's different when you're out in the field), and you get a quite different idea of what work is. For instance, in civilian life you may have thought that as well as work being a necessity in order to live, it is also an honourable occupation; but when you spend all day from eight in the morning to five at night, apart from breaks, sweeping out corridors and bed spaces like we do, your basic attitude to work undergoes a transformation. It's not helped by the fact that we know, and everybody else knows, and what we're doing is as good as useless, and that one man could do it in a third of the time six of us spend. After all, the only reason we're here is that, although nobody has any use for us in the military production line, we have been called up and we can't be allowed home until we've completed the prescribed number of days' service.

This demoralization process also includes our attitude to card games, cheating, and loyalty to our wives. All the interests we used to have are not fun any more, you become indifferent to everything apart from finding new tricks to avoid doing the cleaning, new ways of wasting time, and new ways of borrowing money. The only thing that isn't undermined is comradeship. On the contrary, you never feel such a strong bond as you do with people you've told lies and made mischief with, been caught and punished with, and cursed and suffered with.

This lenghty parenthesis is necessary in order to understand properly how desperate we were when the shock hit us that morning. We were already a bit desperate after the long, sleepless nights, and this is all that was needed for our top show to be undermined. We were just hanging around and the parade was almost over when the duty NCO came clumping down the corridor in his jackboots. We all realized it was us he was after, and we weren't disappointed. He was a sergeant, neither young nor old, or at least you couldn't tell by looking at him. You had to feel sorry for him, because he was one of the few who was convinced the caste system was as widespread in Sweden as it was in India, and the military caste was next in rank after the maharajahs, or whatever they're called.

Anyway, he shouted, "Ten*shun*!" exactly as if there'd been a full regiment of us instead of just twenty or so. Then he picked out all of us in billet number two and, sure enough, all the others grinned and looked down their noses at us. Then came the shock. We'd expected a good telling-off because we couldn't keep quiet at night, and when it came we weren't all that bothered. But when he announced he was going to move his bed into our billet and sleep there until we learnt how to hold our tongues, we all sat up and took notice and it gradually dawned on us that it meant another long, sleepless night for us, a long night of solitary silence and that faint, suffocating smell of fear.

We grew desperate, just a little bit mad, although it didn't happen all at once. During the day, though, we worked up a head of steam and by the afternoon – it was a Wednesday, when we were due for a late pass – we were all dangerous, as dangerous as completely normal people can be when something happens to them, something of the kind that had happened to us. It was nothing more or less than fear seeping into us and taking possession of us, and is there a person more dangerous than a frightened one?

We worked as usual that day – actually we'd long since ceased to call it work. After the parade we put on our overalls, which look like miniature flour sacks and are the only dress a conscript is allowed to wear on entering His Majesty's mess. The custom of dressing for dinner is observed even in the army. Then we ambled over the square to the mess in a group, all eight of us – Gideon was with us as well: we'd forgotten what had happened to him. We talked as little as we normally do in the mornings, but what we didn't say was different in tone. We went up the stairs in silence and our footsteps echoed on the stone floor of the ocean known as the mess – it was an enormous room with dreary walls and grey columns and long rows of tables with benches, and they looked incredibly lost in the big, bare hall. Along one of the walls was a barrier of the type usually erected around dangerous road crossings, and a long queue wrapped itself around it as far as the counter where the food was doled out; the long queue looked like a grey snake since everyone was dressed in identical overalls. At the start of the barrier was a corporal who was tearing off a coupon from every card handed to him by the participants in the queue. This corporal was also supposed to make sure everybody was sporting the regulation grey overalls and that everyone was washed and shaved, since the military machinery wouldn't work if that weren't the case. It was also important that the only hair to be served up in army soup should come from the cooks.

It was when we lined up to the right of that barrier that something happened which we realized could never have taken place on any other day. All of a sudden the mess corporal, the one with a silver badge on his chest reflecting his fat chin, bellowed out: 'Hey, you! Go and comb your hair before you come in here to eat!'

He's referring to Dandy, who's at the end of the queue, and we all turn round and look at him to see what he says. We watch as his grinning face slowly becomes serious, turns deep red, and he pushes those in front of him to get past the corporal, saying: 'Bugger off!'

The chin reflected in the corporal's badge turns bright red and he spins round on his heel and motions to the duty NCO standing by some distant window keeping an eagle eye on everything going on in his territory. When he notices the corporal's upstretched fist, he comes flying straight over like a rocket, his gilded badge rattling on its chain.

We look uneasily at Dandy, but he winks reassuringly. 'This man,' says the corporal, addressing his superior with due deference, 'refused to obey my order. He refuses to go away and comb his hair.' The sergeant pushes the corporal to one side, leans over the barrier and looks Dandy straight in the eye. Dandy seems a bit nervous, and his muscles start twitching around his eyes. Then he looks down and manages to compose himself by looking at the floor, and when he looks up he manages to seem impressively embarrassed. 'Eh, I must have misheard him. I thought he said I was wrongly dressed, but I've had these overalls on at mealtimes ever since I was called up.'

The sergeant doesn't believe him. We can see that in his eyes, which remain glued firmly to Dandy's skull. But then something happens, something that could only happen on a day like this: Joker jumps over the barrier and marches up to the sergeant, clicks his heels and says: 'I heard him as well, sarge.' The rest of us start walking towards the counter, and pick up a bowl and a spoon. We trudge past the counter as if it were a production line. A series of girls, some of them pretty, others fat and red-faced from the heat in the kitchen, are standing there with dripping ladles, plonking dollops of porridge and lumps of jam into our bowls. They are very accurate. The production line rolls on. At the end is the milk jug, looking like a former white tower that will outlive several Swedish armies thanks to its solidity.

Having collected the last component, we walk the tight-rope with our trays, swaying in and out among all the gobblers sitting behind their grey mugs, chewing away at their grey porridge in their grey bowls, dressed in their grey overalls and sitting at the grey tables standing on the grey cement floor. Nothing in the whole wide world is as grey as the breakfast porridge served up to a Swedish regiment.

Generally speaking, we don't stick together all that much. It's just that, in the early days at least, it feels rather reassuring to have a face you know, no matter how unpleasant it may be,

156

staring at you from the other side of your porridge bowl, rather than a totally unknown one, no matter how nice and friendly it may be. What's happened to us, though, forces us together and forges a chain round us. We can feel it pressing against our arms and backs. 'That bastard,' says Sörenson, spitting out his words like arrows, 'he needs a good thumping.'

But it's all over. Dandy's been out and combed his hair, and here he comes with Joker, carrying their trays. Horses are neighing and thumping their hoofs on the stones of the courtyard below like drumsticks. The faintly acrid smell from the rotting manure heaps drifts in through the south-facing windows and prickles our nostrils. It's so quiet the sound of spoons against the bottom of plates sounds like the clanging of a metal-working factory. We are sitting at the long, grey table like slaves rowing in a galley. They also had to shovel their porridge into themselves while chained to the side of the galley, as Scriber says. He has a knack of pressing everything that happens to us into a framework of similes, and that's the main thing that distinguishes him from the rest of us, who reckon you don't need to know how one thing works in order to understand another. Edmund, who's good at finding the right words for things and likes to discuss matters in long sentences, put it like this one night ages ago before all this happened, before this smell of fear made itself felt: when a bloke like Scriber sees a fire extinguisher hanging on the wall, he says it looks like a bottle of Indian ink. When he sees an Indian-ink bottle in a desk drawer, then of course he has to compare it with a fire extinguisher. But just think if he needs to use both the Indian-ink bottle and the fire extinguisher in the same sentence. How's he going to manage it without mixing them up, without the firemen starting to spray ink on a fire and the artist drawing his sketches with carbon dioxide?

Now the metal-working factory starts to wind down production in the big mess hall, and instead the buzz of conversation starts, quite soft but as vehement as a wasp. Long grey queues form and start wriggling towards the sinks where the last greasy remnants of breakfast are scraped off. The stainless-steel draining boards round the sinks are covered in splodges and dollops of porridge, and are not a sight for weak stomachs. Gideon usually makes the excuse that he's in a terrific hurry and goes straight to the grey counter where the dirty plates are piled up. Sörenson, who's a real sadist with everybody he comes across, generally spends every dinner-time telling Gideon exactly what the sinks look like in other regiments. They have scrapers with wooden handles and soft brushes hanging there, to be used to scrape off the plates what is left by the knives and forks. He especially likes to dwell on the ingredients of the goo that's scraped away, and then Gideon can't face his food. He slinks off and makes do with a cup of coffee at the café in the park.

This morning, though, everything's so very different. Gideon comes with the rest of us to the sinks, and nobody finds it the slightest bit odd. Then we go out on to the square, which hasn't woken up properly yet. The sun pasted diagon-ally overhead makes the barrack walls blush, and a group of lieutenants come bobbing in from their morning ride on their black horses, with their necks all tense and looking superior. Their brasses are gleaming and the gravel rasps under their hoofs, like when a gramophone record has come to an end. The sound from the cars is more like a faint hum. They stand there like bulldogs with their stern, low-slung chassis. The drivers are sitting smoking on the running-boards, their leggings gleaming. The straight blue strands of smoke mingle with the small, trembling clouds emanating from the engines. It's already oppressively hot on the barrack square, and we look down as we salute the mounted lieutenants. The mess doors are spewing out their long grey snakes that wriggle their way over to the various gates. It's five minutes to eight, and the little bugler makes his way to the bunker. His instrument is glittering in the sun like a broad strip of medals across his chest. He halts when he gets to the bunker, does an about turn, bends his head back and put the mouthpiece to his mouth so that his instrument is pointing up at the sky like a bronze snake. The big hand on the mess clock is trembling for the last time before it comes to eight o'clock, and, as if by magic, the whole gigantic barrack square is suddenly empty – apart from a few grey laggards left in splendid isolation in the middle. They run like mad to get away but it's like running through a lake of pitch and they're caught by the first rough notes of the bugle call and are petrified at the attention as the flag slowly creeps up the pole on the chancellery roof.

Meanwhile, we're walking in silence up the broad staircase that's covered in spit. The bugle call is strangled halfway through a note, because a skilful bugler stops blowing the moment the flag reaches the top of the pole. Grey figures with snub-nosed rifles and bulging ammunition pouches come racing towards us down the stairs, and nearly crush us under their weight. We escape into our corridor and gather round a window. As if somebody had opened a dozen gigantic taps, a flood of grey figures comes cascading out of the barrack-room doors. Then splendid flowerbeds shoot up from the gravel, beds of gravel-flowers watered by the sizzling saliva from spat-out commands, according to Scriber (the one with all the similes).

The grey canon of commands is sung in accordance with the ritual, and the first columns trudge away towards the training ground. Other groups, less advanced, march in tight circles around the bunker; it looks like an unrelenting cattle drive and clouds of dust rise up slowly from the ground, making it look as if they're walking through clouds of gas. Down below us is a group of conscripts who've been back-squadded, their hands behind their backs and their right feet advanced, listening to instructions. Ten feet to the left of the left marker is a bloke generally known as the Parrot, partly because of his voice and partly because he looks like one. From sheer wickedness, the officer in charge has separated him off from the others and he can't understand why, because he's dedicated his life to a battle with those around him, and his big, staring idiot-eyes ruthlessly peck out all the shortcomings of his fellow men.

The Parrot is shorter than the shortest drummer-boy and broader than the most sturdy of majors, without quite deserving the word fat. He looks as though he's spent a long time being pressed between two buffers. His voice is thin and squeaky, and all you can make out in his grotesquely compressed face is an enormous, semicircular, shiny nose. We stand nonchalantly at our window, watching his gigantic red, freckled hands dangling from his wrists like weights. But Sörenson has that grin of his, that sharp grin that you can't see without feeling ill. He spits at a creeper outside the window and strokes his belt buckle as if it were a revolver. Now we can hear the back-squaddies clicking their heels, getting into line and processing out on to the gravel. Only the Parrot plods slowly and awkwardly, his hands clutched to his chest like an outsize heart, towards a bench directly below our window, and he stretches out on his back. Heat is showering down through the enormous sieve of the sun. The dust climbs higher and higher around the cattle drive and muffles the barked commands so that they sound like half-choked cries. Two heavy lorries pulling anti-aircraft guns drive cautiously across the square as if over glass, and disappear out through the park gates, their rear ends bobbing up and down. Sörenson whistles through his pointed front teeth and drops a cigarette end on the Parrot. It misses the back of his swollen head by an inch and its glow slowly fades away in the burnt-out grass.

A door slams behind us and the sound of creaking jackboots is an alarm bell for us. When WO Boll enters the company corridor and peers round with his owl-like eyes, we're all hard at work. Sörenson, Dandy and Happy-Go-Lucky have slipped into the urinal and are busy with the rubbish pail. Cheerful Charlie's in the stores, thumbing through lists of equipment, while Joker and Edmund are pretending to shift a locker from one side of the corridor to the other. Gideon and Scriber go out to town to buy a newspaper: their working day doesn't start until nine.

And so the day plods on, yellow and spotted with dust, and with red flames from the barrack walls licking through the corridor. The air is stuffy and heavy under the sweaty ceilings. The furious machine-gun clatter of the typewriters seeps out and hits us. Female secretaries pass from office to office. Then we bend deeper over our sweeping brushes and discuss them as possible meat for our beds. We walk like sowers and sow wet sawdust over the corridor floor from our buckets. Then our brooms dip their wigs on to the meticulously rationed areas of floor, meticulously rationed as they have to last for a whole yellow day. In the urinal icy-cold squirts of water from black hose-pipes lick the carefully closed windows, which look as though they're covered in spiders' webs, and we burn paper and damp sawdust in the iron stove standing stiffly to attention in the corridor, until the acrid smoke seeps in through the major's keyhole. Towards midday we pat our worthy corridor lockers lightly and respectfully on the head with a dusty duster, and, bloated by all our work, we walk as a tightly knit group, in silence and with angst in our pockets and round our necks, over the barrack square where the clouds of dust raised by the twirling heels of the soldiers have not yet dispersed. Teams of horses pulling the big guns blink at the sizzling midday sun with weary, negro eyes. Every noise is wide awake and halfway to being a scream. The horsese are in their stables, the anvil is clanging in the smithy, and a circular saw bites frantically into the day's throat. A row of rifles chained together stands chewing the cud in the dust. And the day progresses, the golden, copper day gradually turns to aluminium. We play poker-dice on the barrack-room window-ledge. Sixes twinkle like newly born boys' eyes, the regular full houses with their bland symmetry seem deeply melancholic, and the giddy fives gape in amazement beneath our sweaty palms. But we play in silence, and our lips are more tightly sealed than usual, and more quickly than ever

161

before it grows serious. An enemy is standing by our side, and the five dice are rattling in his cupped hand. We know it's our fear that does it. Our angst drips bitterness and suspicion into our reactions. We stare greedily at the dice as they drop from the palms of our hands, even though it's only ten öre a throw. Then we stand ruthlessly and cruelly round the gaming machines in the café behind the church, directing bullets into our opponents' goals with our cruel index fingers. And the day staggers on. The disc of the sun slides down behind the rooftops. The dull, dignified afternoon sinks as silently as an owl. Buzzing lorries drive into the courtyard. The angry clatter of blank shots rattles in from the range and acrid wisps of pale smoke float down through the greenery. Empty containers are clanging away in the kitchens. In one of the wings well-filled bags of washing are being flung down from the top floor on to the back of a lorry parked beside the main staircase. As flabby as puffed-up seals, they fall past the three floors and hit their target with a light, nonchalant thud. The first squads are returning from the training grounds. All heads are tired and are drooping like flowers that haven't been watered for ages. The whiplash commands bounce back off their thick-skinned weariness. The aluminium day slides towards leave time, and the big flat-iron starts glowing in the window-panes. We carry our ironing board out into the corridor; without the usual jokes, and standing guard watchfully over our possessions, we press the creases into our dress uniforms. We miss the usual sprinkling of water and the friendly jostling, and all of us are wearing masks as if we'd exposed a cheat with false dice in our midst.

All of a sudden the whole barracks is filled with the harsh rattle of breaking-up noises. Rifle butts thud against the stone flags where heels had been grinding sand. Sweaty horses, their flanks glistening as if with dew, skip gracefully and cheerfully over the muffling gravel, their frisky neighing blending with the drone of broad, warlike lorries growling as they lunge between the stables and the kitchen towards the square.

Orderlies, bent low over their sturdy army-issue handlebars, whistle as they swerve round the corners of the barracks and bump over the pot-holed courtyard, where pot-bellied cannons with legs wide apart like feeding canaries and slim-limbed anti-aircraft guns, sketched subtly into the afternoon air, stand side by side. The grey queues start growing outside the mess.

It's time to collect our late passes. These are disturbed by WO Boll, who is enjoying one of the highlights of his military career. WO Boll is a dangerous man, like everybody else who takes himself seriously. Since the amount of danger is in inverse proportion to what you have that needs to be taken seriously, WO Ball is as dangerous to those around him as a primed hand-grenade, because he regards it as one of his duties to make sure six corridor-cleaners distribute wet sawdust on the company floorboards in accordance with regulations and with deep, fervent, almost religious seriousness. When a late pass is due he looks like a high priest: ecstatically red-faced and with a dignified glint in his eye, his body swelling out over the little desk chair and out of all proportion to the size of the little room, he hands out the late passes to a long, impatient queue. 'Remember that leave is a privilege and not a right,' he says to all the unworthy objects drifting past and collecting their passes, and he hangs a two-ton weight of significance on every word. He adds especial emphasis when it comes to the eight of us.

'Bollocks,' says Sörenson as we come out into the corridor, and retracts his head like a bull ready to be pole-axed. We drift slowly down the desolate corridor, the desolation clinging fast to our throats and almost choking us. Isolated iron-shod heels are beating a tattoo on the silent staircase. The barrack-room windows are glittering in the western sunlight like gigantic cows' eyes. A dog with its belly hanging down melancholically ambles along by the stone wall. Driven by our angst, we step out over the weekend-still courtyard and through the gloomy and guarded exit gate, past the surly, bulldog-like ceremonial cannons and the vast, grass-free gravelled square with its sentry boxes sticking up like islands, and out into our evening leave. The tower of St Oscar's looms like a ramrod over our heads. We cross in silence over Narvavägen, adorned with stiff lady riders and leaning piles of firewood, and come to Djurgårds Bridge. A semi-naked canoeist in a green craft slices the water into brown strips with his sharp paddle. One of us spits far out over the parapet.

Then we suddenly disperse, as if we've been held together so far by a thin elastic band which somebody has just cut through. With indifferent expressions and silent acknowledgements, we go our separate ways, alone or in small groups, according to how our angst drives us.

The Mirror

Regret stems from angst. Some people become desperate when terror strikes. Others become very clear-headed and can observe the circumstances with the febrile clarity of a hunter. What has been important hitherto is now blown up like a balloon. Anybody who's made a mistake is possessed by regret, anybody who's been jealous becomes a monomaniac, and anybody who can't make up his mind dares – thanks to the terror – or even has to abandon his position and take a leap into the unknown.

Dandy and Happy-Go-Lucky had no problems, or at least none that could be solved by thinking about them; nor was their inclination to regret things more highly developed than normal. On the other hand, they both suffered from a perfectly normal tendency to be quarrelsome and to want to start a fight. What distinguished them especially, however, was their adventurous spirit, in its Swedish form: a desire to get involved in adventures with girls and strong drink. Now they were desperate. Their hunger became voracious, a string was tightened inside their bodies which went ding and then continued vibrating.

They were sitting by the water at Funtime Café, watching the city lights glittering like fireworks. They were a little drunk and thought the lights would never go out, but just spread like drops on a sheet of blotting paper until they flared up again. Happy-Go-Lucky shoved the cups and saucers to one side and placed his broad boxer's hand with its battered knuckles in the middle of the table, like a market square. His beret had slid down a lock of hair over his ear, where it now dangled like a rock-climber in an emergency. Dandy had his on his knee, and was less drunk. Inside it was a hip flask of rough spirits bought from a sailor in the gents at Tivoli. They'd whetted their whistles with it while there. Now it was sloshing about in their cups together with the coffee, looking like dirty paraffin.

I've drunk a hell of a lot more than him, thought Dandy, watching one of the stars on the city coat of arms twinkling through the greenery on Kastellholmen Island, and yet I'm a hell of a lot less drunk. The star was stuck on the end of a poker or something, and was approaching fast. Dandy peered at his friend through his superior, bushy eyebrows. He swayed back in his chair and contemplated critically the tense sinews in his neck from behind.

Happy-Go-Lucky was obviously about to start boasting. He stretched his hand voluptuously: it was already boasting as it lay there in the middle of the table, and he crooked his index finger to form a U. 'Anybody care to take me on at finger wrestling?' he asked, realizing himself that his awkward words were a few sizes too small for his gesture, and stared with good-humoured hostility around the table.

The girls giggled, fingering their cups thoughtfully. They had ladylike fingers, slightly pointed like a well-sharpened lead pencil. One of them, Dandy's, was wearing lace gloves made from white spiders' webs. Oh hell, he thought, and it hit him like a stroke of lightning from the mountain of enlightenment, and he thought the booze was inspiring him to think fine thoughts: we're not out in the sticks, this isn't a bloody yokel's wedding party. As carefully as if it had been a delicate china cup, he slid his hand down on to his knee. Then he raised it again towards the cup but missed the handle and, holding the cup in the palm of his hand, emptied it in one slurping gulp.

Lucky was then hit by a whirlwind and transported up to the roof of Tivoli's roller-coaster, where an old man with earphones sat feeding him with bird seed. He had to laugh so loudly he brought himself back to his senses and turned cold with fear and was transported back to the table on a wave of fear. The girl opposite blinked her long eyelashes and gazed revealingly at him through a foggy haze. I'm a boxer and all that, he thought, feeling wretched, and so she sits looking at me like that. Then he heard her say in a cool, chilled voice served up on a plate directly from the refrigerator: 'And him as well?'

Bloody hell, they're talking about me, he thought, trying to get it straight and straining to be interested, swimming up through the shallow water with the thought in his hands. Then he heard Dandy's voice from up on the bank: 'Yeah, he's a bit like that at first, see, but it's not as bad as it seems. First you think he's passing out, but then the bastard comes to again.'

Aha, they think I'm bloody pissed, thought Happy-Go-Lucky, taking firm hold of the table top with both hands, staring hard at it and making an effort to overcome his drunkenness by thinking logically: I'm sober. Ten times eight is eighty. The girl has a red hairband. There are four cups on the table. Here comes the waitress. She has a red handkerchief in her breast pocket.

Then he surprised everybody by saying to the waitress in a loud, clear voice, like you do when you're trying to prove you're sober: 'I'll pay for two coffees, two Danish pastries and a cream bun.' The stars that had been dancing over the orchestra gathered at one point and became a lamp. As they

166

trooped out into the street, pushing the girls before them like shock absorbers, Dandy leaned down and winked and whispered in his ear: 'Bedtime!' They took a taxi to Djurgårdsslätten.

Blue light was now filling the beakers of the streets almost right up to the brim. Happy-Go-Lucky was sitting on one of the tip-up seats and it suddenly struck him that the car roof was his hat. They travelled along a broad, grey-rimmed Östermalmsgatan lined with houses looking like safes in the twilight. All four of them remained silent. The boys because it was all fixed now, and everything said from now on was a bit like overtime. They didn't need to overstrain themselves, because they'd achieved their goal. They could close their eyes and see the house they'd stop outside. The little entrance hall with the trademan's entrance. Then it was usually the first, second, third or fourth floor. An old-fashioned, white-painted kitchen with flowery curtains, a pantry with a hanging lamp and an unwanted still life beside the trays hanging from the wall. Sometimes it was a really big room, with a wide couch and a little tea-trolley with brown, yellow, flowery or white coffee cups. The sponge cake was often burnt round the edges and had too much lemon or baking powder or apple sauce. Occasionally there was a gramophone or a modest portable wireless playing music from a little club in Paris or a restaurant in Brazzaville. It was often just a little box room with a bit of flowery cretonne on the wall, or with a dated guitar with a rosette attached to the strings.

The girls were also quiet. They'd been taken by surprise when the bitter drops at the bottom of their cups had made them feel, just for a short while, a slightly intoxicated affinity with the boys. Now the haze had lifted, and they regretted it. One of them wound down the window and let her hand dangle in the slipstream like girls do when they're in a boat. The other was sitting with her chin in her hands, looking up at her cavalier in resignation. Not long ago she'd thought his chin was forceful, his cheekbones aristocratic and his bushy hair raven-coloured and attractively curly. Now that she was looking at him from below, she could see that his chin was corrugated, his angular cheekbones inflamed, and his eyes rather simple.

The taxi moved in from the centre of the road and homed in on the kerb, where it came to a stop with a gentle curtsy. The boys clambered out and viewed the building with an expert eye. The usual wall-safe façade. They winked knowingly at each other. Happy-Go-Lucky paid for the taxi in twenty-five öre pieces, and it bobbed away round the corner, its subdued headlights peering short-sightedly into the dark blue twilight.

It was a tradesman's entrance as usual, and the boys thought: I expect it'll be the second floor, a big kitchen with a refrigerator, a wide couch and a decent gramophone. But the girls didn't unlock the door. The one with the gloves slowly removed her right one, and her little ladylike hand glided towards Dandy, as white as a vanilla ice-cream, and then on towards Happy-Go-Lucky when Dandy didn't react. But Lucky didn't take it either, because he didn't know what was going on. The girl with the gloves coughed nervously and said as she slowly backed towards the door: 'Well, goodnight, boys. I expect we'll meet again another time.' The other girl turned her back on them and started fumbling with her keys. Somebody on a balcony upstairs was holding a cat in her lap, and it was mewing something awful.

'Shush, up there,' said the girl with the gloves, trying to slip in through the door while the other girl held it open for her, and then let it close and lock itself. Dandy already had his foot in it, though. He took the girl with the gloves by the hand and twisted it, not so hard that it could be called brutal, but with sufficient force for an exclamation mark. He'd been involved in cock-ups like this before and had sorted them out with a dozen fine-sounding words, and in others that hadn't been sorted out at all; but he'd never taken a girl home in a taxi without being invited in afterwards.

If things had been normal, it wouldn't have mattered all that much. There were a few hours left of the late pass, and they could have taken a number fourteen bus out to Djurgården, or simply wandered down to Strandvägen and strolled up and down under the lime trees.

The fear now living inside them had made them desperate, however. They needed to let off steam. It drove them to audacity and ruthlessness, which was normally quite beyond them. It made them desperate, it demanded an outlet. They felt they would burst if they weren't able to let off steam, to push their way into an area they'd only brushed up against in the past. The possibility of missing out on it terrified them. They thought all would be lost if that door closed on them, and the new danger made them excessively hard, both in what they said and what they did.

'What the bloody hell's all this?' said Dandy, shoving the door open with his shoulder. Lucky followed him and took up the same line: 'D'you think we gonna take you home in a taxi and then let you throw us out on to the street?' He sounded pathetic in his eagerness, like many another piss-artist.

He pressed the automatic light switch. A clicking noise echoed through the whole building, and a hesitant light dripped from the ceiling. The girl with the gloves gave up. She shrugged, and you could see her skin trembling like the surface of a pond under her silk blouse. 'All right, then, but you'll have to be quiet because the major will be in bed by now.' They climbed up the stairs in Indian file; there was a faint smell of fried fish and a hint of onion, and the stairs were narrow and highly polished.

'Bloody hell, is he a major now? The bastard was only a company director when we were at the café,' said Dandy, trying to sound bitter about having been deceived. The other girl, who had less of a stiff upper lip, started giggling. Lucky brought up the rear, and now he had the feeling the whole staircase was his hat, and what was underneath was bubbling away like brandy and lemonade.

169

It was just the first floor this time. And there was a still life in the pantry. It comprised an orange, two bananas and a couple of thin fish, certainly not the kind that featured in the feeding of the five thousand. There was a refrigerator in the kitchen, and the girls had their own room – quite large, with a window overlooking the courtyard, but no guitar and no gramophone and no portable wireless. Still, they did have two wide couches set at right-angles, and a sizeable tea-trolley. There was a chicken in the fridge, some gooey paste or other made of tomatoes and vinegar, and some soda water. Lucky took the hip flask from out of his beret and poured a drop into all four glasses. The mood, which had been somewhat on the reserved side, thawed a little. Dandy gave a wink behind the girl-with-the-gloves' back when the photo album was produced from the bureau. His opening gambit was often to slide his arm round the girl's back and help her to hold the book open. Lucky wasn't in the mood for subtleties like that, though. He'd found himself wearing an even bigger hat when they came into this room, and it was fizzing away something awful. He made careful note of the wall light that was plugged in just where the two couches met, and he took a sweet out of the bowl and gobbled it, paper and all. All you needed to do was to pull out the plug when you wanted it dark, and shove it in again when you wanted it light. No bloody problem.

Then something happened to make all the good intentions peter out. There was a knock on the door – quiet and distinctly sympathetic, but energetic even so. All four of them jumped, and their faces took on attentive wrinkles. Then came the sighing of a gentle, soft voice wafting into the room: 'Hello, there! I say, d'you mind if I come in, my dears?'

Before anybody had a chance to reply, a head peered round the side of the door. It hovered there, nodding up and down, as if it didn't have a body but was stuck on a pole, a bit like a hobby-horse. The head was covered in white hair, like wisps of hay, and the face was small and red and smooth, but even so it gave the impression of age – it looked like a doll that had been lying outside in the rain. Suddenly it was followed by a body after all, a thin, slightly twisted trunk a bit like a walking stick, dressed in a nice little doll's dress with lace around the neck and cuffs.

The girl with the gloves looked seriously and enquiringly at the others, but the girl lacking in style said in a stage whisper: 'It's the company director's old grandma.' They all got up from the couch as if their schoolmistress had walked in. The old lady beamed at them in turn and said in a calm, business-like voice which, surprisingly enough, didn't sound in the least like one of those dolls you press in the stomach: 'We were sitting there feeling *so* bored, my dears, and we thought we'd ask you young ladies to come in and keep us company, but now I see you have visitors, so perhaps the visitors would like to join us as well, or perhaps you young people would prefer to stay here by yourselves.'

The young lady with the gloves saw an opportunity of slamming the door closed again and she nodded happily like a young horse champing at its bit, and the other girl, who had already started to fall from grace, gave in as well, albeit in silent protest.

The old lady with the doll's face had already turned her back on them and was trotting along the corridor. They followed close behind her, as if afraid of losing her. The boys brought up the rear, in some disarray, but before leaving Lucky leaned over the wall lamp and pulled at the cord until it came away in his hand. He put it in his pocket and felt a moment's relief.

The corridor was swaying markedly, as if it were high up in a tower. The walls were covered in green paper with a pattern reminiscent of a moonscape. Hanging on both sides of the corridor were so many still lifes you might well have been in a still-life graveyard. They were meticulously sorted: on the left-hand wall were southern fruits and other garden products, and on the other side were fish, angry red crabs, lobsters with enormous claws and shrimps looking as if they were barely a week old.

Dandy was starting to recover from the coup and needed a safety valve to prevent him from bursting, so he said in a loud and emphatic voice: 'This old bloke must be something big in the fish-and-veg line.' The girl in the gloves turned round and looked at him with her big, doe-like eyes, but the other one let a narrow ribbon of giggle flutter behind her.

The green corridor led into a rectangular hall, a strange cross between a hunting lodge and a dentist's waiting room. Two pairs of crossed bayonets were grinning coldly down from the wall, looking like bones: only the skull was missing. High up, almost as high as the cornice, two old-fashioned hunting rifles dangled from broad leather straps.

Just think, maybe the old bugger is a major after all, was a thought that crossed Lucky's weary mind when he saw the rifles. He was staggering a bit, and his hat had become awfully small. A fat little white dog with pointed ears was sitting on a basket chair. The old lady snapped her fingers at it, making a sound like a snapping twig, and the dog rolled down on to the floor like a bowling ball made of feathers. An enormous bone-white door that reminded you very much of your mortality croaked in its sleep as it slid open. The dog bounded in, its tail wagging energetically, and the old lady scampered after it like a mouse and into the gigantic doorway, which was a little room of its own with its own ceiling light. A stuffed elk's head glared down at passers-by with its impertinent, peppery eyes. There was also a mirror made of cheap glass but with a great big antique frame, more antique than antiquity. It was an enormous mirror, and when you saw yourself in it you could imagine yourself being an eighteenth-century portrait. If you had a guilty conscience and looked in a mirror as big as that, you might think your bad conscience was looking over your shoulder, keen to get into the picture as well.

Lucky was captivated by the mirror straight away. It seemed to him that it was some kind of passport control you had to go through in order to get access to the inner room. He'd reached a stage where no thoughts were too mad to be taken seriously by his intellect. That's why he stopped in front of the mirror, and at first he was very surprised at what he saw there. He didn't grasp straight away that it was himself. It must be the inspector, he thought, and searched in the corners of his memory for his army number. While he was searching, though, he slowly identified the man in the glass, a bit like when you make out your likeness in a misty window-pane.

His first reaction was deeply hurt. Bloody hell, is that me? He observed in horrified confusion his large, pockmarked chin with the hint of blue shadows. Then he was overcome with disgust and wanted to smash the mirror, but he was held back by respect for the frame. Before his misty eyes the inflamed tops of his cheekbones grew bigger and bigger until they looked to him like enormous dollops of jam. He suddenly started to be convulsed by the beginnings of sobs, and fell several yards down into the well of self-pity. What he really wanted to do now was to turn round and hurtle down the stairs and keep rushing into the night and perhaps further still into the deep forest. That's how he felt, literally.

But now he was thumbing through his moods as if they were a boring book, and then he was struck by the piano taking deep gulps from the glass of silence on the other side of the heavy curtain with gold braid behind which the others had just disappeared. Duty called and forced its grip over his forehead. Bugger it, he thought responsibly to himself, I can't just stand here, not when they've invited me in.

He bowed smartly to the mirror and started looking for a way in through the wide curtain. He eventually entered a large room, as big as a small market square, but a market square that had been used as a car park. Every square inch of floor was covered by a table, or so it seemed to Lucky's confused gaze, big ones and small ones, made of walnut, oak or stained birch, tables for every purpose imaginable: tables to eat at, drink at, play chess on, play bridge on, sew at, put gramophones on, or flower arrangements; indeed, there was even one with sharp wooden spikes round the edges, perhaps intended for the family fakir.

Where there was no table, there were chairs, and where there were neither tables nor chairs there was a piano. They'd fitted it in somehow in the middle of the floor and it was grinning merrily with its yellow, horsy teeth. The girl with no style was sitting on the piano stool. She had a V-shaped neckline at the back, and by pure coincidence Dandy's hand happened to be resting just there. Notes were clambering up and down ladders under her fingers, sometimes standing on each other's heels and squealing.

In another part of the room they'd managed to find room for three people, the girl with the gloves, the jolly old lady doll, and a fat man in a cloak, with an outsize tomato for a neck and a highly polished cannonball for a bald head: the company director. They were playing billiards. The old lady was evidently the expert and was building big breaks, scampering round the table and jabbering away eagerly. The company director and the girl with the gloves were standing opposite each other, and when it wasn't their turn, he was poking her playfully in the chest with his cue. Oh hell, so that's the way it is, thought Lucky. He was going through a period of sober clarity, and could feel that uplifting feeling of superiority you often get when you turn up sober at a party that's been under way for a while, and everybody else is starting to be a bit tipsy.

He turned his attention to the walls for a few moments. There were paintings everywhere, jostling with each other as if they were in a sauana, queuing to get into the shower from the ceiling light. If nothing else, the display showed the owner's sense of systematic order: there was a group of waterfalls, for instance, which would have cascaded into each other were it not for the picture frames. Bloody shame, thought Lucky, experiencing a minute or two of misanthropic exultation, since nobody had taken note of his arrival yet.

Next to them was a collection of sunrises, with pines, firs, cliffs and meadows full of flowers; there can't have been more than a quarter of an hour between them. Then came a big collection of farmhouses, some of them with mooing cattle with nose-rings in front, and others with well-dressed, clean-nosed children and playful calves. One of the paintings depicted no less than five calves, which was a bit much for a cow-shed the size of that in the picture. Maybe they'd borrowed a few extra that day, so the artist wouldn't be disappointed, thought Lucky with a yawn.

That's when he noticed her. His gaze tumbled down from the frame and fell more or less straight on her. She was sitting crammed against a rickety little table in a dark corner, and almost blended into the chair back. In front of her was an imposing bottle of mineral water and a fizzy glass. She was knitting away eagerly, her needles flying around in the air like flashes of lightning, and all the time she was gazing down into her mineral water.

She was sitting there as if she were the only person in the world, as if her home was that chair at that table by that bottle of mineral water. Lucky suddenly felt sorry for her, because she was so alone. It was his own self-pity that spread to her. He'd worked himself into one of those moods now – everyone round about him seemed to have companions they could exchange ideas with; he was the only one who was so wretchedly lonely.

As he worked his way over to the other lonely creature through a labyrinth of tables and chairs, he noticed through the rear mirror of his mind that the billiard-playing company director was now standing next to the girl with the gloves, and finding it increasingly difficult to keep his hands off her. The old girl was frolicking about in high spirits, her cheeks flushed, and hadn't noticed she was the only one still playing. It dawned on Lucky, just as surely as if it had been written all over her, that the solitary girl was the company director's wife.

The piano was lapping away at the silence. Dandy's hand had drowned itself in the piano-girl's hair, and the skin revealed by her V-neck had slowly started glowing. Lucky suddenly felt very sorry for himself, and hence also for the lonely girl.

She hadn't heard him coming. He sat down on a high-chested, shamelessly mock-antique armchair standing below a big, half-hearted waterfall yawning between two blue-green expanses of wildly romantic forest. She let her needles fall into her lap and said with a directness that surprised him: 'Are you the other soldier Grandma was talking about?'

She had a feeble voice, as thin as a thread, and it needed poking with the jackboot-pounding of the piano in order to be heard. It's only a short step from self-pity to shame, and now he was ashamed of being a giant in dirty, creaking boots who'd landed in a doll factory. The image in the mirror returned and placed itself scornfully on the table between them and in front of the bottle of mineral water. He strained himself to work out how best to hold his lips and tongue and throat in order to ensure that his 'yes' would sound as refined and crystal-clear as her words had done, but when it finally emerged it had turned rusty along the way.

She'd started knitting again and wasn't looking at him, and he was glad about that. He examined her closely and with blue eyes, frightened of soiling her with his looks. He suddenly had a bright idea that astonished him because of its obviousness. He could have started whistling, so obvious did it suddenly seem.

Just think if she doesn't really exist, he thought. If she's just something I've invented, something between me and that chair. A bit of carving on the chair arm that my imagination's breathed life into. It seemed to him her behaviour supported the idea.

He was intrigued to note that there wasn't a soul there who'd registered their existence. An empty chair couldn't attract less attention. He saw that the flabby company director, whose green plus-fours he'd glimpsed under a fat-bellied Chippendale chair, and the girl with the gloves had now withdrawn from the game altogether. Only the old lady, the one the lonely girl had called grandma, was still at it. She seemed to have split herself into two or three parts, each one battling furiously for hegemony over the pockets. With undiminished energy she scurried round the table with her cue, executing a wide variety of strokes one after the other. She was reminiscent of one of those little mechanical toys you wind up, with an unusually long spring.

The pair of them were sitting calmly and quietly on their chairs. They both had wine glasses before them, glinting like newly varnished wood. The company director suddenly raised the girl's hand towards the light, like a champion who'd just won a boxing match. All of a sudden, a large ring was glistening on her finger, disgustingly large, like a phos-phorescent wart. Had she been wearing it before?

'I'm knitting,' said the lonely girl. She was there again, in any case. Suddenly her hand closed around his wrist, like a handcuff several sizes too big. Before that, though, she'd caressed the sleeve of his tunic. She pulled his hand over the table towards her. 'What do you think of this?' she asked, and when he looked down he saw that his hand was alongside her knitting.

What the hell are you on about? he thought, sullen and wide awake. Why did she have to insist on existing when everything had been going so well? He took it like a mathematician who's realized that one of his premisses is wrong.

'I'd be so pleased,' she said, 'if you'd be so kind as to try it on and see if it fits.' 'Fits?' he said. He picked up her knitting and bent one of the needles until it formed a little bay. 'On my hand, do you mean?' 'Of course,' she said, 'on your hand.'

It was something that looked like a misshapen child's sock in blue-green. When he stretched it, he could just get two fingers into it. 'It fits smashing,' he said, throwing it at her.

OK, he thought, joke's over; and he moved on into a brutal period. It felt as if he were surrounded by water on all sides, and had to struggle with a boat-hook in order to get to the surface.

Then he looked up into the waterfall, and let his gaze swim around among its green stones, resolved not to let himself be won over any more.

'That was great,' she said. 'That it fitted, I mean. You see, I'm knitting for the soldiers. Making some mittens. You're sure it was OK?'

'Of course,' he said, and thought to himself: OK for dwarf soldiers, if there are any. Why should she believe my wrist is no broader than two fingers? Maybe she doesn't believe in anything at all, come to that. There are folks who believe in far dafter things than that. He felt his sunburnt wrist, came upon his watch, and was thrust brutally into a context he'd come close to losing track of.

There was just one hour left of the late pass. One more hour before the fear returned. On the other side of that border stood terror itself with its pitchfork and its green torch, and, suddenly isolated from all connections with reality and comradeship, he experienced a moment of brief but penetrating horror.

When he came round it was almost dark inside the room. The ceiling light was out, and the old lady was muttering away at the billiard table. She couldn't see to play, and kept tapping her cue on the side of the table like a conductor. In the end she gave up, and left the room complaining, leaving a little trail of ill-will behind her.

The company director had switched on a table lamp, but apart from that he and the girl with the gloves were hiding in the darkness. From time to time a whisper sauntered through the room. The lamp on the piano was wrapping a melancholy blanket round the piano-girl and her admirer. Lucky felt very lonely.

Why, he thought, why is it just me who has to go through

this? He felt a violent need to annoy or scare somebody. He wasn't as tolerant as he had been shortly beforehand when he'd thought the lonely girl should be allowed to maintain her belief in his wrists. He switched on a lamp under the waterfall. It projected a little cascade upwards, and exposed it as soapy lather. A cone of light balanced on her cheek, and light dripped down through the hair on one of her temples.

'Do you really believe all that?' he asked.

'All what?'

'That crap about supplying the whole of the Swedish army with wrist warmers, or whatever it was you said.'

'Yes,' she said. 'I think that's something worth believing in. But maybe you have a better suggestion?'

'No,' he admitted. 'But has it occurred to you that it's far too hot just now for your mittens? And another thing: you shouldn't sit here all by yourself in this room, and get too interested in what *you*'re on with. Can't you see what's going on, and *if* you can, why don't you do something about it?'

'A belief,' she said, 'a belief isn't something you keep changing as the years go by. Do you really think I should believe in sandals and loincloths when it's hot and mittens and ski-socks when it isn't? A belief isn't a thermometer, after all. As for the rest of what you said, I don't know what you're talking about.'

'You don't?' he said fiercely, taking her by the chin with one hand and the cheek with the other, but tenderly and carefully, so that she didn't need to be afraid, and he pointed her face towards the centre of the room.

'Look,' he said, 'can't you see 'em, the pair of 'em?'

When he let go, though, her head just sprang back as if governed by clockwork.

'The girl's sitting on his knee now, the fat bloke's,' he went on. 'Now . . . but look for yourself!'

'No,' she said, 'but you tell me.'

'They're sitting there in the lamplight, quite shamelessly. Now he's taking her arm and lifting it up to his mouth. Now he's fumbling for her ear and leaning forward to kiss it. You should see 'em sitting there in the lamplight. You only need to turn your head the teeniest little bit.'

'You can stop going on like that,' she said, quite sharply. 'You know full well I can see him, of course. Oh, how marvellous his hair is! Can't you see it glistening in the lamplight? Just like it did that morning when he came to pick me up at the little boarding house on the Rue Lamartine. The sun was shining, you see, and the landlady had a cage of canaries hanging in the staircase. Oh, how they sang when the sun shone in through the front door! He was sitting next to the coachman up front, and when the horses came to a standstill outside the entrance, you know, he jumped down so nimbly and threw a rose he'd had in his buttonhole up to where I was sitting on the balcony.'

It's now or ever, he thought. I can force her into a cul-de-sac. I can sow the seeds of terror in her as well. All this loneliness will be a thing of the past.

'Yes,' he said, 'that might very well be true, all that. It sounds pretty. I reminds me of some film I've seen, or maybe something I read somewhere. But you must realize it's all over. You're not living on that island any more, or whatever it was. Now you're in a room in Stockholm – bloody ostentatious furniture you've got, by the way – and he's in the same room as well and he's fat now and he's more or less as bald as a coot, and you've got to face up to the fact that he's here in the same room, messing around with a bit of skirt.'

'Ah,' she said, and her voice had acquired a noticeable edge that the lazy notes from the piano cut themselves on. 'I know you. I know your sort. You're a liar, just like the rest of them. Don't think I don't know you. You're no better than the rest of them, not one bit better. I know all of you by now. Let's take her for instance, the one you reckon he's messing about with but who in fact is helping him to improve his business letters in French. You see he's always had trouble with French, and I could tell you all about what he does for me. I sit here knitting, day in and day out, and when I've finished a garment I say: Miss Brant, would be so kind as to send this to Save the Children – you see, these aren't mittens for soldiers at all, I just said that to see whether you at least could resist lying to me, but you couldn't, because you said, as you might remember, that it fitted you perfectly. Anyway, when you leave I'd like to draw your attention to a carton standing in the hall next to the shoe stand, a carton they thought they could hide away from me, but I found it even so.'

Good God, he thought, and suddenly felt absolutely calm, I feel sorry for the girl. She's in a cul-de-sac, just like me, but not the same one. He thought he could see the tragedy of her situation straight off, and was filled with a violent desire to defend her against all these louts filling the room. He hoped they'd attack her, with taunts, with invectives, or with sticks and fists. Suddenly his hands remembered her cheeks and her chin and he leaned over the table to caress her.

'If you like, I'll sing you a little song he used to whisper in my ear when we separated every night at the corner by the tulip-seller's stand – but you must promise to drop all those silly fantasies you tried to make me believe just now.'

Without waiting for an answer, and without changing her expression or her posture, she started to sing. She sang through his hands, and he could feel her pulse beating under her delicate cheekbones:

> Au clair de la lune,
> mon ami Pierrot,
> prête-moi ta plume
> pour écrir un mot.
> Ma chandelle est morte,
> je n'ai plus de feu.
> Ouvre-moi la porte
> pour l'amour de Dieu.

'Yes,' he said after a while, and now the piano had stopped

dripping and the room was filled to the brim with silence. 'Pretty. But I didn't get much of it. I only understood the bit about "amour" at the end.'

Now he knew what could save him. Not a bit of hot passion with the piano girl, not chasing after the lonely girl with words that stung like whips, not sharing his pain with somebody else.

I must tell her, he told himself, forming his hands round the countours of her cheeks, that I like her. I won't do anything else, that's all I need to do. She must know I'm not lying to her like the girls do, or deceiving her like the fatty. I need to know when I leave that she knows that I like her.

He didn't feel he could say it to her straight out, though. He realized she would look at him, the liar, with eyes full of distrust. And his voice wouldn't be able to bear that distrust. He had an idea. He carefully detached his hands from her face and dived down under the table where there was a newspaper shelf. He discovered a thick fashion magazine, and in a big white gap between two pictures of models, he wrote in pencil with big capitals: I LOVE YOU.

'What are you doing under the table?' she asked when his hand brushed against her leg. He withdrew his hand timidly, but didn't answer. Instead he put the magazine on the table in front of her, unhooked her hand from her knitting and placed it just below his words.

Just then the light came on. It was the old lady coming back. Now she was looking for trouble and carrying her billiard cue like a sword. 'Now I want a game, dammit,' she shouted. At the same time the company director and the girl with the gloves and the piano girl and Dandy all got to their feet. Lucky noticed the suspicious vigorousness of their movements and the heartiness in their voices. 'Well, sir,' said Dandy, 'I hope you don't mind if I pack up now, sir. We have to be back at the barracks in half an hour's time, and I'd rather like to say goodnight to my little girl first.'

The piano-girl giggled, a giggle that was hard to translate.

The girl with the gloves was standing in front of the company director like a sort of shield, stretching her long fingers. Lucky glanced down at the lonely girl. Now when it was light the big letters in the fashion magazine leapt up off the page, but her hand was still lying just as motionless as before, directly underneath them, like a box she'd put there because there was no other place to put it. She was gazing at the glass of mineral water, which had stopped fizzing.

Then the company dirctor said, in a voice that was swollen up and festering: 'Of course, gentlemen, do leave, if you must. I dare say we'll manage without you for a while. Ha ha!'

His swollen-up, mushroomy laugh mingled with the piano-girl's giggling.

Then it happened. The lonely girl got to her feet. She put her hands on the table in front of her, as if she were about to deliver a lecture, and her scream sort of cut through the cloth of impure words and furtive actions: 'Don't you see, you idiot? I'm blind! Blind! Blind!'

Then he stumbled out. Forced his way through the curtain like an actor unused to leaving the stage that way. In the hallway beyond he was confronted by his image in the mirror. It was looking at him through a grey mask. His stomach churned and he wanted to be sick. Why didn't I say it to her? The words hammered through him over and over again. Now she'll never know. All at once he hated this pitiable shadow, this down-and-out standing opposite him. In order to shake himself free, he beat it again and again with his fist until it died.

He continued out through the door which was still creaking in its sleep. He leaned over a carton standing in the hall. He opened it, and under a double layer of tissue paper lay the things the lonely girl had been knitting, layer after layer of grossly deformed blue-green children's socks.

Now he could hear the voices behind him – or was it just one, the company's director's fat, asthmatic roar: '. . . the thanks you get for inviting them in . . . in the middle of the night . . . respectable folks . . . bloody thugs . . . better pay for the mirror . . . a hell of a price . . . bloody antique . . . irreplaceable . . . get out of here . . . bloody yobbos . . . don't dare show your faces . . . report you to your regiment . . .'

They searched for the light switch on the stairs. Dandy found it first. They walked slowly down the steps with a handrail supported by solid, brown, roughly carved pillars. On the step level with a gaudy stained-glass window, Lucky felt an arm on his shoulder. When he looked round he was blinded by his friend's gaze and the next moment his surprise was shattered by a series of stings on his defenceless face. With a faint echo of surprise left inside him, he sank to the ground, slowly, like when you're folding up a collapsible bed.

With a quarter or less of himself still there in the camera world, he felt the driving rain ease off after a while and give way to an enormous wave of pain, and then he felt someone lifting him up by his shoulders, slowly, almost tenderly.

The Iron Band

Late on in the evening they finished up at Norma's Bar. It was raining outside, a thin, steady drizzle, and everybody coming into the bar left shiny watermarks on the brick-red floor. They arrived during that slack period when the regulars have run out of steam and the bumble-bees of conversation have lost their wings. At first they stood inside the door, looking for a table. They could occasionally distinguish shrill, individual voices among the dull drone of noise, and thin wisps of smoke were rising up from the smokers as if from sacrificial fires.

A window table looking out on to the street became free. The window-frames cut off just the right amount, and you could sit there and think you were observing life. They sat down and looked out, somewhat casually. The rain had made the evening darker. Outside the cinema opposite were gaudily coloured shadows under the lamps, which were greedily carving out sections of dusk for themselves. The neon light outside the cake shop on the corner was glistening in the blotting paper of the street. A car would occasionally draw up at the pavement's edge and people would get in or out without slamming the doors. They watched people stride by their own illuminated window. Most of them were just profiles. From that angle they could distinguish neither weeping nor laughing. Perhaps the owner of that laughing profile would burst into tears at the next crossroads. They didn't need to know that, though; they could content themselves with what they saw through their window, and take it for reality. It was simply an idealized picture of life they were watching, a life without sounds, in which all actions were benevolently meaningless, and the usurer's grip on the arm of a client gave no impression of evil because of the speed with which the scene flitted past.

They'd wandered from bar to bar all evening without getting really drunk. They'd started in daylight and now it was dusk. They'd started at one end of town, and now they'd reached the other. They'd seen the Carnegie stout advert, the jovial gent with a pipe sitting with his bottle, a dozen times, and the jovial chappie showed no sign of being the slightest bit tipsy. They'd been down so many streets that all the streets eventually fused into the Street, the average street, just as they'd already formed a picture of the average bar and the average bouncer.

Their long, uneventful walk had made them feel jaded. They thought: this is what life must be like, the same grey streets and the same red-faced bouncers with gold buttons. The same cramped tables with the same stains from the beer glasses. The time for metaphysics and speculation on the meaning of life was fast approaching. They set the slender bottles coughing up into glasses on unsteady, drunken feet, and sensed a mystical connection between that action and life. They'd tried putting it into words. Saying, for instance: life isn't something that comes to an end, it's like a liquid, it just moves on from vessel to vessel like a beer, and when it seems to have said goodbye for ever, in fact it's just reconstituting itself in a way that gives support to the highest form of life: life free as air.

But all their words were tired and had gone to sleep in their sleeping bags. They had to give the sleeping bags a good shaking in order to make them release anything at all. Maybe the only thing that would really help was a big bucket of water. And so they sat there in silence, as motionless as blocks of marble, watching the street as if it were a film. The rain had withdrawn to the clouds, leaving just the darkness behind. But that was still stretched out over the streets and pavements like a yellow skin in the lamplight.

Earlier in the evening, before all the words had gone to bed, they'd been talking about the state. 'We all think we're living our own lives, but are we bollocks,' said Edmund. 'We're not?' asked Cheerful Charlie. 'Whose bloody lives are we living, then? Old Man Carnegie's, or that bastard Hitler's, or Joe Blogg's?' 'As I see it,' said Edmund, 'you can only live if you look after yourself. For God's sake, I mean, we've mortgaged ourselves from the very start. People sell themselves every day for a bit of security, a shitty little bit of security, a bit of cheap insurance to make sure all's OK in the larder and the drinks cabinet. And then you accept without a whimper the really big piece of insecurity. The fact, for instance, that the state that's supposed to be giving you security is shoving a live grenade in your hand, and meanwhile you can go to hell with all your tax forms and your insurance policies and your pawnshop receipts and all the rest of it.'

'I feel pressurized,' said Edmund, 'I feel as if there's an iron band pressing into my skull when I find there are laws nobody's asked me if I'll accept that make me practically defenceless. Of course it's true that in theory I can hire myself some public square and a loudspeaker and nobody's snipped through my vocal cords, but the fact is, I'm just on loan. At any moment they like, the big security supplier can take me back again, because there's no fixed time for the loan, that's part of the lender's conditions, you see, because now I'm needed in Manchowko. I've got to go there and shoot a few camels that are threatening the security of my security supplier. Or maybe I've got to go to Kenya. There's a crocodile there that's said something rude about my status as a citizen and my security supplier suddenly discovers I'm upset about it and I've got to go there and get eaten up by the crocodile.

'All this means,' said Edmund, 'that I feel threatened, I feel bloody well threatened by my security supplier. I feel much more threatened than if I lived in a gangster district. There I'd be confronted by big pots I recognize. There I can reckon on assistance from my pals. But there's nobody there demanding I should grab hold of a pistol and shove a black mask over my face and toddle along to Östermalmsgatan and shoot some company director who's started encroaching on the gangsters' territory.

'But the security supplier,' said Edmund, 'is in part a threat to my personal safety, a physical danger. Another thing is that the security supplier offends my personal dignity, in that he robs my will of its integrity. In the eyes of my security supplier, my will is nothing more than a balloon I obligingly blow up on national holidays in order to give myself the illusion it's my will that's being manifested.

'Since I regard my will in principle as the finest instrument of my ego,' said Edmund, 'I naturally have to regard this offence against it on the part of my security supplier as an extremely serious business I owe it to myself to sort out. In theory that can happen in a quite simple way that's painless for both parties. I can go and knock on my security supplier's door and say: "Mr Security Supplier, I've been noting your aggression against my person for a long time in both fear and astonishment. In order to get things put right, as I expect you no doubt know, I've been sending you quite a large number of letters. However, for one reason or another, none of them has been answered. And so I've written to the newspapers and published stern articles pointing out the facts. They've had no effect. In the end I rented the town square and exposed your plans as they affect me in front of masses of people. I can also mention that I had loads of leaflets printed attacking you, and had them distributed free. None of this has got me anywhere, however. There's only one possibility left. I assume, Mr Security Supplier, that you have no serious objection to my taking out the revolver I have in my trouser pocket and shooting you through the head. I take it you realize you've brought this action of mine upon yourself by your provocative silence, and that's my excuse."

'That's what could happen,' said Edmund, 'provided of course the security supplier was a person with a fixed address, his own telephone and an account with the Scandinavian Bank. Unfortunately, though, it ain't like that. I go to some government department, and I meet a civil servant or a deputy caretaker. I say: "I'd like to speak to Mr State, please, also known as the security supplier. And quick. I'm in a hell of a hurry. This revolver," I say, tapping my pocket, "is borrowed from a friend who wants it back by one o'clock at the latest and it's already a quarter to." "I'm sorry," says the civil servant or the deputy caretaker, "I can't help you. There's nobody by that name on our register, but if you really want to shoot somebody, here I am at your service." "Aha!" I say, and I'm interested by this. "But what good would that do? Would the state put a stop to its aggression aimed at my very existence? Would I no longer run the risk of having my rights trampled underfoot?" "Unfortunately, sir," says the civil servant or the deputy caretaker, "everything would go on just as before. The only visible outcome would be two notices in the next morning's paper." "What do you mean?" I ask. "Why two notices?" "Oh yes, one in the Deaths column and another in the Situations Vacant, for men."

'So that's the way it is,' said Edmund, 'I want to be aggressive, I want to stand up for my basic human rights, but I come up against a brick wall. The possibilities open to active anarchism are suddenly exhausted, and the iron band tightens round my skull. It's not 1937 any more and it's not Spain, where I joined the fighting in order to save my soul. After Spain, though, it became impossible. That was a road that was blocked. If I joined the fighting after 1939, it was to save my body.

'As far as I'm concerned,' said Edmund, '– and in spite of everything I'd be happy if I knew my position wasn't unique – there are a few escape routes, if I can call them that. For instance, I can just leave the iron band where it is and pretend I was born with it. Or I can say: "Look here, my friends, I have the honour of presenting the planet's latest fashion for men – an iron band à la state. No other headgear is needed. It's a miracle of comfort. It doesn't need any sweat-bands. You don't need to take it off when you enter a restaurant. You can keep it on when you go to the cinema. You can fix a candle to it at Christmas, or a flag on the Swedish national day. It adjusts automatically as the temperature varies. It keeps you nice and cool in winter, just when you need it. It's as hot as an oven door in summer. Another advantage is that it grows. It could well be the only headgear in the world that grows. Before long ear-muffs will be a thing of the past. Headbands will be unnecessary, sunglasses as well. You'll be able to throw away your nose warmers and your moustache brushes. You won't even need a chin strap, nor a woollen scarf. You'll be able to save on buying clothes. Give your shoe coupons to somebody who really needs them. You won't even need arch-supports once your iron band has had a chance to grow properly. When you reach that stage, you suddenly realize this must be Happiness. Happiness must have been stuck on the inside of the iron band, or been linked with it in some other mysterious way. You feel very, very secure, you've never felt so secure until you acquired this marvellous iron band, and now of course you have to recommend this item of equipment to your friends.''

'But,' said Edmund, 'this solution seems immoral to me. Once you've felt the iron band in place, I think it's not right to flaunt it. True enough, having felt it is marvellous compared with never having noticed it, but when you don't feel up to it and can't bear to wear it any longer, it's more honest to pull it off, even if there's a risk your scalp might stick to it, than to pretend it was a marvellous jewel. You don't change your attitudes like you change your clothes – even if some people think you do; you have them forced upon you, and have to be grateful for that.

'But there is another way of looking at it,' said Edmund, 'and in this case the way of looking at it isn't the same as an escape route, because there's no question of that. To be sure, it means accepting the iron band – not in the positive sense of making it a part of your fancy-dress costume, but as a burden that has to be borne as long as there's no way of putting up active opposition to it. Remember this, though: don't wear it as if you were a martyr, as if the iron band were a crown of thorns. You're not wearing it because you deserve it, but because of so many people's cowardice and your own inadequacy.'

All of a sudden a shadow appeared on the table, an elongated image of the bouncer. Edmund had been speaking too loud. His words had warmed him up, and he'd discovered how he seemed to be able to make new discoveries and new conquests without any apparent effort. 'But,' he said, as if he hadn't noticed the shadow at all, and maybe he hadn't, in fact, 'as long as I'm wearing my iron band, my angst is the biggest in the country. Nobody's angst can possibly be greater than mine.' He was shouting now, almost as if he'd just discovered some new natural law. And he really felt angst, not just as a word, but as a brand-new reality. It was as if he'd stuck his head in through a familiar window and suddenly been hit by a new and unfamiliar smell. The iron band suddenly became a reality. He could feel it pressing against his cranium. It was getting tighter and tighter, and he felt it was impossible to force a single finger between his skull and the band. It didn't last long, in fact it only lasted for the brief moment it took from the first appearance of the shadow on the table to the bouncer grabbing him by the shoulder.

They'd been shooed out like dogs, and they'd then wandered through the streets like dogs, poking their noses into every hole that looked interesting, driven by their anxiety. They were carrying their fear around with them like you do the beginnings of a fever, without really knowing what was going to happen next.

Now they were in the bar. They could observe the street through the window as if through an aquarium wall. Big buses appeared briefly in the asphalt mirror as chunks of red, the occasional cyclist flitted past like a firefly, the audience flowed out from the cinema like lava, and the lamps at the entrance were switched off. A blind man walked along the edge of the pavement, tapping his stick against the kerb. Directly in front of their window was a parked bicycle, head down like a bull's, and they would have knocked on the window to warn the blind man if doing so wouldn't have attracted too much attention; anyway a young man took him by the arm and guided him past the obstacle.

They sighed with relief, and emptied their glasses.

Now came the flurry of activity before closing time. The bar door was half-open all the time, and men with unbuttoned jackets and watery eyes peered in, looking for an empty table. The level of conversation moved into a higher gear. Things were buzzing, and cheeks suddenly decided it was time to liven up and straight away they took on a brighter colour. Hands thought so as well. They carved their way through the thick air with sharp gestures. If mouths didn't immediately feel happier, they wouldn't be filled with great words of wisdom.

Edmund and Cheerful Charlie and Joker were carried away by the general excitement. Joker felt something very strange now, something quite new to him. He'd turned his gaze into the room. Cheerful Charlie was picking his teeth with a toothpick. Edmund was hammering out a march on the foot of his glass. And Joker thought to himself: I've got to say it now. Now's just the right moment. I can't wait any longer.

He opened his mouth to let the words out. He'd had them inside his mouth for so long now, he thought they ought to just shoot out of their own accord. But they didn't even twitch. And then he felt the iron band fall into place all of a sudden. It was such a physical feeling, he was surprised he couldn't hear the sound of the sledge-hammer bashing it into position. The half of his ego that clung stubbornly to the idea of achieving clarity, that wanted to be liberated, was strangled. Conversely, the other half of him had much more room for manoeuvre. The half that said: that's no business of yours any more. It's just a lot of daft bloody mad ideas. Let 'em go. Kick 'em up the arse. Send 'em to hell. That was the half controlling his tongue now. There were holes in the iron band, and meaningless words he didn't need to think about before saying came spurting out through them. He started prattling on about bus connections in the Gothenburg region, then about a make of roofing tiles that were much worse than any others, and finally about a builder from Södertälje who'd got beaten up one night for being found sitting back in an armchair in the house of an ironmonger's wife in Enskede.

Edmund and Cheerful Charlie nodded and laughed at the punch lines if there were any and suddenly Joker started dreaming he was in two different rooms. Literally two different rooms, with pictures on the walls and armchairs and divans on the floor. In one of the rooms the wireless was broadcasting a cabaret, and half-drunken, cheerful people with brandy glasses in their hands were sitting round, roaring with laughter. He was quite a sensitive room, and the laughter tickled his wall hangings and he dreamed that he started hiccuping and the pictures and the embroidery (HOME SWEET HOME, four feet by nine inches) started jumping round the walls and some of the drunks who noticed felt frightened and were convinced they'd got the DTs.

In the other room, though, which was adjacent, the mood was one of great fear. The people in it couldn't afford a lamp, never mind a wireless. Two people were sitting in opposite corners. They were as quiet as mice and they sat swaying backwards and forwards in their chairs and when the arms hit the wall it hurt him, being the room, and it felt just as if his nerve centres were at precisely that point. So much angst gathered just under the ceiling, the ceiling would have loved to jump up and float into the attic if there hadn't been a grand piano on the floor above.

Now the room that was himself started hiccuping with laughter, and the other room that was also himself was filled with extreme fear and the walls staggered back and would have run out of the house if only they could. As one of the rooms, the angst room, he thought: I must turn the walls and the ceiling and the floor inside out and creep in through the door to the wireless room with the cabaret, otherwise I'll just burst as a room. Then roars of laughter started coming from one of the angst chairs and a white face with two pointed torches instead of eyes stared up into his own, which were on the ceiling. 'Ha ha ha!' said the chair. 'You think you'll burst! Ha ha ha!'

Then his eyes, which were now suddenly fastened to the floor with gigantic picture hooks, noticed the walls and ceiling were being held together by a massive iron construction, a monstrous skeleton with iron clamps, and enormous amounts of angst could be held there before they started to give way. The iron band, the iron band, he thought.

Then he woke up. It was Cheerful Charlie laughing. Oh, how he hated it. He'd have loved to fling his hands across the table and choke it. But instead he remained where he was, perfectly calmly, and he heard his voice saying: 'In this case I'd

prefer bloody cement, I bloody would, Blue Circle cement.'
In which bloody case? he thought. Maybe one of them was
going to build a house, Edmund or Cheerful Charlie or even
himself. Maybe that's what they were talking about. He didn't
know. He suddenly felt very tired.

It'd have been a lot better, he thought, but for that bloody
iron band. Then nobody could have stopped him saying: listen,
lads, I'd like you to help me now. I want you to listen to me
very carefully, and when you've finished listening I want you
to say: 'You don't need to have a guilty conscience. Was it
your fault he was dead when you got back with the water
ladle? Do you think he'd have thought badly of you just for
that? Don't you think he'd have thought: this is a mate who
ran to get me some water, a mate I've learnt to trust. I know
he's running like a greyhound to get back straight away. He's
a smashing mate, I know that. Even so, I don't know if I'll
bother to wait. Fact is, I'm not a bit thirsty any more.'

But while the buzzing voices were being cut off like string
by the clock's pointed hand and the bar gave a heave and spat
out into the night a crowd suddenly struck dumb, he could feel
the band tightening round his temples. They walked through
the identical streets, echoing emptily, and it grew tighter and
tighter all the time. They walked over Slussen, where the
adverts lit up in neon were shuddering hysterically; they
strolled along Skeppsbron, where sharp, defoliated lamps hung
over the road; they crossed over Gustav Adolf's Square,
where someone had placed a half-empty bottle of beer under
the heroic king; and they came to Strandvägen, where they
followed a drunken prostitute and an elderly gentleman with
his hat askew, and the gentleman was slapping the girl's
bottom with his cane until she started singing for him; they
passed flashy Narvavägen, which was lying asleep with its
shirt unbuttoned; and they trudged over the sandy wastes in
front of the barracks: and the iron band just pressed and
pressed. It dug deeper and deeper into his cranium, stopping it
from splitting.

When they got to the iron gate and pressed the bell push, he suddenly felt extremely frightened. He grabbed hold of Cheerful Charlie's arm, ruthlessly, like the beak of a kite. He wanted to shout out: save me, quickly, before it's too late! But the iron band prevented any words from passing his lips.

'Hey, Edmund,' said Cheerful Charlie, 'givvus a hand. Joker's passed out.'

Oh, how he wished he could have bitten their sweaty, helpful hands.

The Rag Doll

Two little boys came out of the alley. They were carrying a rag doll between them. Its limp body was dangling and its long, thin legs were swinging grotesquely. One of the boys took a rusty mouth-organ from his trouser pocket and produced a few shrill notes. The other boy giggled, and looked around cheekily. Both of them were barefoot and wearing long, baggy shorts made out of old overcoats. One of them had on a long, black jacket with holes in the elbows. He took a standing jump over a pile of horse dung lying steaming in the road. In a window opposite the school was a red-haired girl, feeding the pigeons with an old loaf of white bread. Some bits fell down in front of a tall, stooping chap wearing Jesus-sandals; he waved his fist at the window, and hurried on his way.

The boys ran with the doll into the gardens in the middle of the square. In the middle of the doll's swollen nose was a shiny safety-pin, which was out of place with the rest of its shabby appearance. The girl playing in the sand-pit with a green tin spade screamed when she saw the safety-pin. The boy with the mouth-organ took the spade off her and flung it into the street. The girl started screaming as if she had colic. Then came a voice sounding as if it was from heaven, but in fact it came from a narrow, leaning block of flats in the corner of the alley, instructing that 'them bloody lads had better be bloody nice to that bloody lass'. The girl fingered her nose at the boy with the mouth-organ, ran to fetch her spade, and disappeared like a mouse into the entrance-hole of the old building. She had long, thin, spidery legs that pointed inwards somewhat. The boy in the jacket swung the doll round and round like a slingball and let it go at the top of the arc. It flew through the air and with a gentle thud hit a window-pane where nobody was at home on the first floor of the narrow building. It slid headfirst down the pane and lay on its stomach on the window-ledge, like a man that's been shot. Fini.

A long, high, pink school building formed one side of the little square, which was not much more than a puffed-up alley. Angry round trumpet blasts came bouncing out of it and smacked against the house-wall opposite. They died with a final moan as they slid down to the street. A pale girl with a fringe and wearing a gym-slip was standing in a window on the top floor, beating a blackboard cleaner with a pointing stick. The chalk formed a pillar that reached right down to the asphalt yard below.

'Tell that bastard to stop torturing the poor bloody bull,' yelled the boy with the mouth-organ. 'That's a dusty wig your old lady wears,' screeched the boy with the jacket, filling the whole playground with giggles. The girl went to fetch another blackboard cleaner. She seemed quite unmoved. 'Come down here an' I'll give yer summat nice to suck,' shouted the boy with the mouth-organ, taking a bag of sweets out of his trouser pocket. The girl slammed the window shut with an annoyed bang. 'That gottcha!' screamed the boy with the mouth-organ, sticking his tongue out at the school.

Now the trumpet started sobbing as if nobody wanted it, and in the end it fell silent altogether: you could imagine it lying bent double over a bench with tears streaming from its keys. After a while a boy in frayed long trousers emerged through a hole in the iron railings. The trumpet was hanging from his back like an elephant's trunk in a black case. He took a short cut through the gardens and playground in the middle of the square, walking quickly and resolutely, his eyes glued to the ground.

When he was opposite the sand-pit, the boy with the jacket yelled: 'Hunchback of Nôtre Dame!' and flung a handful of sand at him. The boy with the mouth-organ jumped up on the edge of the sand-pit and sang in a bawling, provocative voice:

> Dad's down at the Feathers,
> Mum's out in all weathers,
> Screwing with her bloke.

The verse evidently referred to the boy with the trumpet, because when he'd disappeared down the alley the other two sat down in the sand and began squabbling over a penknife. They soon reached agreement and started playing the knife game. They laid one hand in the sand in front of them with their fingers spread out wide, and stabbed the spaces between them at lightning speed. The knife blade glinted in the sun that was cascading down over the little square and making the school wall blush. It looked as though they were holding a struggling lizard in their hands.

After a while they changed over to the less pointed blade, and the boy with the jacket stabbed himself in his middle finger just below the nail. Howling like a dog, he raced across the square, over the road and disappeared down the alley, his injured finger wrapped in the lining of his jacket. The boy with the mouth-organ spat in the sand and went on playing for a while with the blunt blade.

The two pensioners in their ragged cloth caps who'd been sitting on the bench next to Sörenson got up and went for a little walk in the sunshine. It enveloped their threadbare figures like shiny armour. They stopped in the doorway of the narrow building and peered inside with their sinewy, bird-like necks. One of them gave himself a secretive little pat on the chest before they disappeared into the shadowy entrance. Shortly afterwards came the sound of a cork being taken out of a bottle.

The pointed gable of the narrow building cut out quite a lot of the sun. The sunlight took its leave of the little oasis in the middle of the square and started climbing up the school wall. A stray seagull screamed as it glided over the schoolyard, sketching in an invisible chalk-line between the school's flag-pole, and its dipped wing-tip. Pigeons were clattering on the window-ledges and dropping breadcrumbs on the pavements. The sparrows, those winged rats, were chirruping away around the piles of horse dung. Somewhere down the alley somebody was kicking an empty tin can over the cobbles. A few little girls in summery dress were playing rounders in the schoolyard: bong! . . . the hard thud of bat on ball, the pattering of little feet, the gentle bouncing of the ball, suppressed giggles, then the shrill screech of 'Home!' The boy was still sitting all alone in the sand-pit, playing with his knife.

But suddenly, in the middle of this little oasis of calm, Sörenson had a vision of horror. The alarm bells started ringing and he thought he could feel himself jumping up from the bench and racing over the grass in a reckless dash for the dark entrance, fumbling for friendly door handles. In fact, though, he remained seated, watching the bare-headed man in black walking past the house opposite. He suddenly realized he must have seen him coming long before his consciousness sounded the alarm. He was walking slowly and hesitantly, close to the wall, like a blind man who's recently got his sight back. It looked as if he had an errand for every window and every doorway, indeed, for every paving stone. He stopped on the pavement directly opposite the sand-pit, and Sörenson suddenly noticed the man was being pulled by his shadow in front of him. He could see quite clearly how the shadow sprang forward from the sole of his shoe, leaned forward over the gutter, took the man by the arm and started to drag him over the street, keeping watch with its dusty steel-bullet of a head.

Everything in Sörenson's world suddenly changed quality. The green blades of grass shrank to form little, painful, shiny, black fingertips. The busy chirruping of the sparrows bombarded his ears like cruel darts, and the shrill 'Home!' of the girls playing rounders became a grim, ominous warning cry. A mechanic's ring of horror closed in round the sand-pit and the boy playing in it. The man and his shadow were now approaching from two sides, from behind and from in front. Sörenson wanted to shout: run for it, run for your life, but he knew the boy wouldn't be able to hear anything through the ring. He suddenly started to feel cold, and with a loud clang the roof of the narrow building touched glasses and drank a toast with the school.

The man in black was now standing in the sand in front of his shadow, taking a long knife out of its sheath. He tested its edge thoughtfully against his thumb. Then he stabbed his shadow with it, and it fell headfirst on to the sand between the boy's knees. The boy looked up, and the man shoved his shadow to one side so that their eyes could meet. He sat down on the edge of the sand-pit and started talking to the boy, softly, quickly and urgently. All the time his eyes were straying towards the houses, up the street and down the alley.

Now the shadow was dead, though, and everything was back to normal in Sörenson's world. The blades of grass recovered their original colour, the houses straightened themselves up, and the girls playing rounders no longer shouted out symbols. The ring of horror caused by the uncertainty burst open, and suddenly Sörenson knew what was going to happen. The man in black had no secrets from him. He reckoned he knew all about him. He was not surprised when the man and the boy got to their feet, the man quickly and the boy hesitantly. Nor was he surprised when the man in black stuck the long knife in its sheath in the boy's pocket, and took the boy's hand and pulled him towards the street. The boy's hand hung loosely from his, as if stuck there with chewing gum, and his feet seemed glued to the pavement. A pigeon took off reluctantly and glided down into the gutter. A ball whistled over the square and landed like a bomb in the middle of a flock of house sparrows. They squeaked hysterically, and the boy turned round to look at them with sad eyes. The man smiled and patted the knife in his pocket, and the boy's will finally gave in. They swung round the corner of the school-house, and disappeared quickly down the alley.

Sörenson got up and followed them slowly.

When he got to the corner of the alley, he could see them in the distance, as if they were at the bottom of a well. The boy was walking tentatively over the cobbles, like one does over a field of newly sown corn. The handle of the knife was sticking out of one pocket. The man was a pace or two ahead, walking with a gait suitable for cobble-stones, and it occurred to Sörenson: that man's a sailor. He's bought that knife in Lovisa or Turku.

Without Sörenson knowing it, his identification committee was already meeting. It had booked a room and hung a blue notice up on the door mirror saying 'Unnecessary noise and ulterior motives forbidden'. Red-cheeked errand boys were running up and down corridors carrying trays of material for identification, and the files proliferated and the committee members were already rubbing their hands at the prospect of the final report. Meanwhile a few delegates were out in the corridor, boasting about conclusions already drawn so as not to make the boss impatient. That business about the sailor and the knife were words he had picked up in this way through the crack in door.

The walk was proceeding along the big stony river of Slottsbacken. The index finger on the obelisk was trembling in the evening breeze. They turned towards the water's edge, all three of them, cut across Skeppsbron Bridge and round the corner. The last of the sun was drowning in the windows of

Skeppsholm church, and the beginnings of twilight were already starting to dress the avenues in Kungsträdgården in a blue hairnet. The boy took the sheath from his pocket and scraped it along the stone wall along Norrström. Well-dressed people turned round in distaste and stared at the ragamuffin of a boy in his bare feet. They resented having the tranquillity of their evening walk shattered.

Just for a moment Sörenson lost contact with them in the mass of people on Norrbro. A platoon of infantrymen was just passing the bridge, sticking a cork into the bottleneck below the palace. Traffic was piling up behind them. The tram bells were ringing like wall-clocks behind the drone of motor-car engines. Cyclists weaved in and out of the cars, their mudguards rattling. Sörenson pushed and shoved his way through to the southern end of the bridge and paused under the statue of the lion, staring out over Gustav Adolf's Square and down the Strömgatan promenade. The red lanterns were glittering with a dull red glow outside the Opera House. The last rays of sun were drowning in Riddarfjärden, a ferry was creeping over the water and seemed to be balancing on it. A gull with blood on its wings sailed over the parliament building and swooped down at a steep angle towards the Strömparterren terrace.

He could see them approaching the bridge. He could glimpse the boy's bare legs behind a pair of bow-legged officer's jackboots. He leaned over the railings and stared down into the water to avoid having to greet them. A man fishing for smelt was doing battle with the current, oars straining, as he tried to pull in to the quayside. He closed his eyes and heard the jackboots clumping by. Then they brushed past him, so close that he could have grabbed the boy's arm and rescued him.

But he couldn't. I can't do that, he thought, it would attract too much attention. Maybe the police would come, and then there'd be trouble. Everybody's got their eye on you when you're just a conscript. But there was another voice – he often had a whole army of voices jostling for position – and this voice said scornfully: don't give us that. The plain fact is, you're a coward. Pack it in, instead, because that's what you really want to do, and go and have a beer somewhere.

But he kept following them. The man had bought an ice-cream for the boy at the stand at Norrbro Bridge, as a final payment. It melted in the boy's sweaty hands, and white drops fell on the black blotting paper of the asphalt. People who weren't looking where they were going rubbed out the drops with the soles of their shoes, and turned them into a crooked grey line that didn't come to an end until it reached the kiosk. They paused there, and the man bought something for the boy, who stuck a dirty index finger in through the opening. He'd let go of the man's hand now, and it would have been so easy for Sörenson to whisk him away and start running up Strömgatan with him and disappear into the crowd.

Instead, he kept walking slowly along the quay. He was walking a tightrope on the very edge of the stone kerb. There were just two boats moored at the far end outside the Grand Hotel, without smoke in their funnels and with empty portholes. The quayside immediately opposite Kungs-trädgården was bare, and there was no sign of the usual herring boxes and crates of strawberries. Sometimes there was a thin layer of herring scales there, glistening on the cobbles. The water down below was a mass of mysterious eddies, and the current had carried away the tidemark of soggy paper, eggshells and used contraceptives that always clings to the sides of boats in big harbours. He looked out over the water and watched a ferry creeping over the blue millpond of the evening. Its cabin lights were glittering in the water like bubbles of carbon dioxide. He kicked gently at a mooring ring, and it made an unexpectedly loud ringing noise like a bell.

All the time he was walking he kept his ears skinned, and when he heard the boy's high-pitched voice just behind him, he bent down over the mooring ring and tied his fear to it.

After a while he started following them again, but at a greater distance now. They went past the first white boat, where a precarious heap of herring boxes was piled up on the quay.

Thank God for that, they've gone past, he thought, because every postponement was a blessing as far as he was concerned now. The sound of violin music came wafting out of the windows of the Grand Hotel veranda, and strollers were wandering up and down outside. The ferry in the distance came up against the choppy water coming in from Saltsjön, and jumped awkwardly over the hurdles. Seagulls were screeching around the other white boat's funnel and pecking at the stained covers over the lifeboats. They're surely not going there, he thought, and went all cold. But the quay came to an end and there was no choice and he realized he'd been hoping all the time the quay would go on for ever so that he didn't need to act. He realized that had been his hope right from the first moment he started following them. He'd never believed they would actually get to where they were going, and he'd been pushing his action before him like a wheelbarrow. Now he wanted to let go of the handles on a downhill slope, and jump into the ditch to be safe. But when it came to it, he was even more scared of the ditch.

There was no gangplank and the deck hatch was closed and the rails chained off. Twilight started piling up shadows over the foredeck and the intensely white bodies of the seagulls flashed like lightning past onlookers' eyes. They stepped over the hawser, which was hanging loosely but tightened like an enormous muscle when the current slapped against the stern. The man vaulted over the rail, then quickly lifted the boy after him. They walked over the deck, which was newly tarred and reluctant to let go of the boy's bare feet. Now that they were there, the boy was frightened and started whimpering because he'd also believed the quay would go on for ever, for the sake of the knife. He threw back his head and looked up over the quay with big, scared eyes. Just at that moment the lights came on illuminating the façade of the palace, and a green flash from the tram wires welded the tops of the trees on Logården.

Sörenson's eyes fled there in order to avoid meeting the boy's, and they flew like Mauser bullets across the water to Skeppsbron. The white cloud of seagulls flew up from the top of the boat and glittered for a moment under the blue sky that was being tightened like a steel hoop round the temples of the city.

Like a man at peace with himself on an evening stroll, heading back home for a cigar, Sörenson walked past the boat and continued towards Skeppsholmen Island. He thought he ought to have been shaking in every limb and yelling out in protest because his legs wouldn't carry him over the rail, but all he felt was a faint sense of disappointment. It was just like when he'd been on his way to a friend's wedding once upon a time, and when he got there he couldn't summon up the courage to go in and had walked past the house. Just walked past, as easy as that, and been disappointed afterwards and endlessly surprised. Now he was just disappointed.

However, he continued walking along the deserted quayside, his thoughts doing a balancing act on the slack rope of the violin music. A bunch of rain clouds put up their umbrellas over the Skeppsholmen sky, and an irritating wind started screwing itself in from the big, empty square. The water rapidly grew dark, and the quays at Skeppsbro and Skeppsholmen tipped large mattresses of shadow down into the water. The jagged skyscape of Söder above the Stadsgårdsbergen cliffs disappeared under the black umbrellas, and it gradually started to rain. Lengths of dark-blue silk were wrapped round all the clumps of green trees, and even the occasional gull was enveloped. Sörenson followed the quay until it came to an end at Skeppsholmsbron, and it was when he turned round and looked back that he experienced it.

The white boat lost its outline in the rain driving slowly in from Strömmen in blue clouds, and the colour dampened its light and the big black flunnel became slim and toy-like, but behind the flag-pole, as bare as a defoliated branch, from a porthole at the stern of the boat, he could see two eyes looking at him. He was intrigued, and started walking back along the quay towards the boat. Courting couples were crowding on to the steps outside the National Museum, and others were running there, their feet slapping against the pavement, to get out of the rain. He wasn't alone, but he was the only one who could see the eyes. He thought they were glued to the porthole, and only when it was too late did he realize he would have done better to dive straight into the sea and disappear rather than meet their gaze.

The steel band was pressed hard around the city's brow that was his own, and he could feel the clamps aching with each heartbeat, and he suddenly realized he was running down a long street that had no end, and there were shop windows down each side. The display in all of them was exactly the same. Those cruel boy's eyes were dangling on hooks along the whole of the street, which was in fact just the side of the boat with its misty portholes. He ran and ran through the drizzle, taking the street with him until the quay came to an end. Then he paused and rubbed the water from his face, and was surprised that it didn't taste of salt when it ran into his mouth.

Now the umbrellas were coming down, one after another, and the roof was raised by several miles. The rain stopped, and the wind swished it away. Seagulls' wings peeled off out of the darkness and cut their way through the blue with their knives. The bowls of the streetlamps were filled with light sloshing over the sides and slowly dripping down on to the asphalt. He watched his shadow taking a rest in front of him, and leaned over it as if over a barrier, observing the women, their backs mainly, in gleaming raincoats and with glittering legs, scuttling down Strömgatan. Even so he knew all the time that the street with the boy's eyes was behind him, and he only needed to turn round a tiny weeny bit and he'd cut his own eyes on them.

He was walking quite quickly, but not so quickly that it seemed he was running away.

When he got to Norrbro Bridge he thought: what do I really know about it all? Maybe it was a relative of the boy who just wanted to show him the boat.

As he crossed over the square at Riksdagshusplatsen, he remembered the knife and he thought: how do I know what he's doing to him? In any case, little boys have to learn to be careful.

As he walked over the bridge near the Chancellery, his memory told him he'd followed them as far as the boat even so. Still, I have my own free will, he thought tetchily, and I'm not responsible for what the bloody kid gets up to.

When he turned into Västerlånggatan, his memory asked him straight out why he'd been so scared when he suddenly remembered the boy's look that he reacted by doing something remarkably like running away. He shook off his repugnance so that part of it fell down into the street, but quite a lot was left hanging by copper threads. All his waiting-rooms were now being filled with expectant murmurings from typists chatting away merrily and photographers cursing non-stop behind their buzzing cine-cameras in the identification committee.

Yet as he walked up Storkyrkobrinken he thought: it's about time I had some fun tonight. It was a thought that came to him compulsively, just as a drowning man thinks when it's already too late: I'm going to have swimming lessons to-morrow in any case. Tonight, he was going to have some fun. He blew the message out into the alley like a fanfare from a trumpet filled with water.

When he came out into Stortorget Square, however, he started following a well-padded back in a vivid red blazer. It disappeared behind a big front door which immediately clenched its teeth. In any case there was a wild boar on the door, with a threatening snout.

Then something very frightening happened to him, something very strange. He was walking along a long street and it was so narrow that even somebody with his arms cut off at the elbow would have to keep them pressed close to his body for fear of scraping them against the walls. He suddenly felt as if he were asleep and dreaming, and in his dream he could see himself going down that narrow street, slowly, with his hands in his trouser pockets and with a strange sort of gait he recognized but which wasn't his own. And in his dream he suddenly became extremely scared and wanted to start running, and the one lying asleep in bed yelled at the one walking down the street to turn round and run away. Nevertheless he just kept on walking down the street, as slowly as before, and in any case he couldn't turn round because the street was closing in behind him. His sleeping self became even more scared, but it looked as if it was all too late. All of a sudden he stood still in his dream, and now the houses threatened to swallow him up in their black gullets. Instead, though, they moved back, and he felt agonizingly lonely. He was standing in an open square where lamps were sprinkling and trees glistening. He was standing on a pavement, and straight across the street was a sand-pit and he could see it when he was a long way away from himself.

Now the moment had come. The responsible members of the identification committee, all of them in morning dress and smelling of the same brand of after-shave, knocked at the door of his consciousness, and then lined up in order of seniority in front of his desk and, with the worried expressions of officialdom, handed over the result of their work. Then they bowed deliberately, and withdrew in their considerate, felt-soled shoes.

A feeling of fear that petrified his ego to such an extent that he couldn't move a muscle overpowered him now. He watched the man lean over the boy playing in the sand-pit and wanted to run, but at the same time he could feel his breath on the back of his neck as he turned on the ladder in order to get a better grip of the block. Then he had him next to him as they ran over the hot quay to fetch a doctor.

Now, though, there was such a narrow gap between fear and happiness. He suddenly realized he was alone, and there was nothing but an upturned tin bucket with a broken bottom in the sand-pit. He woke up, and felt the relief you experience after a nightmare. For God's sake, what had happened? Nothing of what could have happened had actually taken place. They hadn't met. They hadn't needed to vomit together, or to call the police for each other. They hadn't needed to go through it all together one more time. They could keep on going their own sweet way, dragging their happiness behind them, or at least their composure, their relative composure.

As he crossed over the street and approached the bench in the gardens forming the little square, he experienced a certain amount of quiet contentment at having sacrificed the boy. But why use as harsh a word as that? He thought: what happened was no doubt all for the best. Somebody always gets the short straw after all. Might it not be best if it's the one who least understands what it's all about? He didn't bother to recall that he himself hadn't known as much about what was going on when he followed them as he did now. It's so easy to exclude things. After a while you forget everything that doesn't help you to keep calm.

Then he heard a rustling behind him in the bushes and turned round, expecting to see a dog or a rat. Light was dripping from the leaves, which were still shiny from the recent rain. He peered cautiously between the branches, which were shaking off the last of the raindrops. They ran down his neck and made him shiver. He could hear somebody calling quite softly, and thought it was someone calling a dog and stopped investigating. Instead, he tried to guess which of the buildings the boy came from. He didn't feel any regret, it's true, but he was still not totally uninterested in the boy's fate. He thought of him with a certain amount of sympathy, as you do about someone walking along a street in front of you who gets a tile dropped on his head when it might just as easily have been you. He hoped they wouldn't be getting anxious about him, whoever it was that looked after him.

But then it was all too late after all. Someone grasped him by the shoulder and he whipped round on the bench ready to defend himself. It was just a little old lady, bare-headed and with a black furrow on her forehead, looking him straight in the eye and asking: 'You haven't seen the boy, by any chance?' 'Which bloody boy?' shouted his conscience, which had been awakened after only a light slumber. 'Am I supposed to keep an eye on all the kids in this town?' The old lady came out of the bushes and sat down beside him on the bench. He looked at her hands as they slowly lay down to rest on her lap, and saw they were like stones, flat stones like the ones you play ducks and drakes with when you're little.

She didn't say anything at first, just sat there, her head drooping so much it could easily have dropped off. He tried to make use of her silence in order to build up storm barriers between his cowardice and his fear. He sat trying to work out where she was going to direct her thrusts. In the end she said, and he wasn't sure if she was talking to him or not: 'I'm the boy's grandma. And now he's gone. I've been looking for him all night. I've been to Matsens down the alley, I've been to the warehouse, and I've walked as far as the palace. I've been all the way down Skeppsbron and back. I've been looking in all the doorways and I've made enquiries at the school. For God's sake, what am I going to do? I'm so frightened.'

He'd finished building his barricades by then and said consolingly, as consolingly as you can afford to be with an enemy you know you can beat: 'Take it easy. He's probably just gone to town with some pal. Maybe they've gone to that new circus that came earlier tonight. There was a procession through the whole town and they have settled at Stall- mästargården. You know what boys are like.' (For Christ's sake, circuses don't come to town like that any more, he thinks, and breaks into a sweat.)

But he could see from her hands – he didn't dare look her in the face – he could see she was grasping at that straw. Of course, she didn't believe it, no more than he did, but they helped each other by believing it. 'It's like the gentleman says,' she said, 'of course it's like the gentleman says. You can't trust little boys. But even so I'm so frightened, so frightened of being alone.

'I say,' she said, looking up into his eyes, but he couldn't manage to see any further down than the black furrow on her forehead, 'would you be really nice and come up to my flat and wait there till the boy comes home? Just to help me while I'm waiting. You've been so nice to me. Maybe that's asking too much, though.'

Too bloody right it is, he wanted to yell, have you ever heard of anybody asking somebody else to come up to their flat and hang themselves? But then his fear went a mysterious, roundabout route and he went along with it and thought: well, why not? I've sacrificed the boy. I'm buggered if I'm going to sacrifice her as well. Isn't that what she's saying to me? You can save me. Shouldn't I do just that? Sacrifice what has to be sacrificed, save what can be saved, isn't that the way to do it?

And so he went with her. It was on the first floor in the narrow, leaning building in the alley. There was a smell of mildew and old newspapers, the stone steps were concave, and they had to step to one side to get past the girl who'd been feeding the pigeons. She was drunk now, and her knee was bleeding. She'd probably fallen on the stairs. Somewhere upstairs the little girl with the spade was screaming. She'd no doubt been left on her own, and was screaming as loudly as she could.

Where the old lady lived was just one room which you came into directly from the landing. It smelled of unwashed dishes that had been standing there for day after day, the pile just getting bigger. He felt sick, and when he felt at his sickest he realized she'd got used to it. They had an iron bed each to sit on, by the window. 'I sit here day after day, watching him play in the sand-pit. He makes sand-pies on the edge of the sand-pit day after day, and he's so pleased with his nice new tunic. One day he got a nice new green spade from that nice gardener, but that nasty girl took it off him and threw it out into the street.'

He had to press his weight down into the iron bed and hear it creak in order to make sure he was awake. What kind of rubbish do we all manage to convince ourselves is the truth? he wondered. What's all this nonsense? There followed a long silence, and the water tap hanging over a big metal sink at the other end of the room was dripping away merrily. There was a commode next to it, with a gas ring standing on it; the flame coming out of it looked like a modest little blue flower some sadist had shoved into a pile of scrap iron. A coffee-pot was standing over the flame, blowing smoke out of its beak.

She pushed a chocolaty-looking cardboard with cheerful red lettering over to his side of the table. As she was laying the table, he opened the box and found it contained photographs, as he'd expected. There was a bundle of them half a finger thick, and all of them were of the boy. He was called Lars-Göran, and he recognized him even though all the snaps were taken when he was little. On a lot of them it said 'Varberg 1939', and he was either standing on a jetty or building sand-castles on the beach. In one he had the sun in his eyes, and was peering out from under a fringe. In another he was sitting at the wheel of a car, laughing. He was no older than five at the most in any of the photos, and it dawned on Sörenson that he'd never grown any older than that as far as she was concerned. She hadn't noticed, or didn't want to notice, that he'd grown up, adopted some nasty ways, started swearing, saying rude words, hitting little girls, fighting other boys. In a way he thought that reduced his guilt, because he could sometimes feel it was still there after all. What difference does it make to her, he thought, if he's ten or fifteen, or if he grows five years older in a single evening, this evening?

They had their coffee, and meanwhile it grew darker

outside. He laid the photos out on the table like a set of patience cards, and she helped him with eager fingers. A car came swishing up the alley and stopped in front of the house. She opened the window and guessed who would get out. But it was only the red-headed bird-feeder and a man with a swaying hat. They were laughing raucously all the way upstairs. When she closed the window again, she brought in the little rag doll.

'Look,' she said, putting it on top of the photos, 'isn't it pretty! He got it last Monday for his fourth birthday, and now he takes it to bed with him every night and he can't get to sleep until he's given it a goodnight kiss. Isn't it sweet?'

He stared in disgust at the filthy rag doll with the shiny safety-pin in its nose. Now he could see the head was made of webbing, and somebody had cut it with a knife so that the stuffing, some kind of vegetable fibre, was sticking out. Where has all the innocence gone? he thought. Here's somebody sitting holding grimly on to it and refusing to see it's disappearing drop by drop, day by day. And I don't feel sorry for her. Hasn't she sacrificed him even more than I have? She's the one, the guilty one! He started to feel sorry for himself, who'd had to put up with all the suspicion without good reason.

Suddenly she lay down on the bed and looked up at the ceiling through half-closed eyes. 'Please wake me up when he comes back from the circus,' she said. 'Promise me, won't you! I'll be so happy then.' She fell asleep the very next moment. He sat listening to the dripping tap and her breathing. Once the tap was drowned, he took his leave like a coward. He left the door ajar so that she wouldn't be woken up by him closing it. Everything was going full tilt upstairs. The red-haired girl was screeching and the gramophone playing. He longed for somebody to be caressed by and to tell everything to. But he'd rediscovered his tranquillity: he thought he was carrying a pair of scales in his chest and they balanced exactly. The weights (stamped with both cowardice and suppressed fear, although he didn't know that) weighed just as much as the commodity of well-being.

He met the boy in the hallway. He was standing fumbling with the light switch, although it was already on. Their eyes met, and the boy would have rushed past if Sörenson hadn't stopped him. He didn't do so because he'd sacrificed him. He just wanted to thank him for being allowed to do that. It's not every day somebody sacrifices themselves voluntarily in order to help your peace of mind. You've often got to beat somebody into doing that. Anyway, he pulled him close and stroked his hair gently. Would twenty-five öre be enough, or would a crown be more appropriate?

As he stood there wondering, he suddenly noticed how the thin little body went limp and just hung over his arm. Then it doubled up like a cramped muscle and its head fell as if it had been broken off. He started vomiting in the hallway over Sörenson's arm. Sörenson held his hand under the boy's chin and felt how violent the eruption was inside him. Eventually he turned him round carefully when it was all over, and that was when he met the boy's gaze for the second time. As the hall light was still on, he couldn't avoid seeing in those eyes why the boy had vomited. It had nothing to do with wine or greasy food. It was due to disgust at the nasty adult world, the treachery involved in every action, and the cowardice, that is, the fear of being afraid. He'd vomited at Sörenson, who'd thought it was OK to run away from his fear about what was happening to somebody else, just as you can run away from a bill in a bar.

Sörenson ran over the square, and although it was a cool evening he was drenched in sweat. He brushed past the Obelisk, and looking down into the water at Strömmen was like looking into an inkwell. He saw quite clearly that everything had been a cowardly retreat. He understood perfectly that the industrious identification committee hadn't dared to come up with any other result when their boss was cowardice itself. He ran along Skeppsbron, but when he got to the corner he was so weary he almost collapsed. He leaned against the railings and watched the water writhing in agony down below. The little fishing boats were coming into the quayside, and the musicians in the Strömparterren café had no doubt packed up and gone home. The lantern on the hot-dog stand at Norrbro was flickering behind the curtain.

When he could eventually bring himself to look down towards the Grand Hotel, he could see a light in a porthole in the boat farthest away. The light was streaming down the side of the boat, and stretched quite some way over the water. That's where it had happened. He tried not to look, but when he looked at the Opera House there was the lit-up porthole, and even when he looked towards Skeppsholmen, where all the trees were black as soot, it was still there in his eye. How dangerous it is to have a porthole in your eye! He tried to remove it from his eye like you do a piece of dirt, but it was no good.

When he was on the point of leaving anyway, he felt the rag doll in his pocket. He took it out and examined it in the light from the shining porthole in his eye. He applied a burning match to where the stuffing was sticking out, and then he flung the blazing torch into the water. He could see through the shining porthole how it glittered like a firefly over the water just for a brief moment. Then it went out and floated away with the current. Perhaps it drifted in to the quayside and got caught up among all the empty matchboxes and used contraceptives. Finis.

The Snake

When night falls and naked lamps start shining over the big, dirty barrack entrances in the yard, with the broad stone steps spat out in front of them, there comes a moment when the inmates of the barracks, walking across the yard in the dark towards the light, suddenly get the feeling that every step that's echoed round these walls, every blank shot that's gone off, every shout, command or scream of desperation that's been heard in the barracks in days of rain, dazzling sunshine, hailstorms or thick snow since 1890, lingers on, hanging there in the form of high, mercilessly oppressive clouds pressing down on their heads. Perhaps the conscript feels frightened and wants to run away from it all, but he has nowhere else to go, only towards the lamp. Then he runs past it and up into the day-room, which is half of what used to be an apartment, with Charles XII on the wall, a piano that was broken as early as the first year of the war, and six rows of brown benches to sit on when you're being lectured at. There's a wireless on a table next to a pile of regimental magazines that you stop reading after you have read one issue. The glass in the wireless's dial is broken, and the tuning knob doesn't work. He sticks a ruler in through the back of the case and knocks the tuning pointer until he hears music playing. Then he can forget everything, if he likes, because it's nearly time to go to sleep.

He's inflamed with fear, though, when he goes out into the corridor, which is long and wide and dirty. Ten thousand pairs of boots have left their mark on the wooden floor. Ten thousand pairs of hands have made the locker doors ill-fitting. Ten thousand pairs of eyes have stared, defiantly or in desperation, at the corridor's ceiling, which is grey and full of broken bulbs. Surely all those eyes must have left their mark on the ceiling! He goes over to the window, where ten thousand pairs of elbows, or possibly even a hundred thousand, have stuck into the window-ledge while all those eyes were gazing out over the barrack square, full of horses and carriages or full of cars and lorries, in broad daylight or at night, as now.

All this – Charles XII on the wall and the marks on the

floor – is called tradition. It's called that by all the powerful types with pips on their shoulders, those phrase merchants who, when they wake up the troops in the morning, puff up their chests with thoughts of the parade in order to avoid having their ribcage knock against their spine. But for this man who's scared and who is walking down the corridor all by himself, waiting for the late passes to run out, tradition is something to be afraid of. He wants to shout out, but anybody who's got the barrack-room willies doesn't shout out, because he's got a clamp round his throat.

Then comes the moment of barrack-room willies when tradition means the memory of all those dead men from 1890 onwards who hanged themselves or shot themselves or jumped from the attic window. Then the frightened man suddenly thinks he can see bodies dressed in uniform hanging from the ceiling over by the lockers, or thinks that bodies of men who've taken poison are lying stiff on their stomachs in awkward positions on the corridor benches, or that bodies are sitting on the corridor floor in murky corners with their heads hanging down, their backs against the wall, with blood pouring from their wide-open mouths and rifles lying over their knees, their polished leather straps shining in self-satisfaction.

Now he starts running, but where can he run to? There are clouds on the other side of the courtyard and he can't go out because he hasn't got his late pass with him and lights-out will sound before long. With trembling fingers he opens the padlock dangling from the office door and when he goes in he's very quick to switch on the ceiling lights. There is a smell of sawdust coming through the gaps in the floorboards looking like the slits in money boxes as he stands looking down over his shoes.

At first the smell made him feel sick, and so did the dirt on all the floors and all the stairs, and the dust on all the tables and all the shelves and all the documents he had to copy. And he could have vomited at the thought of all those people round him who'd stopped taking anything seriously, or maybe had never even begun. They'd roared with laughter when he offered to scrub the office floor with a scrubbing brush, and they'd reacted with a scornful smile when he asked how the underclothes should be laid out in the lockers in the corridor. The day he'd scoured the glass top in the warrant officer's desk with white spirits, he'd had to eat alone at dinner.

It wasn't long before he gave in, however. Discipline, he tried to tell himself, isn't discipline the most essential thing of all? But nobody listened to him. That's what he believed himself, and that's why he'd learnt to tell the time so early on; indeed, it seemed to him he'd always been able to do so. He didn't think he could live without knowing the time, and the days when his watch was being repaired were completely ruined, in a way. Everyone he knew in the town he came from also had clocks: grandfather clocks at home, and wristwatches with stainless-steel straps or birthday-present watches they took with them wherever they went. At their bridge sessions on Fridays twice a month they tried to fool their clocks after drinking three whiskies – they never drank more than that – but anyone who did manage to do so became an object of envy and never tried it again.

Sometimes Mum was still awake when he got home every other Friday, which meant the home help had gone home and so he had to help her to bed. 'I've been so lonely since Daddy died,' she said, despite the fact that he was always at home. She often wanted to go out as dusk fell, and had done so for as long as he could remember. She'd been on the threshold of old age when he was born, so when the time came for him to take her out for walks she took very short steps for fear of falling. They would leave behind their little detached house with its ledges and iron railings and walk along the right-hand-side pavement down towards the garden village; they always left the big, newly built concrete boxes behind them. Actually, she was the one who always said they were newly built; but he would count up the years since they were finished, with their big, damp, frightening walls, and felt the years were running away from him. When they went out in winter they would talk about the snow padding out the gardens, or the icy roads that nobody put sand on; in spring they'd discuss the coltsfoot or the danger of melting snow and ice invading the basements; in the summer it was the scent of the hawthorn bushes or the oppressive heat or the man they'd found dead in the rhubarb patch five, or it was it eight, years ago, who was husband and father to them.

He remembered how, after the funeral, the boss had come up to the pair of them as they stood with their relatives and close friends at the coffee table in the parish hall, and repeated what he'd said at the graveside, namely that both the firm and the family could be proud of having had such a well-organized and loyal (loyal sounded much better) comrade. Afterwards one of the family cynics had winked and said quite loudly that Gideon could now expect a rise, because his late father's boss was Gideon's boss as well. In fact, he was gradually promoted to the rank of deputy-chief clerk, which was as far as his father had got, and he felt a little flush of satisfaction at the thought that he was sure to go even further.

In the autumn they would check the apples in neighbours' gardens and thought their own were better. Then came the snow, and with a slight feeling of bewilderment he would note that another year had gone by, that he hadn't undergone any hardship during that year, and had a good chance of becoming chief clerk in the coming one. What he didn't notice was that the length of his stride became shorter with every year that passed, and that his mother was the only person he could walk beside without fear of stumbling. He started to venerate the firm's books, and imagined life to be a beautifully written, dead-straight and accurately calculated column; when his was over, whoever was left could count up the sums, check the entries and ring up the accountants, because he was convinced that a conscience was not something you needed to have until everything was finished.

Then came the war. He'd never bothered about politics, the only thing a well-organized and placid person can ignore, and he continued not to bother about politics. Mind you, he was upset about the Finland business, and donated quite generously to the collections. Then he started talking about his Country, because he'd suddenly discovered his own Country was so incredibly much more right than any other. That discovery pleased him, because up till then he'd never been quite sure how one could believe in one's Country without getting political. He was filled with a marvellous sense of relief, which came at about the same time as the fall of Paris. He felt something similar shortly afterwards. Meanwhile he'd invested in a number of defence bonds, thinking it was everyone's duty to their Country, and in any case it was so very attractive to a well-organized person to have the opportunity of buying shares in the fatherland.

Then it became quite clear that Germany was going to lose the war, and it dawned on him all of a sudden that it was possible to hope the Allies would win without actually getting political, because this happened quite a long time before he started talking about 'those bloody Germans'.

Then one day he was called up, and a lot of people thought it wasn't a day too soon. He regarded it as his duty to his country not to feel upset about being called up, and he typed out lists of items he ought to take with him. He would be serving as a clerk, because there was something wrong with his heart. He arranged a home help for his mother, and was feeling happy and expectant when he set out.

When he arrived, however, he found that nothing was what he'd expected. He'd always thought that a state of readiness meant going around in a state of constant readiness, your rifle always loaded, your index finger on the trigger, and your eyes alert, always on the lookout. He'd been reading stories and poems about this state of readiness, and had been under the impression Swedish soldiers never needed to eat or sleep, still less to think, and never did anything but stand guard by a bridge or a precipice, and, for the sake of their country, had replaced their wallets with the military instruction book in their inside pockets.

He wasn't even issued with a rifle when he arrived. He had to sit waiting all day in order to get a pair of underpants and marching boots, and almost as long to be allocated a bed in the barrack room. The third day he was given a desk and a chair in the office, and the fifth day, which was a Monday, he was given something to do. Meanwhile he'd been wandering around the camp and had been amazed to find how everything happened on the basis of pure chance; how those whose job it was to sweep out the corridors spent half a day doing one hour's work, in order to avoid having to empty the dustbins; how those whose job it was to empty the dustbins would carry them backwards and forwards between the WC and the staircase half a dozen times before they actually went out, in order to avoid being assigned to sweeping the corridors. In the offices, clerks would set out files dated 1940 or 1941 beside their typewriters and always had the same half-finished letter in their machines in order to give the impression they were working. In fact they would sit playing dice in an open folder, or reading a book. That was easy, because the ones who were supposed to be giving them work to do were constantly having to remind themselves of how important their function was, yet were not as truly convinced about it as they ought to have been. No doubt it was not completely irrelevant, either, that because of the feeling of superiority they seemed to have been born with, they all managed to inspire in their subordinates even higher levels of idleness and obstruction.

What shocked him especially, as someone who had supported the idea of defence bonds, was the attitude that it had been so popular to decry during the Finnish Winter War and dismiss as defeatism, but which seemed to have taken hold of more or less everybody there. Quite a lot of war posters were ripped down from the company noticeboard before he realized that what he and many others had called defeatism was nothing more than a necessary defence mechanism against all forms of unholy naïvety and all kinds of collective pomposity masquerading as support for the fatherland; such attitudes were especially objectionable to anybody whose job was to hang around the military back yard and do the cleaning up.

At first, he tried nevertheless to lead the life advocated by the posters: austere, determined, punctual. Those characters in the posters often found their main impact was as advertisements for gentlemen's wristwatches, but nothing much went according to the clock in the military back yards. He kept a strict timetable for three weeks, perhaps a little longer; returned to work after the lunch break exactly one hour after leaving, and never spent longer than half an hour at the café in Banérgatan, where the conscripts played the football machines if they had any money, noughts and crosses if they didn't, and dice if they did but wanted more. He didn't play anything at all, because he was busy writing his letter home to Mum or reading the local paper he had sent on.

When the incident occurred, though, something had already started to happen to him without his noticing; but then his fear made him start examining himself carefully, and when he noticed he was starting to change he became still more afraid. He realized that this man, who'd been in the habit of walking around the little town back home, going past all the gardens with his mother or along the road to work or to his bridge evenings, and discussing the advantages of the various seasons in restrained and dispassionate language to himself or to his companions, could now come out with a swear-word without even thinking about it until afterwards. He also noticed that although he'd never needed to make an effort to be what his mother and, eventually, himself called clean-living, he had now started having secret desires to try out his body with somebody else's and later stand in front of the mirrors in the washroom in the evening and boast about it, like everybody else did. With a touch of irony, or was it regret, at the corners of his mouth, he was able to claim, in a rather good analogy, that so far he had disported himself like an accurate wall clock in an American saloon, which stubbornly goes on displaying the correct time even though the pendulum has been on the receiving end of a few bullets and the glass has been shot to pieces and the drinkers are unconscious under the tables.

It started one day when he came into the corridor from the stairs. It was a hot day in August, and a big cloud of sand hovered motionless over the yard. The combatant section of the company had just got back from a three-day manoeuvre with a brigade located in a barracks some miles further south. They'd been marched back from the Central Station through the heat, carrying full kit and rifles, and hence there was a big cloud of sweat under the corridor ceiling. Their voices were loud and cheerful, as they always are when you get back after having a rough time and think it was the worst experience in the world. The kit was piled up in jumbled heaps on the floor, like the droppings of some gigantic animal.

At the far end of the corridor was a little group, silent and still, watching a tall lad who was showing them a black tie. Gideon picked his way through the kit lying around and breathing out its heat, and wondered at first why they were all standing so still. Then, when it was too late for him to find an excuse to run away, he saw that in fact it was a snake hanging over the boy's arm. That was when he started feeling frightened – no more frightened than one can easily cope with, but nevertheless for somebody not used to being frightened that did mean something. Then he heard the story behind the snake. Somebody had finished up with the wrong haversack during the manoeuvre. The last evening when they got back to the camp somebody had started yelling and screaming about having his nice new haversack pinched and replaced by some some bloody rubbish with broken straps. Everybody came up to have a look, but nobody recognized it. Then the frustrated soldier opened the haversack and looked inside and turned as white as a sheet and dropped it like a shot. There was a snake lying at the bottom, and a lad who studied zoology in civvy life got three crowns to look after the haversack. He didn't kill the snake, though, but took it away with him because he wanted to try a few experiments.

Now he had the snake in a box in his locker. It stayed there all day and all night long, and everybody thought it was remarkable how different that locker had become since the snake arrived in it. It was as it were a new locker altogether, and everybody could have sworn it was taller and more threatening and ominous in colour than all the other lockers in the corridor.

Although Gideon was more scared now than he'd ever been in the whole of his life, that fear was nothing compared to what came later, which he thought was definitive. One day when it was raining and everybody had been given things to do indoors it so happened that the zoologist was sitting with his box in Gideon's billet. There were a few more who'd slunk in and were playing dice on a blanket spread over the window-ledge. Suddenly there was a disturbance in the corridor. WO Boll had noticed some people were missing and was on the war-path. They were in the middle of their game, though, and so they grabbed a few blankets from the beds and went out into the corridor and said they'd been ordered to give the blankets a shaking. The zoologist was more nervous by nature and just ran out, and he got a good telling-off, well deserved, too, because he'd failed to observe the most elementary of a soldier's skills: to be able to put even the most grotesque and impudent actions down to obeying an order, irrespective of whether it is made up or not, because the very word is the key to all military thinking.

Afterwards, of course, the zoologist maintained he'd put the lid back on properly and fastened the strap; but in any case, when they got back into the room the lid was on the floor and the box was empty. Everybody was scared to death. At first, of course, they tried to bring their fear under control by taking it out on the zoologist, but when they suddenly realized they couldn't manage to shout away their fear, they started searching. They searched in the way very scared people do, poking at the blankets and lifting the mattresses tentatively and looking underneath. They got down on their knees, having first made sure the snake hadn't sprouted wings and was threatening the backs of their necks. At the same time they were all speaking in very loud voices, just like some tribes of natives who beat drums in order to scare away the evil spirits. They shouted and yelled in an attempt to chase their fear away. They searched all evening, getting louder and more scared all the time. But their search was in vain.

The first night was bearable because there were so many of them feeling scared. They shared it around, taking roughly equal portions each. Those who lay awake tried to raise their arms as high as they could in order to keep it as far away as possible, but unfortunately they couldn't raise their arms out of their consciousness. Those who fell asleep took their share with them into their slumbers.

The next day the combatants got their marching orders. They disappeared through the barrack gates in the back of big lorries brumming away indifferently. They sat crammed together on benches, the barrels of their rifles poking up from between their knees, hunched and with their deportation faces screwed into place.

Then came the first, the second and the third nights when nobody could get to sleep. There were too few of them left to make it worthwhile dividing the fear into shareholdings. Their comradeship now underwent a surprising development. Previously they'd stuck together with the greatest reluctance and only because it was the done thing to stick together with somebody or other; but now they were scared of being on their own. As there is no more effective way of making friends of people than mutual fear, what could be more natural than the reaching out of tentacles to Gideon as well?

Gideon lay awake the first, second and third nights. The

first night he thought he could hear the dry rustling of the snake's body sliding over the floor. He crept into his blanket as if it were a bag, wrapping it around himself so tightly there was no room between it and his body for any fear. The second night he thought he was much less frightened. He even smiled an amused little smile as he listened, but the noise he was expecting never materialized. Still he couldn't sleep. The third night, though, when the third of the story-tellers had finished his tale, he realized to his great and genuine surprise, possibly the most genuine he had ever felt, that his fear continued to pulsate inside him, even though he'd forgotten all about the snake. He'd sorted that out. He'd thought: it's all a bluff, of course – the zoologist just wanted to have a joke at our expense and hid the snake in his trouser pocket, because we'd have found it otherwise. His self-discipline – that is, his capacity for deceiving himself – was so great he actually believed that.

When he discovered his fear was still there, it finally dawned on him – although it cost him a large portion of what he'd always believed before – that the snake had just been a symbol or an excuse. Sooner or later it would have had to happen anyway. He looked out into the darkness, and a memory seemed to emerge from it: they were eating, he and his mother, and it happened during a very dark period of his life when there were no such things as birthdays; maybe he was eight or ten or eleven. They hadn't said a word throughout the whole dinner, and now came the stewed rhubarb, which was tough and hard to chew and it irritated the throat. 'Eat,' said his mother, although he was trying his best, '*you* must eat at least.' There were three chairs round the table, and one of them was empty. On the table in front of the empty chair was a plate of meatballs and a dish of stewed rhubarb. He'd felt so little like eating, he felt sick when he looked at them. All the time he was eating he could hear his father's footsteps thumping on the floor of the room over his head. His father was walking so quickly the boy's head started swimming if he tried to follow. At last they came to a stop. When he clasped the arms of his chair tightly, the silence suddenly became unbearable. The man upstairs has stopped moving, and the boy daren't move. He felt as if his father had climbed down through the ceiling and was now balancing on the top of his head. It hurt something awful. Then came the scream, his father's scream, and liberated him. He heard his parents talking about it one evening, but he couldn't grasp that anybody as big as his father could be that scared.

One evening long afterwards, however, when they were out in the garden watering the nasturtiums, his father suddenly said: 'One of these days you'll be very frightened. You'll feel so frightened you don't think you can bear it; but you always can. Before you can keep going, though, you have to execute yourself.' He was so excited the water sloshed about in the can and splashed over his shoes. That was not long before they found him in a heap in the rhubarb bed.

What's the point, he thought now, what's the point of knowing what time it is, of being precise, of being careful, well-organized, loyal, industrious, when none of that can cure you of this? Why isn't one a clockwork motor, when so many others want to be just that? Why can no insurance comany in the world guarantee immunity from this? We'd be prepared to pay anything for the premiums!

Suddenly he discovered a way out. He could have yelled out loud for joy. There was an insurance after all. He thumbed eagerly through the prospectus. Incredibly cheap premiums, just one tenth of the insured as a payment every quarter. All dissatisfied clients can have their premiums back if necessary.

And then he realized he'd already taken out that insurance, that he was already paying the premiums every day. But that wasn't enough, he'd have to bump up the payments. The company was suddenly demanding he should pay everything he had, otherwise there could be no guarantees. He'd have to pay in all that was left of Gideon by postal order, and he realized that was necessary even if he screamed when he was parted from him.

When the reveille sounded he thought he knew how he should go about it. Being immune from fear meant becoming like everybody else. Take bigger strides, shouted the agent to him, start swearing, play cards and dice, forget all about the clock. Learn to deny the possibility that discipline has any significance for your happiness. Admit to yourself that anybody who acts in an exemplary manner, who rakes the gravel paths in his garden and dusts his leather-bound books, only does so because he's a coward: he knows there are other things to do but he closes his mind to that in order to avoid being forced out into unknown territory. Look at all those neatly clipped hedges and beautifully arranged stamp collections, Mr Insured, and think how much fear lies behind them.

Hey, lads, he wanted to shout out after the reveille had sounded and they were all crawling out of bed with their irritated morning grunts, just listen to me, lads! From today onwards I'm going to be a changed man. I'm going to pull down all the barriers and come over to join you. I want to be one of you, please accept me. Be glad I'm coming. I executed myself last night, and that's why I can be different today. But of course, it couldn't happen like that. Nobody can become friends with somebody else, enter into somebody else's circle, by being as blunt about it as that. No, you have to creep in, trick your way in, move carefully. You don't want to risk being laughed at and made a fool of when you're on such delicate business.

When they attacked him, he wanted to shake them all by the hand and say: 'I didn't scream. I acted like one of you, didn't I? I was brave, wasn't I? You just wanted to test me, didn't you, to see if I was good enough for you?' He tried to believe that, he spent all day trying to believe that, he never left them alone, he was at their heels all the time. He circled around their heads like a persistent bird, trying to land on their heads or their shoulders. Sometimes he thought he'd managed it perfectly, and nobody could be better than he at diving after a welcoming gesture or gobbling up a smile turned in his direction.

When evening came, he thought to himself: now we'll all go out and have some fun. Maybe there'll be a pub crawl and you can be sure I won't be outdone by the others. They left the barracks and marched as a group past Oscar's Theatre before crossing over Narvavägen. He wanted to shout to all passers-by: 'Look, this is the gang from billet number two on the first floor at the Göta barracks. We've got a late pass, and we're going to have some fun.'

But all of a sudden he was on his own. Nobody said: 'Hey, Gideon, you're coming with us, OK? We're off to the pub or maybe we'll take a taxi and go into town. Pick a card to see who pays, so that it'll be cheaper.' He walked back, over Narvavägen and towards Karlaplan Square. As he went past Linnégatan he saw one of the female typists from the office. He used to help with the stencilling machine because he'd noticed what pretty hands she'd got. She was with a warrant officer, and he tried to smile at her. She looked at him like you look at a full bus.

The little insurance agent who was the only one in the whole world who knew he'd sent in a postal order to cover the whole premium ran after him and told him not to be upset. He couldn't expect to join the club just like that, surely he could see that. Just wait a little bit, later tonight maybe, after the late pass runs out. Now they're out on the town and might be talking about Gideon, wondering if they should accept him as a member. 'Yes, of course,' says one of them, 'he's such a good bloke. You could see that this morning, didn't say a word, even though he got a right good bollocking.' And so they vote him in.

He allowed himself to be comforted, calmed down and almost felt happy. When he got to Karlaplan he went into the telegraph office and ordered a call to Västerås. When he heard his mother's voice, thin and out of breath and almost drowned by the crackling, he first felt very worried and regretted ringing. She shouted 'Hello!' three times before he could bring himself to answer. But then it went more easily than he'd expected. 'No, Mum,' he said, 'I can't come home. All leave has been cancelled, and nobody can go home for the weekend. You'll have to try to manage without me.'

It was remarkable how easy it was to tell lies. All you needed to do was to stop listening to yourself. 'Goodnight then, Mum,' he shouted, pleased that the conversation was coming to an end at last. 'See you in a fortnight, perhaps.' Then he sat in a bar in Karlavägen until it got dark. He was full of confidence, telling himself that ridiculous game of hide-and-seek between himself and fear was definitely at an end. Now he was a member of a big and powerful club of souls who enjoyed salvation.

Why is he so very afraid now, then? Why is he sitting in the office with his head in his hands? He's not crying, that's true, but he doesn't dare to look up, doesn't dare or hasn't the strength to look the room in the eye. A barracks isn't something you can pat on the shoulder and chat to when you're feeling lonely. It's so horribly silent everywhere that he thinks he can hear this heart tickling like a clock. Perhaps it's hanging on the wall, ticking the time away. He daren't look.

Then he hears voices from the other side of the locked door, and the insurance agent who's been keeping at a discreet distance tiptoes up to him and whispers in his ear: 'There you are, you're not on your own any longer. The moment has come, make no mistake about that. Out you go, and you can collect your membership card for the club for people who are not lonely.'

He leaves the room, puts the light out and relocks the door, then walks towards his barrack room. Ah, they're all back again. They're standing in a big circle in the middle of the corridor, just like a formation dancing team waiting for the signal to start, even though they know the violinist has an ulcer and won't be able to come. Is there room for him in the circle? He finds a gap and fills it. Why can't he shout: 'Here I am, then! I'm in the middle of your circle. Touch me so that you know I exist.'

He looks at the silent, uncommunicative faces all around him, without saying a word. Why are they all closed, why haven't they rolled out the carpets with 'welcome' on them outside somebody's door? Let me in, let me in, he begs, fearfully. But how long will it be before somebody sets the dog on him?

Then he looks at them again, and now he notices the horrific fear in their faces. They're so immersed in their own fear, clinging on to it so tightly, that they're not aware of anything else. It's only by chance that they happen to have formed a circle in the corridor just here, because they can hardly see each other.

'Me and Dandy,' says Lucky in the end, and leans forward and focuses on the toes of his shoes – but then Dandy nudges him in the ribs and he falls silent. Everybody is silent now. Why won't anybody let him in? If shared fear is not a reliable link to bind people together, what can be?

Then there's a shout from the far end of the corridor, and somebody comes running up, running past them and belting with his fists on all their closed doors. They open up reluctantly. Cheerful Charlie, who hadn't been in the circle, is standing in front of them. He has a boot in his hand – they recognize it from the poker game, it's where the pot usually ends up. They all stand staring at a common or garden marching boot, shiny and in good shape thanks to all the polish, and with a big, greedy mouth. Now the big mouth turns round and spits out something on to the floor. They all stare at the floor with covetous eyes and now all the doors are wide open, albeit from curiosity. The snake is lying there, its back broken. It's as stiff as a rod, as straight as a ruler, as if it were in the process of measuring the floorboards. Somebody fetches a cardboard box, somebody else brings a shovel, a third person wraps a bit of string round the cardboard box and puts it in the dustbin.

How odd, he thinks, in Charlie's boot, the poker boot. It must have crawled there and kept still all the time we were hunting it. Maybe somebody stood on it and killed it while it was still in the billet, and that was why Charlie didn't notice anything when he carried the boot back to the store. 'I'd put the cards in the boot toe,' says Charlie, 'and then I comes across this lad from Svea who had a few tenners he wanted to get rid of. I shoves my hand in the boot and you can bet yer life I was shit-scared when I felt that bugger there cold as ice.'

They'd forged a circle round Cheerful Charlie that was pretty solid, based on admiration, and one of them in the circle was Gideon. He watched in amazement as all the previously tense and boarded-up faces opened wide like a set of ballroom doors, and anybody who had designs or wanted to borrow money or something like that could hear the orchestra tuning up as a sort of welcome. Now, he thought, now's the moment for it to happen. Just look how inviting all those faces seem when they turn towards me: all I need to do is to take their proffered hands and offer them shares in my fear.

Oh dear, he doesn't yet know, the one who's still carrying his fear around, that they've all shoved theirs in a cardboard box and thrown it away in the dustbin. He can't possibly know that, unlike him, they've been injected with small doses of fear for as long as they can remember, and they've gradually grown more or less immune to it. He can't know that the only reason they've put out their 'welcome' mats is that they've been afraid of the snake, this dark-coloured two-foot-long measuring tape, simply because it's ceased to exist except as a memory. You can bet your life he doesn't realize either that the idealist's worst opponents are all those former idealists, or that anybody who's still living in a state of fear can expect the greatest threat from all those people who've got rid of theirs. The greatest scoffers are all former believers, the ones who see a hidden threat in the fact that some representatives of their former ideals still dare to exist. Fear is an ideal for anybody who is sufficiently afraid.

Now they're all so pleased at the prospect of giving a travel pass to their fear that they don't even flinch at the thought of denying three or more times all the things they've done and all the thoughts they've entertained while they had the iron grip of terror around their throats. They all join in laughing at those ridiculous figures who were actually themselves. They're all so cocksure now. 'By God,' says Dandy, 'Lucky got one hell of a biff from that sailor-boy, just look at his chin. But you should've seen what happened next – I grabbed the bastard and gave him such a beauty, he's probably not come round yet.' Lucky nods and roars with laughter at the poor little sailor-boy.

What comradeship, thinks the man who knows nothing about it, what marvellous comradeship!

'Bloody hell, Joker, but you were dodgy on your pins all right. I thought you were gonna land up on your arse outside the guard room,' laughs Cheerful Charlie. 'Yeah, I were a bit bloody pissed,' says Joker, laughing dauntlessly, or was it with embarrassment? 'I met a mate from Bermuda,' brags Sörenson, 'a specialist in black girlies. We got ourselves a litre of the hard stuff, and you should've heard the stories he had to tell about the Congo and the States. Bloody hell, it really made a poor bugger's mouth water.'

These are the lads, thinks the only one who's afraid but doesn't know that yet, these are the lads the weak and the lonely must join forces with, all these men of great courage who are possessed by fear but even so have got used to the thought that it's inevitable and have learnt to cancel it out through their mutual friendship. He doesn't know that what they're frightened of more than anything else is actually feeling frightened, and they only accept as friends people who can persuade them that fear doesn't exist.

Now he's walking down the corridor in their midst and all round him are flashes from the crossfire of their smiles and the sound of firework-words exploding in the air. He suddenly notices that Scriber is missing. Then they're all standing at the sinks in the washroom and nodding as they renew acquaintance with their calm, happy faces in the wall mirrors. It's the first time they've seen them for several days, which is why they're especially pleased to meet them. And he barges into this moment of happiness like an elephant in a flower-bed. 'We've got to be mates,' he says, raising his voice instead of grabbing himself by the throat and keeping quiet, 'we've got to be mates now that we're all so frightened.'

It's terrible how sound can echo round a room. They think their ear-drums will burst, but when they discover they've survived, they set on him like a pack of wolves. They hold him down as if he were on an anvil while the jets of water smash against his body like lashes from a whip. They don't need to hold him down, in fact. He can't move a muscle anyway: what's happening to him is so far beyond his comprehension he's paralysed by surprise. They let him go and wander off, but it's a long time before he's able to move again.

And it's longer still, not until the morning sun stretches its red veil over the topmost windows, before the penny drops. Then he screams. It's not a long, drawn-out scream, just a short, shrill one like a quick blast on a trumpet that wasn't intended. It doesn't wake anybody up, but it penetrates their slumbers and sets them off dreaming. Somebody might dream of a pheasant shoot and see a pheasant hurtling down into the reeds, screaming shrilly, with lead shot all over its chest. Somebody else is standing on a railway platform in the rain, waving a black handkerchief at his dead sister. A whistle blows through the rain, and the train disappears into its own smoke.

What does he know of other men's dreams?

The Flight that Didn't Come off

That same evening, though, Scriber was sitting on a bed in a hotel room in Klara. It was a real showpiece of a room, with two enormous beds. The bedknobs were gilded, and because of their size were reminiscent of the shiny foreheads of rich businessmen. The bard's hat was dangling from one of them. The bard himself was sitting in the window, fiddling with the mauve-coloured braid on the curtains; the chair he was sitting on was an unusually cheeky forgery of something Gustavian. On the other bed lay a currently fashionable cultural critic, struggling with his thoughts. It was part of his aspirations always to deal with thoughts in that way.

Scriber raised his beer glass until he could see the golden knob on the flag-pole sticking out from the hotel on the other side of the narrow street bobbing up and down in the liquid like a float. 'I maintain,' he said, wiping the froth from round his mouth, 'I maintain without any doubt at all that my fear is the greatest in the world.'

He'd only just said that, but, strangely enough, nobody had believed him. The cultural critic refused to do so because he was suspicious on principle of people who said things he'd have liked to say himself, and the bard likewise because his unspoken conviction was exactly the same with regard to his own fear. Still, he let go of the curtain braid and slowly turned his white, mirror-like face in towards the room. 'Would you mind justifying that claim,' he said. 'Everyone is no doubt convinced he lives no more than a couple of miles from the worst bog in the whole world, but when you ask him to actually go there and examine it without any preconceived ideas, he suddenly discovers the bog wasn't a bog at all, but a most appropriate place to construct a tennis court or a miniature golf course.'

The cultural critic was only half-listening. He'd decided it would be all right to use Scriber's sentence in his next essay in any case.

'Oh, yes,' said Scriber, 'of course we agree there are bogs for everybody, both in this country and in all others. All the same, I think my good friend's observation about bogs that can so easily be converted into tennis courts or golf courses doesn't correspond to the way things actually are. Ask any bog or swamp owner you like, and you'll find he has no idea he's got anything of the sort on his land. He might blush when he admits it, or he might not, but that doesn't matter. We must surely agree, though, that the present time provides us with an unusual aptitude for fear. This might seem a remarkable fact at a time when even the simplest of people have their own radio-police and nobody who doesn't really insist on it needs to be alone with his silence at night. But nevertheless, even the keenest of denigrators has a marsh to go to when it gets dark enough.

'Unfortunately the invention of searchlights wouldn't help anyone who wanted his bog illuminated right down to the bottom. Some people might possibly have been tricked into thinking so, or even quite a lot of people, if you really think about it. They run around in the fields on tiptoe, and some of 'em might even play football without letting on they're carrying their fear around with them like a cannon-ball chained to their feet. They might imagine you can be vaccinated against fear just as you can against smallpox. But then comes a day when a snake disappears in your room. You get desperate and look all over for it, but you can't find it.

What can you do then? You realize of course that fear is a disease that's always lying latent within you, and it finds its way along the finest threads of your consciousness and stings 'em till they start glowing and burning. Then you also realize you have no choice: what you thought was freedom from fear proves to have been nothing more nor less than a convulsive attempt to eliminate it from your existence. In your desperate situation you might even find everything is balancing on a column of fear, and so you start making arrangements to live in the light of that knowledge. But then it can happen that the snake suddenly turns up again, and that's when the deplorable situation arises: the impudent denigrators stand up and say, "We were never actually afraid, really; it was just him that shat himself, ha ha!"

'And this,' said Scriber, contemplating the gold knob swimming in his beer glass, 'is deplorable, but it's also tragic. It's the tragedy of modern man that he no longer dares to be afraid. That's disastrous, because the consequence is that he's forced to stop thinking. That's only logical because anybody who doesn't dare to be afraid has to stop doing things that make him feel uneasy and can let him through the back door into a situation where he's frightened. Isn't that why it's so easy for anti-intellectualism to become popular, isn't that why all kinds of blood mysticism and sex cults are taken up so eagerly by all those people whose cowardice leads them to blame all problems on guts and glands?'

'Objection!' said the bard, getting to his feet. He put his glass down on the window-ledge and paced up and down like a Red Indian on the shaggy Wilton carpet. He carried his brow as if it were a little mirror of ivory, and the oncoming twilight was reflected in it. 'Have I misunderstood my role?' he asked eventually. 'I thought the job of the poet was to liberate others from fear, to demonstrate how remarkably little cause there is to feel frightened. Should not the ideal for every person be security and well-being – you claim to be a socialist, and ought to be fighting for a system whereby everybody according to his needs is assured of at least a minimum of security and well-being.'

'That's right,' said Scriber, 'that's quite right: I am a socialist, but not in the sense you seem to think I am. It's a widespread assumption, in fact, that so-called spiritual balance, i.e. freedom from fear, should play a part when it comes to the requirements of social justice. Of course, this is due to the fact that many people regard spiritual well-being as something worth striving for, perhaps the most worthwhile thing to strive for. I don't. I'm striving for social justice all right, by which I mean a system in which there's no longer a slave market, in which people no longer feel gratitude as a matter of course towards their employers, a bank or a lottery for giving them the right to live. A system, then, where the right to live is taken for granted, and where you can provide toy shooting ranges and efficient popguns for all these war-mongers, who form the core of reactionary outlooks. On the other hand, I have absolutely no desire to see well-being as a part of this system. It has transpired, unfortunately, that quiet contentment has a certain tendency to degenerate into belching and super-satiety. In a world full of secure belchers it could be that the most essential elements of all are the possibility of being knocked about and the ability to feel fear. That's why I want to pull down all the chicken-wire we've put up around our fear, open up all the entrances to the snakes in the snake sanctuaries and put broken glass in the bathtubs of all those who claim to have sought and found happiness, because striving for security and well-being is a cruel occupation in a world where there are so many lonely people. As a writer, I certainly don't consider it one of my duties to calm people down and build breakwaters. On the contrary, I regard it as my duty to do all I can to cause unease and to break down dykes. Only those who are on familiar terms with their fear are conscious of their worth, only they don't feel any need to close their eyes when they walk past either bogs or tennis courts.'

The cultural critic's bed creaked. He still hadn't forgiven Scriber for stealing such a good phrase from him. He concentrated on an abstract patch on the ceiling, a bit like Georg Brandes or whoever it was that used to do that, and said a bit grumpily: 'I think I heard somebody say his fear was the greatest in the whole world. It would be interesting to hear that said person expand his ideas a little on that theme.'

'That's right,' said Scriber, deciding the gold knob had lost a little of its lustre and giving it a bit more water to swim in from the bard's bottle. 'I'm just about to do that.' The bard opened one of the windows and looked out into the gathering dusk. At that very moment there was a flash in the street below: it was the streetlights coming on. In a doorway opposite the hotel was a girl in a red beret, staring up at him. Perhaps she was expecting him to invite her up. He didn't look at her all that closely. He sat on the window-ledge with his back towards her.

'Maybe you thought it sounded as if I was boasting,' said Scriber, 'when I claimed my fear was the greatest in the whole world. That wasn't the intention. Because I'm a writer it's quite natural for my fear to be greater than anybody else's. It's natural because, in my view, a writer ought to be a symbol for all people all over the world who are not tempted to try to suffocate their fear. Just as, for instance, a worker is symbolized by somebody whose work is harder than anybody else's – a miner or a navvy, and not a strawberry-picker – and reactionary attitudes by an arms manufacturer rather than a deputy clerk, an angst-ridden person must be symbolized by somebody who's got to the bottom of his fear, somebody who knows most about it and is least scared of it because he is used to going around in its presence all the time. I'm talking about a writer. Might it not be that being a writer means your fear is automatically greater than anyone else's in the whole world?'

The bard emptied his glass and marched up and down the room. All three of them were starting to get a bit drunk, and this had its effect on the room, which seemed to be getting smaller as its walls closed in and pressed up against each other. A cloud of goodwill was drizzling down from the ceiling. The cultural critic smiled and started to forgive. He might perhaps be able to use the phrase in his next essay after all. The bard came back to his window and looked down into the street. The girl in the red beret was still standing in the doorway. What if he were in fact to invite her up? He filled his glass, and pretended to drink a toast to her through the window. She didn't move a muscle, but continued staring at him just as sulkily as before. Somewhat put out, he turned back to face the room.

He was starting to have some trouble keeping his thoughts under control. They were a bit like keys on a string that's come undone. They kept falling on the floor with a clatter one after the other. He had to try to thread them back on, carefully, one at a time. That's why there was a pause before he said: 'Isn't my good friend romanticizing fear just a little bit? Is it really as necessary as all that to be on speaking terms with one's fear as my friend claims?'

'I don't know about that,' said Scriber, 'but I do think it's much more dangerous to romanticize security and well-being. I seem to remember that the harmony philosophy, whose most common instrument is anti-intellectualism, has suffered its greatest defeat just now, during the war. Because of a fear of losing one's peace of mind, a fear of being afraid, even those who knew better came out in favour of military service. Well-being and security before anything else – and if you can achieve it so easily, just by spitting in your own face, then why not! Out came all the old slogans, dressed up in the 1937 and 1939 fashion and equipped with automatic pistols and machine-guns – but was there anyone who dared even to whisper about the emperor's new clothes? People had already given away the right to think in connection with the propaganda for the ideals of security and well-being, and so it was only natural to put your brain out of gear once again, and woe betide anybody who dared to do anything different! It wasn't only their own faces they could spit at! Don't you see how wretched the whole bluff is for somebody who's experienced the inflation of all the slogans from the back yard of a conscript's existence? He of all people has to be convinced that the solution, or maybe not the solution, because there could well not be any solution as such, but the possible way forward, is a new epoch of intellectualism which can give people at least some courage to look their angst in the eye instead of away into the infantile caves and bedrooms crawling of mysticism. Perhaps it is necessary to run away, but certainly not in the naïve way advocated by the hard-boiled school.'

'Sorry to interrupt,' said the cultural critic, getting up off the bed, 'but my good friend mentioned the hard-boiled school.' At least an hour before the others, he'd reached the stage of intoxication when goodwill runs out and the desire to start quarrelling takes over. 'I take it, sir,' he went on, provocatively, 'that you have read my essay on Hemingway, Calderón and the Greek subaltern in the New Weekly Post? What did you think? In any case, it was much better than that snooty twit Westin's piece on Faulkner and the Mesopotamian lizard – what the hell does he think a Mesopotamian lizard has to do with Faulkner? Ha ha!'

Scriber was well aware that the cultural critic would go through the whole list of scribblers he considered to be inferior to him, a hundred or more of them, unless he put his oar in, and he continued as if the interruption had been no more than a parenthesis: 'You see, I can't help thinking it's a bloody naïve method of running away to jump out of a room through one window and then creep back in again through another. But isn't that just what certain hard-boiled mystics are trying to do?'

'Hold on,' shouted the cultural critic furiously, 'don't you think, sir, you should stop short of plagiarism?' He walked over unsteadily to Scriber's bed and took hold of the bedknobs and held the bedposts under his arms like crutches. 'You've pinched that from my essay, haven't you?'

Scriber emptied his glass. He looked at the gold knob afterwards and had the impression it was actually swelling up and was now about the size of a child's head. Just then there was a swishing noise, as if from a giant wing. Then raindrops started patting on the window-sill. The bard looked out. The girl in the red beret was still there. Aha, she's waiting until I'm on my own, he thought, and felt flattered. He wrinkled his ivory brow and looked to see if there was enough brandy left. But Scriber was looking the cultural critic straight in his inflamed, bull-like eyes. It was remarkable how light-headed he felt. It was as if his head had been filled with gas and had acquired an almost irresistible desire to fly away. He felt ready to make very important decisions. 'You're right,' he said without a moment's hesitation, 'the sentence is in your essay, word for word. On the other hand, you didn't take the thought to its logical conclusion, which is what I was about to do when I was interrupted.' The cultural critic bowed sarcastically. 'How are you going to do that, if I may be so bold as to enquire?'

A wild, fantastic thought emerged like a flash of lightning from Scriber's brain. One second later he knew exactly what he was going to do. That would put paid to that jumped-up little prat. 'If you'd like to come over to the window with me, sir,' he said, 'I'd like to demonstrate how I intended to carry my reasoning to its logical conclusion.' The balloon got bigger and bigger. He pushed the bard to one side and clambered up on to the window-ledge. 'What the hell?' wondered the bard, but the cultural critic hushed him. Scriber looked down into the street. Almost directly below him on the pavement was a big white bag, with rain pattering down on it as if it were the skin of a drum. They were bloody high up, in fact. In a doorway opposite the hotel was a girl in a bright red beret, looking up at him. He gave her a wink, although he realized she couldn't see it from that distance. She was probably sheltering until the rain stopped.

He carefully swung round on the window-ledge until he

was facing the room. He looked over the top of their heads and fixed his gaze on a miniature on the far wall. Then he slowly stretched out his arms and embraced the wet wall, at the same time stretching his left foot back on to the cornice. Very slowly he edged his way backwards on to the cornice until he was standing there like a man crucified, albeit facing the wrong way, between the two windows. He slowly turned his head and there was something that caught his eye, and although he knew it was a very dangerous thing to do he just had to turn his head a little bit more in order to see what it was. It was the gold knob on the flag-pole, just lying there and licking the rain, so close at hand that he only needed to take ever such a little jump and he'd land right on it.

He shuffled his way along the cornice and soon he was on the sill outside the other window. The pair inside the room both thought he would come in now. When the bard realized he was intending to go on, he shouted to him: 'You bloody idiot, come on in now before you fall off.' 'No bloody fear,' said Scriber, and the all-embracing, contented, balloon-light feeling of peace was still resting inside him. 'I'm not one of those who think running away to where you started off is a radical solution. If you're going to run away, you've got to find somewhere new to run to. You tell the cultural critic that.'

When he turned his head he could see the cultural critic hanging out of the other window. He just seemed curious. Scriber looked down at the beret girl over the road. He raised his hand and waved to her. She didn't move a muscle, just went on staring at him. He felt a twinge of unease through all his tranquillity. Then, as he prepared to edge further along the cornice, he discovered that it came to an end, because the building also came to an end with the window. There was a drainpipe, and on the other side of that was a new cornice on the next building. It had recently been covered with shiny tin plate, and sloped gently downwards. Above it was an open window, with a white lace curtain hanging out of it like a dog's tongue. That's where he was going to go. It would be OK, it would have be OK if he took one long stride and clung on to the drainpipe all the time. It was too late to turn back now. He looked down at the girl once again. She was leaning against the doorpost and had crossed her hands over her stomach and was staring straight up at him. He suddenly started to feel cold, although there wasn't the slightest sign of a breeze. Far down below he could see a big shop sign, its curved, shiny black top looking like the back of a buffalo. A couple of matchsticks came floating along the gutter, and it seemed to him he couldn't have seen them in more detail if they'd been tree trunks. Water was gurgling along the gutters like mountain streams, and the rain was giving him sneaky pin-pricks. Somebody far away in Drottninggatan burst out laughing uncontrollably.

To stop himself feeling cold he leaned forward and formed his hands into a knot around the drainpipe. It was cold and had sharp edges. Then he took a long stride past the drainpipe and reached the end of the other cornice. Then he let go with his other foot and put all his weight on the drainpipe. His foot waggled around in the air and it seemed ages before he managed to put it down on the other cornice. It slipped on the new, shiny tin and he started sliding down and could do nothing to help himself. His body was pulled inexorably outwards, and in the end he had to let go of the drainpipe or his arms would have been torn off.

He fell backwards towards the edge of the pavement. It all happened so quickly he didn't even have time to grab at the flag-pole, which was too far away in any case. But he heard the prostitute scream, and the scream ceased to exist for him at about the same moment as his ability to feel the rain.